An Unfinished Memory

CROCUS VALLEY, BOOK 3

MARIE JOHNSTON

LE PUBLISHING

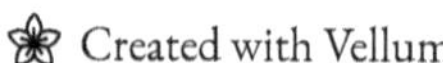 Created with Vellum

I never keep secrets from my best friend, but I'm not sure how to tell her I'm sneaking around with her brother...who's also my ex-husband.

I might be single, but I'm not ready to mingle. I should've stayed home from the street dance. My feet are barely surviving the two-step, and my dance partners are looking for dates while I'm only interested in forgetting the man I was once married to.

The night's about to end with bruised toes and a rainstorm when the guy who swept me off my feet years ago cuts in right before the downpour starts. Wilder Knight has always been the best dance partner I've ever had. Just not the best husband.

Once the storm hits, we take refuge in his pickup, but that isn't all we do. After steaming up the windows and losing my underwear, I make a habit out of hooking up with my ex-husband.

Only the longer we continue, the easier it is to see why our marriage fell apart. I couldn't get over him the first time, and losing him a second time might destroy the secure life I've built for myself, leaving me to ask... Were we better left an unfinished memory?

One

WILDER

Saturday nights used to be for drinking, fishing, or fucking, depending on my age and marital status. At almost forty and newly divorced, I wasn't doing any of the three. I was on the doorstep of an elderly couple, two people who'd known me my entire life and had lived in this small, square home since before I was born, and the guy looked at me like he'd never seen me before.

Saturday nights could be goddamn depressing these days.

I tucked my trusty ballpoint pen in my uniform shirt pocket. "All right, Mr. McCormick. I'll keep an eye out and give you a call. Don't worry, we'll find your truck."

Guy McCormick's lined face was drawn, worry thick in his eyes. "Thank you, Deputy Knight. Maybe I can—"

"No, sir." I didn't need an elderly man with dementia roaming town for a pickup that was sold years ago. "The best thing you can do is stay here. I need to know where I can reach you in case I find it."

Delilah, his wife, nodded and tugged at his arm. "Go sit by the phone, Guy. I'll show the deputy out."

Guy turned into the house. He stopped and nodded in my direction. "Thank you, Wilder."

Just like that, I was back to being Wilder to him. One of the Knight boys. To him, I was probably still eighteen and racing too fast through town in an old ranch truck. To be fair, I could still be that guy, only I could get away with it now.

"Sure thing." I stepped back, and Delilah crowded onto the stoop with me. The top of her silver-haired head didn't come to my armpits, but she looked at me as if I was nothing more than the four-foot-tall little boy who skipped a rock right into her camper window.

She glanced behind her. Guy disappeared around a wall. The kitchen and their landline was on the other side. I could picture him at the mighty oak dining room table, waiting for a report from me. Later, Delilah would coax him into bed, and in the morning, he'd forget about thinking his pickup was gone.

"When do you want me to call?" I asked her. Sometimes a call reassuring Guy we were in full investigation mode calmed him. I usually checked with Delilah. She knew him best and how these episodes went.

She shook her head and squeezed her eyes closed for a heartbeat. "God, I don't know, Wilder. In five minutes, he might forget about it all and remember why the pickup's gone."

Or he might go out and search for the vehicle. Our little slice of Montana was in full summer, but an elderly man shouldn't be wandering the county searching for a pickup he hadn't owned for years. Delilah used to go with him, but after he harassed an unfamiliar teen boy who was in town visiting relatives, she tried to keep him home.

There were times Guy still confronted me about that window I busted. I'd paid for a thirty-year-old broken window five times in the last three years. The next day Delilah would always return the money. The best way to deal with Guy was with routine. Guy had Delilah. Delilah had me.

I had this job. "Shoot me a message or call dispatch. Let me know what you need me to do."

She let out a gusty sigh. "I don't know what I'd do without you." Her pale-blue eyes misted over. "This is so damn hard."

I gave her shoulder a gentle squeeze. Delilah was a proud woman, and she didn't want a fuss made when she teared up. "You know how to reach me."

I got back into my black SUV with the standard word "Sheriff" emblazoned across the side. I wasn't the sheriff. If I was, I'd have today off, and I wouldn't be watching the clock. I'd have seen my niece and nephew perform their second-annual dance recital instead of missing it when I said I'd be there. My oldest brother Cody's new wife was doing a dance number, too, and given she was seven months pregnant, I would've liked to have seen that. I would've liked to have seen Cody's reaction to watching her. The guy was stupid in love, and I never thought I'd see him so happy. Which sucked to say when he was a widower, but he and his first wife had been more like resigned partners, and when she passed away, I'd worried about him.

Now he was worried about me. My brothers wouldn't tell me, but since my divorce, they texted more.

They called. They left messages. My sister too. My siblings were a pain in the ass. Every one of them.

As I pulled away from the McCormicks' place, my phone buzzed. Since it was my personal phone, I ignored it as I called in my encounter with dispatch.

When I was done, my phone buzzed again. I looked at the caller. Eliot, my youngest brother. "Yeah?" I answered, irritated because he was going to give me shit about missing the performance.

The drive to Crocus Valley was just under three hours. Two and a half with no pee breaks or road construction and going a few miles per hour over the limit.

"Where the hell are you?" he asked. Laughter filtered in from the background. My family. Having a great time.

"Working."

"I thought you were coming?"

"I told you I had to work." I was a broken record, but it was the truth. I didn't have a job I could just walk away from.

"You're missing the barbeque. What about the street dance?"

"I don't know, man." I checked the time again. Hadn't I been making calculations in my head the entire day? *If I left now, I could get to the recital.* That time came and went. *If I left now, I could make the family cookout.* That time was rapidly passing. *If I left now, I could make the street dance.* To be determined.

"Get your ass home and then come here."

"I'm trying, Eliot, but I'm on the phone with a pushy bastard—"

"Smart-ass. You should've ridden with me."

I should've, but I often worked over my shift's end

time, and we both knew it, which was why Eliot had proposed the idea. I should have said from the start I couldn't make it. I was less of a bad guy if I opted out instead of canceling. "I'm almost done. Maybe I can make the dance."

"Sure. Hey—" he hollered, and I held the phone away from my ear. "That's my steak, not yours, dog."

I laughed, picturing Cody's dog going after a distracted Eliot's plate of food. "Save your meat. I gotta go."

I looked at the time again. The nights I met up with family to grill were some of my favorites. I'd missed too many of them over the years. My shift was nearly over, getting off early didn't happen, but maybe if I left as soon as I got done...

To finish out my shift, I took another lap through Buffalo Gully, the small town I grew up in and continued to live in. Outside of town a few miles, Knight land sprawled for miles, full of cattle and horses my brother ranched. I often helped him. Since I was on the payroll and all. Since I had to be.

A guy in a yard flagged me down, and my stomach sank. Jeremy Miller. I liked him enough, but Eliot's call stuck with me. Got my hopes up. If something was wrong, I'd have to stay and help.

I pulled over. Jeremy was an old classmate of mine, happily married to his high school sweetheart, with a kid in college and a set of twins in their senior year of high school. The fucker was my age, and he'd lived an entire lifetime while I went home to an empty house to scratch my balls and watch ESPN.

I flashed him a tight smile and rolled down my window. "Whatcha need?"

"Nothing right now, but if you're around this weekend, mind helping me tow Emily's car in?"

Emily was one of the seniors. I hadn't heard anything was wrong, but relief cooled the back of my neck. He didn't need anything now. "What happened?"

"Transmission went out on Quarry Road. Leonard's got family over this weekend. I hate to call him."

Leonard had worked as a mechanic since I came back from college. Leonard was like me. Someone needed him, he went out to help, and everyone knew it.

"I'll call you before I go out to the ranch." Whether I was heading to Crocus Valley or staying, I had plans to meet Eliot in the afternoon. He'd probably drive back at dawn. I should have time to give Jeremy a hand and let Leonard have time with his visitors. "I've got a tow rope in my pickup. Maybe I can get Ray to come out with me."

Jeremy grinned. "Nice. I get to have the sheriff at my beck and call. I was going to call him, but then I saw you passing."

Ray Dahlen was my boss and mentor, an all-around nice guy, unless you were breaking the law. He took the safety of this county personally, and since he lived and worked in Buffalo Gully, he took special care of every one of its residents. I strove to be as respected as him.

Jeremy rimmed his hands around his khaki shorts, giving his striped polo shirt a good tuck. The New Balance shoes on his feet were white. He was in his middle-aged-dad glory.

An ache reignited behind my chest wall. The dad ship had sailed for me, and I was okay with it. Then I saw guys like Jeremy working in their yards with houses full of family, and the what-could-have-beens hit harder than usual. "See you tomorrow."

"Thanks, Wilder. I owe you. Hey—are you going to be the resource officer at the school again this year?"

I smiled and tamped down the impatience his small talk was causing. I looked forward to the start of school in a little over a month and the distractions working with the students brought. The town was small enough I knew each kid by name, and being around that much teen spirit was a nice break from the cases that kept me up at night. "How else can I see all the games for free?"

He laughed. "I know, right? With two kids going all year, those entry fees add up. Thanks for stopping. See you tomorrow."

I waved and pulled away. Two blocks later, I was stopping again. Frustration ate at my stomach lining. I normally wasn't this salty about being helpful, but the school librarian, Annie, was in her driveway with her ten-year-old son, trying to load a push mower into the back of her pickup. They picked it up, one end dropped, and I worried the boy would lose a foot if he dropped the front end.

I got out and jogged toward them.

"Oh, Wilder. Thank goodness." She grinned, sheepish. "I overestimated all the strength I built up hauling books all day."

"Not a problem." Between the three of us, we tossed the mower in the back like it weighed two pounds. I withdrew a tissue from my pocket and brushed the grass bits and grease residue off my hands. I made little progress, but I was grateful the mess wasn't either of their body fluids from an emergency call. If I wanted to get to the dance and spend any time with my family, I'd have to leave now. As it was, they'd all be heading out for the night, and I'd only get snippets of conversation between dances. I wouldn't get to see as much of *her*.

"It's my father-in-law's," Annie explained. "Ours broke down, and Dorian's at guards this weekend. I've gotta return it so he can mow before the rain forecasted next week."

Dorian was her husband. Her father-in-law had back surgery last year, but I doubted it'd stop him from trying to unload the mower. If I left her to deliver the mower, one of them might get hurt.

There was no way I wouldn't feel responsible.

But the dance?

I resigned myself to missing the damn thing. I shouldn't have tried to plan on leaving town. "I'll follow you over there and help unload it."

"Are you sure?" When I nodded, she patted my arm like I was one of her pupils. "What would we do without you, Deputy?"

Her appreciation was a thin bandage against my disappointment. "That's what I'm here for."

She laughed. "Deputy Wilder, your job does not include loading lawn mowers."

It did. I had big plans, and if I wanted to become sheriff one day, this grassroots assistance would go a long way in my campaign. I'd been working toward that goal for years. Almost since the beginning of my career.

I followed Annie and her son and unloaded the mower. Another tissue wipe down later, I was back in my vehicle and heading home. Looked like it was another beer-and-ESPN night.

I maneuvered to the other side of the road to avoid Carla Bosworth, jogging in shorts short enough to disappear in the crack of her ass. She had on a yellow sports bra, and I knew her front was as impressive as her back.

There were no sidewalks on this stretch of town, and the road led past my house, which Carla knew. My disappointment at how predictable the night turned out morphed into irritation. All summer, if I was on duty, she was out for a run. She'd been through two husbands, got the cars and the houses to show for it, and was on patrol for a third.

She looked over her shoulder, her expertly dyed blonde hair swinging in a ponytail. She slowed to a walk, a sultry grin spreading across her face.

Was she wearing lipstick? Wasn't she catching gnats in the stuff?

Walking across the road, she flagged me down. I stifled a groan. My job was to protect and serve. Not sit and flirt. I rolled down the passenger window after making sure the door was firmly locked.

"Heya, Wilder," she purred.

"Evenin', Carla."

She draped an arm on the edge of the window. "Done with work?"

Yes, but I'd rather she didn't know. She was becoming more forward in her flirtations. "Not yet."

Her pout was expert level. "You work too much."

Acid churned in my gut. I was acutely aware of how much I worked and what it'd cost me. "You know me."

She propped her chin in her hand, her brown eyes dancing. "Do I?" She dropped her arm, somehow invading the interior of the car with the door closed. Her floral perfume billowed into the cab, but it registered as wrong in my brain. It wasn't the smell of coconut-pineapple lotion—for a hit of summer every day when our winters were so long.

Fuck. Would there be a day I'd get over *her*?

"I'd like to get to know you," she said playfully.

My phone buzzed again. Her gaze darted around the computer and radio equipment that made up my console, searching for where the sound came from. Taking advantage of the interruption, I eased off the brake. My personal phone had been vibrating with missed texts since I was at the McCormicks', but the newest call was on my work phone. "Duty calls. Have a good night."

She slowly pulled back, like she was doing me a favor. I didn't speed away, but I was tempted. I'd been single for a year and a half. A woman like Carla should be exactly who I was cuffing to my bedpost. My dick nodded, tired as hell of my hand.

I glanced in the rearview. Was I sure I didn't want to interview for husband number three? Yes. I had no desire to be left by another woman, but fuck, my ex had even taken the dog.

My hours weren't stable enough, and if shit went down in the county, I could be gone all night. It had made sense for Oreo to go with *her*.

I was tired of shit making sense.

Was Carla being extra bouncy? Whatever husband paid for her tits wasn't getting to enjoy them.

Hell, maybe he was. Maybe other divorced couples didn't force smiles and make sure to stay on the other side of the room if they happened to occupy the same space.

Frustrated with my lack of interest and my growing pity party, I returned the call from my boss.

"Hey, Ray."

"Wilder." Ray's gruff greeting was full of affection.

He'd been the school resource officer when I was in high school, and he'd taken me under his wing. He cheered me and my siblings on at games, yet understood when we were wild little pricks and redirected us with a stern word and the threat of calling our father, Barnaby Knight.

I would've traded Ray Dahlen for Barns any day.

"You around this weekend?" he asked.

"Yes, sir. I'll be at the ranch, but do you wanna help me tow Emily Miller's car to town? Jeremy stopped me tonight."

"Give me a call when you head out." He perked up. As sheriff, he didn't have much downtime, and when he did, he didn't know what to do with himself. He'd rather be out lending a hand than sitting in his house.

I did a few more laps around town to give Carla time to clear my block before I pulled up in front of my place. The two-story house had been built ten years ago with a front porch and a fenced-in backyard. The grill sat on the back deck, unused for more than a couple of years. The yard was neatly mowed, the bushes in the front precisely trimmed, but the flower beds were empty. A dream home for a family. The big house a young couple had planned to spend the rest of their lives in.

I pinched the bridge of my nose. Coming home was the worst part of my day.

I logged out and let dispatch know I was officially done for the night.

I went into the house and didn't bother with the lights since I'd grab a longneck and sit in front of the TV until I fell asleep. Maybe I'd eat something for dinner. Maybe I'd stand at the fridge and wonder why I never had more than beer. Delilah would bring a pie by tomorrow and claim it was for the trouble. Dealing with her and Guy was no trouble. Depressing, but I was glad to help.

In my bedroom, I dug my phone out of my pocket. Eliot was texting updates. I tossed the phone on the bed, uninterested in hearing about what a good fucking time they were all having.

She'd be there too. A big reason why I didn't pass on the trip in the first place like I should've.

I changed out of my uniform and stayed in my boxer briefs so I wouldn't have to get undressed to get back into my uniform. I wasn't on call tonight, but being asked to help with something like a bar fight wasn't unusual.

I grabbed my phone, got a beer from the kitchen, and sat on the couch with a groan.

Fuck's sake, I wasn't even forty yet.

In a few weeks, I would be.

Another groan escaped. My thirty-ninth birthday had been...exactly like right now. A beer and ESPN, fielding calls and texts from my siblings that were really *How are you?* check-ins.

I looked around the house. I'd taken the pictures off the wall when the ink dried on the divorce papers. Just like I'd left my ring in my sock drawer.

My phone buzzed again. Eliot's name flashed on the screen. I'd expect incessant texts from my brother Austen about what I was missing, but he wasn't able to get leave from the Army. What the hell did Eliot want?

I took a long drink from my beer and read the first message.

ELIOT

You still have time. The street dance goes until 1.

Should I try—

No. Goddammit. I knew what I'd be going for, and I wasn't one for torturing myself beyond the boring nights in front of the TV.

Fucking street dance. It was better I sit my ass on this couch. I didn't need those memories, fuck you very much, and Eliot knew it too.

The next message was a picture. In the middle of the image was Cody looking like the brother I'd grown up with in a black T-shirt, jeans, boots. The wife who'd gotten the stick out of his ass, Tova, was wearing a giant grin and a bright pink dress that highlighted her baby belly. I was about to flick out of the picture when I spotted a couple dancing behind them on the roped-off street.

I set the beer down with a thud and enlarged the image.

Some cowboy asshole I'd never seen before had a delighted grin and was gazing adoringly at his dance partner. The woman was goddamn smiling at Cowboy Asshole while cinched to him. Her dirty-blonde hair was woven into a braid that circled around her head. She was wearing her favorite pair of boots for dancing and a yellow summer dress full of daisies I'd never seen before.

The woman was Sutton Knight. My ex-wife.

I tossed the phone down, the picture still on the screen.

The divorce had been final for months. She was moving on. I should do the same.

I glowered at the image. She was nothing but a speck on the screen, but I suddenly had the eyesight of a bald damn eagle. Her smile. Pink lips with tinted gloss. Legs that used to wrap around my waist.

How's my dog, Sutton?

Oreo was probably living his best life. Sutton was a veterinarian. There was no one better to care for him.

There'd been no one better to be married to. We'd been partners.

And now she was moving on.

Growling, I picked up my phone again. The ache in my chest from earlier returned, turning into a stabbing pain. I might need to call a doctor—or have another beer or five.

I squinted. Was her smile forced? Her hand wasn't draped around Cowboy Asshole's shoulders but flattened. I tipped my head. She wasn't leaning back because they were twirling. She wasn't comfortable being so close to the guy.

Maybe she wasn't moving on.

The phantom pain grew, like Sutton was a missing limb. I could feel her in my arms. The way she molded to me when we danced. Complete trust.

I scanned what little I could see of the crowd. How many other cowboy assholes were waiting in line to dance with the pretty single veterinarian?

The street dance goes until 1.

I looked at the clock for the millionth time today. Crocus Valley, North Dakota, was in a different time zone. They were an hour ahead.

Despite the time difference, there were still hours left of the dance. Hours of men who'd be lined up to dance with the newly available woman in town who had legs strong enough to wrestle a calf and long enough to wrap around a man's waist while he plunged into her. Hours for blue-collar guys with less demanding jobs to woo her and win her over. Hours for her to decide to go home with one of those jackasses.

Fuck.

I had shit to do in the morning.

I read the message again.

> You still have time. The street dance
> goes until 1.

✳

Sutton

I'll take "Is This Night Over Yet" for two hundred.

Street dances used to be one of my favorite nights out. Especially when I attended with friends who were as close as family. Most of them were no longer here tonight, but I didn't leave. My feet hurt in a way they hadn't before, but the ache was better than going home to an empty house. Again.

My best friend and ex-sister-in-law, Aggie Barron, had gone home already with her husband. Her brother Eliot Knight, who was staying with them, had left at the same time, along with Aggie's oldest brother, Cody, and his wife, Tova, who was also a friend. My other good friend, Vienne, was getting swung around to the live band. Her house was only a couple of blocks away, which let her check on her thirteen-year-old daughter often. With Vienne sticking around, I felt moderately less pathetic for being miserable instead of running a bath right now.

Jennings, one of my dance buddies for the night, spun me around. There wasn't enough centrifugal force to push us together, but he used the spin as an excuse to hold me closer.

He tripped over the toes of my boots. "Shit, sorry."

"It's okay." I wasn't the best dancer either. Jennings was admittedly the worst of the partners I'd danced with tonight.

And of course, none of the guys could compare to *him*.

With him, I didn't have to be a good dancer. He did all the work and made it feel effortless to be on the dance floor. Too bad that was the only time it'd been effortless between us.

Except for when it came to sex.

My body jolted. I was thinking of earth-shattering orgasms, but the hold was wrong. The smell of sweat and cheap cologne wasn't right. And the way I was bent almost backward to keep from being flush from chin to toes with Jennings wasn't it.

I sighed.

Jennings stroked his gaze over my face. He leaned close to my ear. I made myself hold still. "Doing okay?"

Survey says...no.

"Yeah." I jutted my chin toward the dark blue clouds visible over the buildings of downtown. "Looks like rain."

Please let it rain soon. The rain would force me to go take that bath.

The song wound down, but Jennings didn't let me go. Vienne appeared at my side and put her hand on my shoulder, her many bracelets falling down to her elbow. She was wearing contacts tonight, her turquoise eyes vivid. It was a wonder Jennings wasn't after her, but all the single men were playing round-robin with the single women tonight. "Hey, I'm heading home."

I broke away from Jennings and gave her a quick hug. "Thanks for staying out with me."

She grinned. "I danced my ass off, and that hasn't happened for a while."

Jennings clasped my hand once again as the first notes of an upbeat country song played. As he tugged me toward him, I gave Vienne a mildly perplexed look. Couldn't he see I was in the middle of talking to my friend?

She sent me a questioning-but-hopeful look that asked if I was into him, but I gave my head a little shake. Her lips turned down. She'd want to rescue me, but I was fine. I'd rather have one night of my weekend be more exciting than finding a project to do around my house.

"See you later." I gave her a wave before planting my hand on Jennings's shoulder to keep some room between us. I didn't want her to feel like she had to stay. She probably wanted to get back to her daughter.

We took a step, and he tangled a boot around mine. "Oops, sorry," he said sheepishly. "I'll do better."

Guilt crushed the annoyance. He really was a nice guy. I didn't want to lead him on, but I hadn't been in the position to give a guy the wrong idea in a long time.

I was out of my element—with men and street dances.

I was ruined.

No. I wasn't. I was a single woman with her life ahead of her. Life-altering orgasms were not relegated to my past.

But I doubted they were in a future with Jennings.

I mentally let out a long sigh. Jennings could be a stud in bed for all I knew. I was trying to piece myself back together, but I couldn't tell if I was still broken or if it was just that my available choices would never measure up. There was more to a solid relationship than amazing sex. If I didn't know that, I would still be married.

The song wrapped up, and another started. I struggled to identify the original singer to take my mind off the decision between staying to dance with men who gave me bruised toenails or going home to an empty house. Was this a cover of one of the Lukes' songs? Dierks Bentley? Who were the new guys these days?

Jennings's hold only loosened a little. "Would you like to dance again?"

He was so dang polite and not as handsy as others I'd spun around with tonight. But the lure of the bathtub was strong. My feet hurt, and I missed...*him*. Yet there were too many memories of going home after a street dance and burning up the sheets. A faint throb started between my thighs. I wasn't going home like this. I'd burn off the energy.

Before I could answer, a man wove out of the dwindling crowd from our right. My desire was still kicked up. The disconnect between my mind and body made my vision go haywire. The height. The broad shoulders. No. He wasn't who I thought he was. I'd danced with that guy earlier tonight. His expression was intent, and his gaze was lasered on Jennings. I was turned on, but not for the man whose clammy grip held mine. Nor was it for the man approaching us.

A strong hand stroked along my back, and I cut off a deep sigh before it slipped out. A large shadow blocked out the lights around the stage.

"I'm cutting in," the new arrival said in a voice that lit up my body better than a spotlight.

My gaze snapped up. Was the confusion clouding all

of my brain? The tall, frowning man with his strong hand on me was an illusion. A painfully familiar one I drank in. "Wilder?"

My heart rate slowed, doing its version of a slow clap. My brain stopped working. My hormones yelled, *Survey says, this is the guy!*"

How could he just appear?

Was I so miserable I was hallucinating?

Was there a guy in Crocus Valley who looked like Wilder Knight? A man with the same strong jaw, dark scruff that defied daily shaving, and flashing brown eyes? Another Wilder who would appear discontent and annoyed that I was in another man's arms?

No. This was my Wilder. Except he was no longer mine.

Behind my ex-husband's shoulder, the guy who'd planned to cut in flattened his lips and shook his head before he changed directions.

"Where'd you come from?" I clung to Jennings like he was my life preserver.

The beat between my legs did not match the song. It matched the man I was looking at.

"Just got here." Wilder not-so-subtly muscled Jennings out of the way until the poor guy stumbled back, an aggravated twist to his mouth. The tempo of the song increased, and Wilder hooked an arm around my waist, tugged me close, took my hand in his solid, roughly calloused grip, and spun me around.

A full-body wave of relief hit me. I flattened my hand on his warm, broad back and let him take charge. The last few minutes left me mentally drained, and I needed a moment to figure out what was going on. His heat seeped through the white button-up shirt he wore, accented with two different shades of brown. One of his good shirts. He had a cowboy hat tucked low on his head, giving me partial cover because I was that damn close to him.

How was he here? He'd missed his niece and nephew's performance. The street dance would either be over soon or rained out.

He'd missed a special occasion. Like usual.

"What are you doing?" I furiously whispered. "You missed the recital."

"I know." A muscle in his rigid jaw flexed. A dark dusting of stubble traced his jaw. I knew what those tiny dark hairs felt like when he ran his chin across my neck or up my thigh.

A shiver traced down my spine, stopping where his arm was banded around me.

He spun me around the roped-off dance area like he owned me.

Once upon a time, he did. But he'd picked his career over me. Every time.

"I was dancing with Jennings." I summoned as much irritation as I could. The claim was supposed to cement the fact that I was a single woman who didn't answer to him, but my hand clutched his, begging him not to let me go.

"You were tripping over Jennings," he growled.

The way he expertly maneuvered me around, spinning and two-stepping, I didn't have to think. He did all the work. All the thinking. In the process, he made me feel cherished, which only stoked how upset I was. These moments were often fleeting. "It's none of your business."

"Nope," he said and didn't elaborate.

I didn't like arguing with him, but I could've used it.

Energy was zinging under my skin. Excitement. Anticipation. For what? I learned with Wilder, those emotions led to a whole lot of nothing.

Unless it came to sex.

The song died down, but he didn't stop moving with me. The guy who intended to cut between me and Jennings approached again, but Wilder shot him a dark look and gave him one curt shake of his head.

The audacity.

The stark relief that I wouldn't have to be pressed against anyone but Wilder again.

I needed to go. I liked this too much, and this man had already broken my heart. I stiffened. Wilder didn't let up. He kept moving us as the bass player nailed down a beat. Dammit, I let him. I was emotionally drained and running on autopilot.

"Hey, folks." The band leader spoke, his hand flat on the guitar strings. "It's looking like rain, and it's looking fiercer than what our little canopy can protect us from. We're going to turn into DJs and keep playing you some music while we pack up our equipment."

A country ballad blasted out of the speakers. Wilder slowed down but kept me pressed close to him.

"Why'd you come? Don't you have work?" I asked bitterly, trying to keep up the resentment when all I could concentrate on was his strong body.

"Not until tomorrow."

"You didn't answer the first question."

That muscle flexed in the corner of his jaw, but he gazed down at me with those fathomless brown eyes I'd gotten lost in too many times to count. He steered us around another couple. I wasn't aware other people were still dancing.

"You answer one first," he said.

"What?"

He brushed that intense gaze over my face, dipping down to the hint of cleavage showing through the top of my dress. "How you been?"

I basked in his question as much as I loathed it. I worked my jaw back and forth. "Fine."

"Really?"

"That's two questions."

"You asked four," he pointed out.

"And you only answered two."

"Three, technically." The corner of his mouth twitched. I was supposed to be mad at him, dang it. I wanted to lick those almost-smiling lips. "So I'm owed one more real answer. How are you doing?"

I caught myself before putting my head on that solid ball of muscle capping his shoulder. For such a strong man, he was a good cuddler. The few times he'd been around to cuddle. "I'm fine. My business is growing. I'm making friends."

He cocked a brow. A spark of worry was in his eyes. I let him think some of those friends were guys. I was friendly with some men I'd met, but Aggie, Tova, and Vienne were who I meant. They were my lifeline.

"So, why'd you come?" I asked again.

He scanned the dissipating crowd. A raindrop plopped into my hair. I blinked up, but there were no more drops.

"Eliot texted me."

"Okay?" He still didn't reply, and I kept pushing. I wasn't even sure why I needed to hear the answer. "Everyone's home already. You had to know you wouldn't get here until close to midnight." What time was it anyway?

"I knew it'd be late."

His stilted answers were aggravating. "Spill it, Wilder."

I was in the tractor beam of his dark gaze. "He sent a pic. I saw you dancing."

I went rigid, but that didn't stop him from handling me like a well-behaved filly. "You came here to cockblock me."

Fire lit his eyes more than the lights getting dismantled around the stage. His gaze dropped to my lips. "No."

Another raindrop hit my cheek, cooling the growing heat of my anger.

I knew when he was lying. He rarely did, and it was usually over stupid shit, like forgetting to take the garbage out. He'd play it off like the garbage guy came earlier than usual, when really, he forgot. And each time he was in the middle of his claim, his gaze would drop to my cheek or my mouth. Like he couldn't quite look me in the eye.

"You got jealous," I said. Incensed, I gawked at him, also hating the thrill coursing through me. "And you came to make sure I didn't go home with anyone."

"You want to fuck Jennings?" he asked, point-blank, like I was a teen, and he was asking me if the beer was mine.

"Remember when I said it was none of your business?" I asked sweetly, blinking against the rapidly increasing rain.

His shirt was turning translucent where rain was soaking the material. "He's not your type."

"You don't know what my type is." *He* was my type. My only type. I was trying to broaden my horizons, but the effort was pathetic.

"I know when you're grimacing because your dance partner sucks."

"I'm not a good dancer."

He snorted. "Neither was that guy."

His attitude infuriated me. He couldn't be bothered to make it to Crocus Valley in time to see his family perform, but he could come interfere with my life?

"I can't believe you." I pushed away from him. Blinking rapidly, I was grateful the rain would mask the tears gathering in my eyes. Why did my ex-husband have to be so hard to get over?

And while I was at it—why'd he have to be so good-looking? Why'd he have to move the way he had sex—in perfect rhythm, knowing exactly what I needed? And why did his dick have to be so big?

I stomped away.

"Sutton." Wilder grabbed my arm, but I flung him off. His boots hit the pavement hard behind me. Good thing he'd snuck up on me. I'd have a harder time walking away if I'd seen him stalking toward me and Jennings in all his rugged country-boy glory. He was in cowboy boots and jeans. The things denim did to his ass should be illegal. They should come with a warning: hormonal disruption imminent.

But then, my hormones were already disrupted. Or I'd have little Wilders running around, and I would've been tied to Buffalo Gully forever.

He caught up with me, lightly touching my elbow, a flash of electricity pulsating between us. "Come on, Sutton."

"Excuse me, sir." Jennings was a few yards away, his concerned gaze on me. "The lady—"

"Can take care of herself," Wilder snapped.

My belly flipped. Wilder knew how much I hated when manly men stepped in thinking the little lady vet needed a hand with the big ol' animal. This wasn't the same scenario, and I appreciated Jennings watching out for me, but I couldn't deny how well Wilder knew me.

"It's fine." I kept stomping in the direction of my truck. A light curtain of rain fell between us and where Jennings was standing. "He'll eventually vote himself out of the game and give up. He always does."

Sympathy crept into Jennings's gaze, and he gave me a nod. He walked away.

"Low blow," Wilder said under his breath.

"Accurate, though."

"I'm not the one who left."

The reminder was a serrated blade right to the left aorta. I knew why I left. Didn't mean I had wanted to.

The rain turned into a downpour, dousing my indignation. I choked on a gasp, sputtering at the sudden deluge. I pushed my hair out of my eyes, looking for my pickup.

"Here." Wilder wrapped an arm around me and pulled me halfway down the block. We splashed over the sidewalk. When we reached his pickup, he yanked the back door open and shoved me inside.

I accepted the refuge *only* because the rain was so strong. I thought he'd get in the front passenger side, since going around to the driver's side would only soak him, but he pushed inside next to me.

I scrambled across the back seat. His big, warm body was tempting no matter how wet he was. Wasn't he going to give me a ride to my pickup?

He turned to knock water off his cowboy hat outside the cab, then shut us in and tossed his hat onto the front seat. The smoky-whiskey-with-hints-of-vanilla smell of him clogged the cabin.

I groaned, not looking forward to a soggy mad dash to my vehicle but also knowing being locked in the pickup with Wilder wasn't good for my determination to move on after the divorce. "This rain needs to let up."

He twisted to face me, so close the heat radiating off him wrapped around me. "Got somewhere to be?"

"Get this—not with you."

"Sutton, goddammit. I came to—"

"Exactly, Wilder. We're divor—"

He smashed his mouth onto mine. I froze, but only for a moment. Maybe it was the chill of being soaked from the rain. Or the spike of lust I had coincidentally just as Wilder showed up. Or the emptiness that had haunted every corner of me since I walked out on him.

Regardless of the reason, Wilder was an excellent kisser, and his mouth became my only sustenance. I twined my arms around his neck and greedily licked between his lips. The familiar salty dill flavor from his favorite sunflower seeds hit my taste buds. I drank him in, and he met my tongue stroke for stroke.

He leaned me back, his blistering hands brushing up the hem of my dress.

Nothing had ever felt so right. It'd been too damn long since I'd had a non-self-performed orgasm. It'd been just as long since I'd been in Wilder's competent, strong embrace, and I didn't want to leave.

I widened my legs. He was half hanging off the seat, his long length cramped in the back, but he still cradled perfectly between my thighs.

He reached between us and rimmed his fingers

around the edge of my underwear. "You're wet for me, Sutton," he murmured against my lips.

I was wet all over, but he wasn't talking about the rain. I whimpered my reply and rolled my hips into his hand. The roughened tips of his fingers skimmed over my pussy, and I moaned. He was so close to my clit, and I was millimeters away from sheer ecstasy.

There should have been more alarm bells going off in my head, but Wilder overrode them all. His fingers were a breath away from being in me. I didn't care. The rain pounded the outside of the pickup, enshrouding the cabin in privacy.

He dragged a finger through my wetness. "So fucking wet," he groaned.

When the tip of his finger hit my clit, I bucked off the seat and into him.

"Do I drive you wild, Doc?"

The nickname alone, a remnant of when we first met, should have flown the reddest flag I had, but it was a balm to my ears. "You know you do, cowboy."

He gave an approving growl and rolled the tip of his thumb over my clit. "You gonna come loud?"

"Yes." I hitched my knees up, propping a boot heel on the back of the front seat.

He circled my swollen nub, and I panted against his lips.

He kissed his way to my neck. The sandpaper stubble on his jaw had a direct tie to where he was touching my clit.

"I need to be buried deep in that pretty pink pussy of yours." He dragged one side of my underwear down a leg. I bent a knee enough to get the scrap of lace over a boot, and somehow the fabric didn't rip.

My heartbeat thrummed through my entire body. Awareness tapped at the edge of my consciousness, but I batted reality away. I wanted to feel good for once in a long time.

He unzipped his pants and barely a second later the thick, blunt head of his cock prodded my entrance. "You need this." He wasn't asking. Wilder never had to ask. He'd always known my body better than I did.

The alarm bell in my head rang hard, but dammit, I ignored it. I needed to be filled by Wilder one more time. "Get inside me."

Lust swamped his face, and he thrust. I cried out. Fullness and pure pleasure. *Yesss*. Finally.

I felt whole for the first time in a year and a half. I concentrated on this moment. Any thought of the past or the future would only make me question how badly I fucked up.

Two

WILDER

I was home. Fucking finally.

Her body gripped me tight, demanding and greedy. She embraced my shoulders, and I pumped away. I knew everything about her body. The way her walls rippled around me—she was close to coming. I hadn't done more than tease her clit, but with how she was folded in the back seat and the scant amount of leverage room I had, her swollen little clit got the perfect amount of friction with each thrust.

Still, I wasn't going to last long, and I sure as hell wasn't leaving her hanging. I put the whiskers on my jaw to good use and skimmed along her neck. The rough groan that left her nearly made me climax.

"You gonna come hard, baby?" I growled in her ear, knowing damn well my hot breath would tickle her and send electricity right to where we were connected.

"So hard," she moaned.

Changing my angle should've been impossible, but I dug my hands into the bare cheeks of her ass and tilted her.

She barked out a cry. "Oh god."

Fucking music to my goddamn ears. "That's it, Sutton."

"Oh god, oh god, oh god," she chanted just moments before she arched, her hard nipples pushing into my chest, our wet shirts highlighting every scrap of our bodies. "*Wilder*."

Her pussy convulsed around my cock, crushing my last restraint. To keep from ramming her head into the window, I braced myself against the driver's seat and the headrest of the back seat. And I exploded.

Squeezing my eyes shut, I gave in to the most shattering climax I could remember. Her body took it all and demanded more, and I was so damn willing to give it to her. This was it. Everything I'd been missing for months. Since she'd walked out. I wouldn't think about the repercussions. I only wanted to bask in the moment. To feel the relief at long last.

When the peak of our orgasms were behind us, I pried my eyes open. Sutton was blinking and swallowing air like I'd suffocated her. She skimmed her gaze over her hands fisting my shirt and then down to where I was still buried inside of her.

"Oh my god. Oh, shit." Her words were colder than the rain that'd doused us.

I didn't pull out. I needed to know what I did before I fucked up more. "What?"

"We didn't use protection."

Pregnancy had been as elusive as the "'til death do us part" portion of our vows. The other concern sunk in, wiping out the cozy afterglow I should've been basking in. The emptiness inside me yawned open again. "You've been with others?"

She slapped my chest, her mouth set in a mutinous line. "No."

Thank fucking Christ. Relief brought the chill of the rain back, but I shared the heat of her warm body. I could've laughed when I realized what she was worried about. "Then you don't have to worry."

"What do you mean?"

I gently pulled out, but as I wedged back to tuck my still-hard dick into my jeans, I spotted her underwear. She'd taken every article of clothing with her, and my house had nothing of her in it. I finished pulling her lace panties off.

"What are you doing?" She drew her knees to her chest and adjusted her dress to sit on since I possessed her underwear and had no plans to give them back.

I didn't answer the latter question but stuffed the garment into my pocket and zipped myself in. The cab of the pickup was fogged, the musky scent of sex filled the air, and I was hungry for more, but the rain was letting up.

The heavens had opened up long enough to give me the perfect window to fuck my wife.

My ex-wife.

Who'd walked out on me.

The complicated mass of emotions pushing against my sternum could wait. I had to straighten out her thinking. "I haven't been with anyone since you, Sutton."

She studied me for a moment, her eyes full of doubt, then surprise. "Oh."

That was it? Eighteen months since she served me

divorce papers, and all I got was an *Oh*. Instead of letting the ever-present bitterness rise up, I'd hang on to her admission that she hadn't had sex since then either. "We both needed this."

She scowled and peered out the windshield. The fog on the glass let in the shine of the streetlights but continued to seclude us. The shadows settled under her eyes and in the wisps of her fine hair that had broken free from her braid during our frantic fucking. "It was a mistake."

I grunted at the verbal potshot. Sex with me was a mistake. Wasn't that hard on the ego?

She caught my expression, a spark of sympathy in her eyes. "It complicates things."

Irritation clawed the back of my neck. "What things? That you and I like to have sex—together? We're divorced. I hardly see you or talk to you. We're civil at family gatherings. We fucked, and we liked it. There's nothing wrong admitting it, and it doesn't have to change things." Having sex couldn't drive her further away from me.

She dropped her gaze to her hands. How long had it been since we talked so closely? So intimately? Before our marriage ended, I would be putting away my sidearm and my gear while she chatted with me after my shift. Then I'd catch up with her when she was leaving for work, or, since she'd been tied to the ranch as the Knight's Arabians and Cattle Company veterinarian, I'd talk with her if I was also there helping Eliot.

That was when we couldn't avoid hashing over the same troubles again and again.

"And at the next family gathering, what are we

supposed to do?" she asked quietly. "Pretend this never happened?"

"We'll act like we always do. You know I won't blow up a party because you won't talk to me."

She lifted that gray gaze to meet mine. "I know, Wilder. You're all about family obligations."

I blew out a hard breath. And we were back to old arguments. If it wasn't for my family's trust binding me to the ranch, it'd be my deputy job. We signed papers that ended those arguments. What happened didn't have to be more, right? We were exes, but we were fire in bed. We weren't seeing anyone else. The idea got brighter the more I thought about it. "Maybe it can be only about sex."

Sutton feathered her hands over the skirt of her dress and pulled her lower lip between her teeth. Hope, the fickle beast, rose inside my chest. She wasn't saying no, and that little furrow in her brow said she was considering what I said.

"What do you mean?"

I put it as bluntly as possible. "We're not fucking around, but we both like fucking. So let's fuck."

Her eyes widened, and yeah, I couldn't believe what I suggested either. But the anticipation mingling with the evaporating rain on my clothing left me cool and calm in a way I hadn't been for a long while. What would I do to keep having sex with Sutton?

A whole fucking lot after that orgasm.

"We can't—"

"Why not?" I leaned toward her, twisting like I was going to crawl over that lithe body again. I could, she wasn't pulling away, but I didn't need Crocus Valley's finest knocking on my window. I'd busted enough car sex in my life to know how much fun law enforcement had with the task. I wasn't going to be the literal butt of the local police department's jokes. "Are you dating anyone?"

She shook her head, disbelief swimming in her eyes.

"Then let's...keep doing this." A thought sparked in my head, and my dick thought it was a *great* idea. "I'll follow you to your place and spend the night."

"I'm guessing you have an evening shift tomorrow?"

I nodded, the spark of hope dimming. Her sardonic tone wasn't encouraging.

"You work on the ranch before you have an evening shift," she said flatly. "Don't you need to get back?"

"I'll leave in the morning. Eliot said he wouldn't get back until the afternoon." He'd return before noon. That was Eliot. I'd figure out when to get the towing favor done. As long as I didn't cross paths with Eliot on the way to Buffalo Gully, no one would know I'd been here.

"Wilder, we can't..." In the faint glow of the street-lights, her flush was visible. That magnificent mind of hers was policing our situation.

"We're adults."

She shook her head. "Your family has been extremely supportive. What would they think?"

My family would be upset with me. They'd think I was leading her on when she was the one who'd left a giant boot print on my heart when she walked out on me.

I stuffed the resentment down. I'd lived in enough regret. I was working on a few non-self-inflicted orgasms now. "They don't have to know."

She cocked a brow. "You want to sneak around and have sex?"

"Why not? If you meet someone you want to date, then we stop."

She drew back. "Just like that?"

I wouldn't be sleeping around in Buffalo Gully. I'd overheard myself compared to my dad enough after Sutton left. Being likened to Barnaby Knight wasn't a compliment. *Inevitable. The man is a lot like his dad, and that girl knew it. Good thing she got out before they had kids.*

The familiar blister on my heart burned. The kids part hadn't been intentional, and I hated to think that Sutton's monthly disappointment was fate protecting her from me inevitably breaking her heart.

Secrecy would be paramount. I was close to getting some relief from utter loneliness, but I didn't want to open the doors to speculation, critiques, or comments. I didn't care to fall short in my family's eyes or in the opinion of the public I worked with every day. I couldn't have everyone speculating about Sutton. After she left Buffalo Gully, I'd walk into the gas station or grocery store and talking would stop. Then there were the comments from well-meaning people.

She's not from around here. She doesn't get our way of life. That was from Ray as if his comments made me feel better.

Good thing it happened now and not when you run for sheriff. That from my coworker Rusty Kaplan. He could be a real dick.

And then there were the random comments in the bar. *She didn't fit in here.* Or *she was so quiet*—not said in a speculative way, more like Sutton's introverted personality was a fault. Or the one I really hated, often said by single women trying to chat with me and Eliot when we were out—*You deserve better.*

I was tired of my family and my personal life being a subject of conversation. An arrangement with Sutton was something I wanted for myself that no one else could intrude on.

"We would stop if we met someone else?" she reiterated.

"Just like that," I said, repeating her earlier words. "And only between the two of us."

She scrubbed her hands over her face. "No. It's crazy. *No*," she said again like she was trying to convince herself. "It's not healthy. We can't be fuck buddies. I can't lie to your sister."

I smothered my disappointment. My sister, Aggie, was Sutton's best friend, and they grew closer each year. Then Sutton had relocated to Crocus Valley, where they could see each other all the time.

"You don't have to lie. Just don't tell her."

"I can't. It's not right." She patted along the door looking for the handle.

It was worth a try.

Yet, after being in her heat, having her come around me, this parting was so much more than a *sorry it's not going to work*. It was the finale. The end. The empty hole inside me from when she left yawned somehow emptier. But I wasn't going to let her do a walk of shame from my pickup to hers in the dark.

"Sit." I opened my door. "It's still raining. I'll drive you to your truck."

Her sigh followed me as I hopped out and closed the door. I jogged around the back of my pickup to get behind the wheel. The street was quiet. I spotted Sutton's Chevy pickup parked two blocks ahead.

Sutton scooted to the side I'd been sitting on. The door would be closer to her ride when I stopped, but the decreased proximity from me was likely the selling point.

I pulled up next to her pickup and propped my left arm across the steering wheel so I could watch her climb out. Might as well get one last look if this thing between us was really over.

The smoldering burn was back in my chest and spreading to my stomach. "See ya, Sutton."

She got out and turned back in the open doorway. "I'm sorry, Wilder."

"No problem. I didn't mean to pressure you." I should've left it at that. I didn't want to coerce her, and I meant it. But desperate men did shitty things, and I was pulling my ace. "Probably time I take Carla Bosworth up on her offer and move on anyway."

Sutton hated Carla and the way the other woman hit on married men and could insult a person ten different ways in one compliment.

She stiffened. Her sharp intake of breath was audible, and I bit back a grin. She slid her gaze away to glower into the distance. When she gave me her attention, determination shone in her dark eyes. "I'll open the garage door for you. Leave before anyone knows you were in town."

"Yes, ma'am."

Three

SUTTON

A ding woke me. Was that from a dream?

I was pressed against a warm chest, and the smell of vanilla-laced smoky whiskey was in my nose. How long had it been since I'd woken up and all was right in the world? I wasn't emotionally lost or doubting my life's decisions. I was warm and cozy and could stay this way for years.

I breathed out a relieved sigh. The divorce was all a dream.

Another chime was followed by knocking. The events from the night before crashed into my brain. The dance. Wilder's arrival. The rainstorm. Blistering heat in a cramped pickup cab.

I flipped over with a startled gasp. Oh, shit. I wasn't dreaming. I was divorced, and my ex-husband was in my bed.

We'd had sex all night.

All. Damn. Night.

So many orgasms.

I glanced down. I rarely slept naked, but I was completely nude. The underwear I wore last night was still in Wilder's pocket, and I shouldn't delight over how seeing him abscond with it made me feel sexy.

His clothing mixed with mine on the floor. Which meant he was also naked.

Just a peek—

More knocking. Dammit! Who was ruining my morning?

Oreo wasn't barking, so he must know the visitor.

"Shit, shit, shit." I pushed out of bed, my pulse racing.

Wilder lazily rolled to his elbow and squinted at me rushing around the bedroom trying to find clothing that didn't look like I brought a forbidden guy home and had wild sex all night.

"Who's pounding this early?" His sleep-roughened voice wasn't any less sexy than when we were married.

A "Sutton" came from the direction of the front door. His eyes flared.

Yeah. It was Aggie. His sister. We had plans today.

"Be right there," I called. I found a robe and slung it around myself. "It's not that early. You were supposed to get up and leave a couple hours ago," I whisper-yelled.

He peered around. "What time is it?"

I didn't have a clock in my room. I waved my phone around. It was after ten.

When was the last time I'd slept until ten in the morning? It'd been even longer since I'd done it with Wilder.

"Shit," he grunted. "I didn't think to set an alarm."

I rushed to the hallway and spun to close the door. "Stay here and don't you dare breathe a word. She can't see you or hear you."

He only cocked a dark brow as I shut him in my bedroom.

I mentally reassured myself as I scurried to answer my front door. His pickup was in the garage. His clothing and boots were on the bedroom floor. We had come inside, gone to the bedroom, and got right down to business. I hadn't wished to rehash whether this thing between us was the biggest mistake of my life, and I doubted he wanted to take the chance either.

Fucking Carla Bosworth.

I opened the door with a sunny grin, blinking at the onslaught of summer morning light. "Oh my gosh. I'm sorry—I slept in."

Oreo tried to rush past me, but I blocked the German short-haired pointer. Then blocked him again. I had to hold on to his collar, or he'd run right down the hallway and stand point when he smelled Wilder was here. Oreo had been sleeping in the small shed that was more a giant dog house I got with the land when I had pulled in last night. My healing heart couldn't take seeing a reunion between him and Wilder today.

A tiny whine snuck out of him as it was. He was sniffing every square inch of me his brown nose could reach.

"Are you feeling okay? Do you need to cancel?" The worry on Aggie's face didn't dissipate. Her hair was pulled back in a clip that let the ends spray out in a fluffy bouffant. She had on a billowy, blush-colored blouse and beige linen shorts with sandals. The clothing wasn't her farm wear.

Residents in Crocus Valley and nearby small towns were having rummage sales this weekend, and local businesses were in on it. Aggie and I were going to hit up some sales and partake in the coffee shop samples and restaurant deals. Aggie had offered to pick me up.

Her goals were to find balls for the horses, old rugs and blankets for her rescue cats and dogs, and any supplies that she could put to use without having to spend money on brand-new equipment that'd get covered in animal poop or chewed apart.

I wasn't missing a day with her because I let an ex-husband hijack my body for several pleasure-filled hours. "No, I'm not canceling, but I need to get ready."

Aggie waited, expectant. I was frozen, wondering if I should invite her in or would that be too risky?

She narrowed her eyes. "Are you sure you're okay?" She waved at my neck. "Did you hurt yourself?"

"No." Damn Wilder and his epic scruff. The guy knew how to use it. "It started pouring in the middle of the street dance, and I think I scraped myself when I ran to my pickup."

She nodded, buying my story completely. Guilt heated the back of my neck. She was my first real friend, and I was lying to her.

I was stuck now, hiding what I was doing. My skin grew itchy like I was allergic to lying to my best friend.

"Come in. I'll get dressed." Anxiety fired a furnace in my stomach, but I couldn't make her wait outside because I had her brother in my bedroom. When she was inside, I managed to shut the door without letting Oreo slip past me. He wasn't a house dog, but he smelled Wilder and wouldn't care.

"Mind if I grab some water?" she asked. "Nursing has made me a thirsty bird lately."

"Help yourself." Even better if she made noise in the kitchen.

"Is Berry hiding?"

My new but old cat. The gray tabby had been dropped off at my clinic to euthanize. Her owner had to move and didn't want to bring a high-maintenance cat with her. Berry wasn't high maintenance, but the long-haired cat needed regular grooming and had been a matted mess when she was dropped off. The owner had only stayed long enough to tell me Berry was twelve, had been an indoor cat most of her life, and hid most days from the new rambunctious kitten the person had gotten.

So, Berry got a shave and came to live with me. "She probably hid as soon as the doorbell rang."

I slipped into the bedroom, my heart racing. Wilder was dressed and sitting on the edge of the bed, his elbows propped on his knees. Heat kindled in my belly, hoping for another night of intense pleasure.

His sister was in my house and clueless. This was so messed up.

I leaned against the door and closed my eyes. "She's in the kitchen," I whispered. "You can leave after we do, but wait a few moments until we're out of sight."

I opened my eyes to find his neutral gaze on me. He ducked his head to let me know he understood. He wasn't one to panic, and I appreciated his mellowness at the moment.

"Okay." I glanced around the room. He'd also picked up my dress and bra and put them in the hamper.

He'd always been fastidious. The house had been

clean and orderly—and even emptier when he wasn't home. I bit the inside of my cheek. I had no business asking him for more, but I hadn't woken up early enough to get everything done. "If I feed Berry—"

He looked at me like *Who?*

Right. Berry was mine. She hadn't been ours at one time. "My new cat. She's probably hiding. Can you feed Sylvester?"

He nodded like it was no issue. I'd gotten my bearded dragon, Sylvester, after I finished vet school, but he'd been my pet. I'd caught Wilder murmuring to him once about how his food would make good bait, but otherwise, Wilder had left the reptile care to me. Yet, he was willing to do animal chores after I hid him in my bedroom and told him to leave.

Wasn't that his thing? To always be of assistance? That was an old issue, and we were in new territory today.

"I'll feed and water Oreo, but you might want to see him before you go." I ran my bottom lip through my teeth. "He sniffed you on me." My cheeks blazed. I had to smell from head to toe of Wilder.

His gaze heated, but there was a beat of loss in his amber irises. "Sure," he said quietly.

"Okay," I said again, darting for the bathroom. I rushed through brushing my teeth, combing out my hair and throwing it up in a messy bun, and giving my face a quick scrub.

Did I notice my face glowed? That the line forming between my brows was gone? That I was pleased to see beard burn? Or that my eyes shone and all the creases I thought I had gathered through the divorce had somehow been fucked away?

No. I refused to.

In the bedroom, Wilder hadn't moved. His hot gaze branded my skin as he clocked me moving around, finding jean shorts and a loose, pink Sutton's Animal Care shirt I had designed in the name of branding for my new vet clinic. I stuffed my feet into beaded sandals so I could match Aggie's summery vibe a little better.

I checked the mirror to make sure I didn't have a sign above my head that said *I had sex allll night.*

Wilder stood and crossed to me. My pulse jumped all over the place. I wanted to run out the door as much as I wanted to sprint toward him. He put a hand on my hip and claimed my mouth. I let out a squeak, unprepared for a minty make-out session when his sister was on the other side of the door. He must've snuck into my bathroom and stealthily cleaned up.

His prowess had always turned me on.

"It's gonna be hot out today," Aggie called from the front of the house.

Did the little sister interfering with naughty times never expire? She used to catch me and Wilder making out around their family ranch all the time.

I broke the kiss, keeping Wilder's fevered gaze as Aggie's voice drifted into the bedroom. "We should plan an ice cream stop."

"Sure," I called and tried to step away, but I was caught in his strong hold.

He put his mouth next to my ear. Shivers zinged down my spine. "When are we doing this again?"

Never, the logical part of my brain unhelpfully answered. The word didn't reach my lips. "I don't know."

"I have next weekend off," he murmured. "I'll come down after my shift Friday."

I nodded, not trusting myself enough to speak quietly. Did I have plans for Friday?

I wouldn't. Not between the hours of ten p.m. and eight a.m. "I have clinic hours Saturday morning."

"I'll be gone by then."

"The, uh, code for the garage door is..." I knew it had been a bad idea. I screwed up my face. "Your birthday." Which was in two weeks.

His expression turned solemn. "*My* birthday?" he whispered.

"No one would expect me to use it." I'd almost done our anniversary, but I didn't need the constant reminder that the date was now an ordinary day.

Sadness dimmed his expression. "Friday, then."

I nodded, brushing my gaze over his lips. He was so close. But I'd kept Aggie waiting long enough. I snatched the excuse to put a pause on thinking about me and Wilder. I left the bedroom, closing the door behind me.

Aggie came out of the kitchen and smiled. "Ready to find some used shit for my animals to destroy?"

"I'm ready."

And all day, I'd try not to think about how I'd have to pretend I'm not sneaking around with my best friend's brother, who's also my ex-husband.

✳

Wilder

I hid from my sister until well after she and Sutton pulled away. I left the bedroom and got a look at her house in the light.

This was where she called home now?

I'd driven past her house once last fall after Cody told me she'd bought a place, and he and Aggie and Ansen had helped her move in.

The home was smaller than our—*my*—house in Buffalo Gully. An older farmhouse, but built within the last sixty years, white with black shutters, small concrete steps with a landing that wasn't much wider than the door. The only back door was through the garage.

I found Sylvester in a bedroom tucked by the guest bathroom. Were there a third and fourth bedroom upstairs? Had she converted a space to an office? Since she had a nice, new vet clinic, she probably didn't need one.

Not knowing bothered me.

This whole house was a strange place I'd never been in before.

I faced the bearded dragon that was perched on his branch like usual. "Hey, old man."

Was it weird I missed feeding him? Sutton had Sylvester before we met, and I was the pinch-feeder. Handling mealworms and crickets wasn't high on my list of shit I wanted to do, but I'd done it so Sutton could rest easy if she was tied up at the ranch during his feeding time.

He didn't move when the crickets started hopping around. This was the time I typically vanished, but I lingered by his large cage. He didn't move. I didn't move.

Was I going to tell him about the mess inside my head? Confess to how last night was the first time I saw the world in color after months of gray? Tell him that I wasn't sure what hole I'd bury myself in if Sutton told me our arrangement didn't work for her because she met someone?

Fuck's sake. "Take care, old man."

I pushed a hand through my hair and carried my boots with me through the living room. Pictures of our nieces, Ivy and Ro, and our nephew, Grayson, hung on the walls next to photos of Sutton's niece, Petra. Would Petra still be considered my niece? We'd never visited Sutton's family. Her sister was a world-class figure skater and was always on the road or in another country for some training camp. The same went for Petra. By the time I met Sutton, her niece had been old enough to dive into training and competition.

Drawings of princesses were hung next to Ivy. The tiny handprints must be Ro's.

She'd taken a risk divorcing me. My family had become her family, and they'd stayed her family. She was still an aunt to my nieces and nephew. If anything, my family had been harder on me through the divorce. It'd been obvious to everyone but me how badly I'd let her down.

I glanced around the rest of the room. A couch with haphazardly piled blankets and throw pillows was placed in a corner. A recliner and a couple of end tables completed the cozy vibe.

A soft chuckle left me. Forget the office. All of her periodicals, various other papers, and a scattering of notes littered her coffee table. Sutton wasn't a slob, but the living room was clearly where she spent a lot of her time when she wasn't at the clinic.

Longing tugged at my heart. I couldn't give in to my emotions. I had an arrangement with her that suited both of us. I went into the kitchen. My stomach rumbled, reminding me I hadn't eaten after work last night, and I'd had a strenuous several hours.

I'd love to feast on my wife again.

Ex. Wife.

The weight on my chest was back. What the fuck was wrong with me? I could do this. Sleep with Sutton and get on with my life. I trailed my fingers over the crack in the counter by the fridge that held more kids' artwork and pictures of a now-teen Petra in a shimmery yellow competition costume and pristine white figure skates.

Sutton hadn't moved on with another man, but she'd gone on with her life.

I hadn't done the same.

Maybe I should sell the house. Let some other person find happiness within the walls.

I could get a fixer-upper. A project house.

And when would you fix it up, fucker?

My mood dived, and I stuffed my feet into my boots and went into the garage. The second bay was full of kennels of all shapes and sizes, and boxes of supplies for when she went out on a call from home.

Not my business.

I hit the button to open the garage door. Sutton had parked behind the other bay last night, leaving space for me to get the hell out.

"Oreo!" I called.

Several seconds went by, then a skittering of claws on concrete was heard. Laughter sputtered out of me as the brown-and-white dog barreled into me. He jumped to lick and sniff me. We'd trained him not to jump on people, but he forgot his manners, and I didn't fucking care.

Oreo danced on his hind feet and attempted to take the first two layers of skin off my face with his tongue. "Down, boy," I said, still laughing.

It took a couple of times before he lowered to all fours. His hind end wiggled as he circled at my feet, happily panting. I gave him pets and scratches, and goddammit, I hugged him.

"I miss you."

His tongue lolled out, and he watched me like he was listening. I used to get greeted as soon as I got out of my vehicle, be it the work SUV or my pickup. Another thing I missed like crazy.

"I didn't want to give you up," I said gruffly, like he knew about divorces and separating assets and deciding where pets went. "I miss you," I said again.

He snapped his mouth shut and glanced out the door, then turned back to me. I bent to give him more pets and the side thumps that he liked.

When I straightened, he whipped around again, going still. A second later, he raced out of the garage, barking at what was likely a ground squirrel. Oreo had a personal vendetta against those things.

Either I'd stand and wait for the dog to come back and make me feel special, or I'd get back to Buffalo Gully. I had to help Jeremy with towing his daughter's car. My luck, Eliot had probably left at the crack of dawn and was hard at work already on the ranch.

I got in the pickup. I had a long drive to ignore the sensation that I wanted more than an exes-with-benefits arrangement. I wanted Sutton back, but her house said she wasn't going anywhere.

After I pulled out of the garage, a pull-behind Coachmen camper was visibly parked next to the garage. I hadn't seen it in the dark last night, or I hadn't cared because I was focused on when I could get Sutton naked.

I put my foot on the brake and stared at it for a good ten minutes.

Sutton wanted to go camping?

Who would she camp with?

Would she be alone?

She could take care of herself, but women went missing on the trails, and it wasn't because they'd gotten lost. She was smart. She wouldn't go alone.

Then who'd go with her, jackwagon?

The questions and any possible answers gnawed at me as I pulled away. I pushed the speed limit and made up excuses in my head for if I were to get pulled over. None of them would be valid. The truth would land like a ton of bricks.

Why, yes, I was speeding. I had a ton of sex with my ex-wife and then had to hide in her bedroom so my sister didn't catch me before I could leave. My brother counts on me to help around the ranch, and I kind of have to anyway because it's the only way I can get my inheritance. Did I mention I'm a deputy in Montana?

Not one sentence of that would help me out.

I calculated when I'd get back. I'd have enough time to grab Ray and tow Emily's car. I voice activated my phone to call Ray.

He answered with his gruff "Sheriff Dahlen" even though he knew it was me.

"I can swing by in a few hours, and we can grab the car."

"I'm just weeding the garden." That explained his breathless speech. Most of his garden was weeds. "Want me to come by and get you?"

"No, I'm..." I couldn't spill the news to Ray after

Sutton and I just promised to keep our families out of it. Lying to the sheriff would leave an acrid taste on my tongue. "I had to run to Miles City for a lawn mower part."

I winced at the echoes of a flimsy teenage excuse. He hadn't bought them then.

"Miles City, huh?" His skepticism was thick.

He saw right through me. The guy had witnessed most of my teen transgressions and gave me a better future than my father had ever cared to.

"I had to get away." That was the truth.

"Gotcha. You're on the road, then?"

"Yes."

"Good, then you've got a minute. Listen, I'm going to retire."

Shock made me glad for cruise control. "Retire?"

"The county board will appoint you as my replacement, and then you can run for sheriff next year. I doubt you'll have much competition."

The shock turned to acid reflux. I had told Sutton when we first met my endgame was sheriff. After we married, I promised her that once I got into office, I would be home more. No more shift work unless I took a weekend here and there to keep up with what was going on in the field.

Ray had mentioned the possibility of retirement for the last several years. *When I retire... By the time I retire... I've been thinking about retirement...* This was the first time he'd stated that he was going to retire. A year and a half too late to save my marriage.

Would becoming sheriff have helped me stay married, or would I have found myself single and alone sooner?

The main problem had been that Ray had talked retirement, but he'd never done it. The other issue Sutton had thrown at me was that I'd still be gone a lot, playing hero to everyone's non-emergencies in addition to being there for real emergencies.

"You sure? I thought you were going to try for another term." The county would never not re-elect him. He was a mainstay.

He grunted. "This is a young person's game nowadays. I can't keep up with social media apps and what's not safe for kids. They're all not safe, but they're a fact of life, and I can barely look up the movie times."

He was more adept than he was letting on, but his adult kids lived in Michigan and Florida and rarely returned home. With his ex-wife in Chicago, it was easier for them to visit her instead.

"We can talk more when you pick me up, but whaddya think? Still interested? I know your circumstances have changed."

"I'm still interested, sir." Being sheriff was all I ever wanted. I would be at the top. I'd done a lot to build up the Knight name, and with Barns's passing and me becoming sheriff, I could do even more. Barns had ruined a lot of goodwill during his life, and Eliot didn't leave the ranch enough to rectify any of it.

"Good. I've been afraid to ask if you changed your mind. It'll be better for you. Less call, so when you meet someone new, you won't hear the same old complaints."

"Right." Sutton's complaints hadn't been the only ones. Most deputies cited the call hours and the consistently short-staffed department as reasons for leaving the department when they found other jobs. The career was hard on families. I'd accepted the facts, but I'd underestimated how much my wife had been willing to tolerate my hours and for how long.

After the issues between me and Sutton and my work, I was looking at a future of being single. I had no plans to repeat a failed marriage.

Four

WILDER

"Where the hell you been?" Eliot sat on the back deck, his boots kicked up on a railing, sandwich in his hand. His usual cranky expression didn't change just because he was chewing.

"Slept late." My stomach rumbled. I still hadn't eaten.

"You never oversleep," he said around a mouthful. The time difference had worked to my advantage. I gained an hour and wasn't as tardy as I feared.

"Did today. Then Ray and I had to help Jeremy move his daughter's car."

"Why the fuck couldn't Jeremy do it?"

"Not everyone has a vehicle that can tow."

"Uh, the *tow truck driver* does."

"He's got family in town."

His mouth full, he gave me an incredulous look. It wasn't that Eliot didn't help others, but he wasn't in town often enough to offer a hand. He didn't always look approachable either. I didn't expect him to understand.

I opened the bottle of lemon-flavored mineral water I'd bought at the gas station on the edge of town. "Got any sandwiches left?"

"Make your own. I already had to do your work."

Guilt gnawed a hole in my gut. My appetite ebbed. Eliot counted on me. Barns had left a financial mess behind. Cody was repairing what he could, but his main focus was the actual moneymaker, Knight's Oil Wells. He'd cut back on his role with the ranch since he'd moved, remarried, and had another kid on the way. Eliot was able to hire a trustworthy bookkeeper at basement rates. To afford him, I helped with the cattle side.

I went into the house, preparing to get hit with the cigar and whiskey smell left over from Barns. Old habits. The place didn't smell the same, and it didn't look the same. Eliot had brightened the paint on the walls, changed out the cattle skull and antler decorations for vivid landscape snapshots on aluminum, and replaced all the furniture with a neat bachelor style that said *single man with taste* instead of *bachelor in the sticks*.

The apple pie scent was new. I found the source on the island in the kitchen. A pie with two slices missing.

Albert Chambers shuffled out of the hallway where my brother Cody's office used to be. The new bookkeeper.

"Hey, Chambers." Chambers used to be our history teacher and football coach, and his wife, Roxie, had taught English. After high school, Mr. Chambers had become Chambers. I saw him around town and never imagined he'd be a fixture in the house I grew up in.

"Wilder," he said, always sounding mildly surprised to see me. "Busy night?"

"You have no idea," I said, poking around the fridge. "Roxie make the pie?"

"Yes, she's determined to fatten that boy up." He chuffed. "I keep telling her the Knight kids aren't boys anymore."

"Eliot could use some sweetness, though." I set my sandwich supplies on the counter and slid the bread closer.

Chambers chuckled. "That attitude's a family trait no pie can run off." He leaned across the island. "I came to sneak a slice, thinking Eliot was back to work."

I pushed the pie toward him. "He won't mind."

Eliot would insist. He was a cranky bastard some days, but he took care of everyone.

Chambers moved around the kitchen like it was his own, getting himself a plate and fork.

"How are the grandkids?" I asked. The Chamberses had two kids. Eliot and I had been good friends with their son. The daughter was younger than both of us, but Eliot had probably known her better since he was closer friends with the brother more than I was. Between the two kids, the Chamberses had three grandkids.

"Good, good. Meredith is bringing Kaden out for a week before school starts." He chopped into the pie. "Unless that idiot husband of hers has something to say about it."

I bit back a smile. Mr. Chambers was a mild-mannered man—unless he was talking about his son-in-law. I didn't know the guy's name. Every time Chambers talked about him he said *"Big shot banker thinks his shit don't stink."* "I'll give Kaden a ride in my squad car again if he wants."

Chambers plopped a large hunk of pie on his plate, then grabbed a second plate. "You can give Mr. Hoity-Toity a ride," he grumbled. The second piece of pie was slid in my direction. He scooped up his plate and held it at chest level while he sawed off a bite-sized piece. "So, how are you really doing?"

I skipped my sandwich and went right for the pie. My lack of truth could use some sugaring too. "Surprisingly well." The entire drive back I fought to keep from pondering whether it was possible to repair my marriage. Then I'd remind myself the marriage was over. The emptiness would return, and then I'd remember we had plans to meet again.

Not only were we divorced, she had her own business in another town. A vet clinic she'd built from the ground up and was already thriving from what my sister and Cody had said. She wasn't tied to Knight's Arabians and Cattle Company like I was, and she'd likely never agree to work for the family ranch again. There was already a vet clinic in Buffalo Gully, and the town was too small to support another. The Cleavers, the owners of the other vet clinic, made sure of it. They were some of the ill will my father had caused, and Sutton's dreams of running her own place had been stalled because of it.

"You look better," he said, narrowing his eyes. "You seeing someone?"

I froze mid chew. "Uh..." I swallowed hard. "No. Why?" I'd stopped at home to change. Her underwear was in my laundry. Seeing her clothing mingled with mine had left me staring into my dirty hamper for far too damn long.

"Just have that look about you. You Knight boys were always shit at trying to hide something."

"You can blame Barns. He was proud of everything he did—right or wrong, but especially if it was wrong. Me and my siblings didn't learn how to handle guilt."

"Well," he said around another mouthful. "Whatever you're doing, keep doing it. Roxie and I have been pretty worried about you."

Seemed to be the theme of everyone around me. They were worried about me. Sutton was right to be concerned. What would they think of her for sleeping with me?

"Thanks." I planned to keep doing who I was doing.

We ate our dessert in silence, and I considered Chambers. Roxie was Chambers's first and only wife. They raised two kids and were half-assed retired and entertained their grandkids whenever possible.

In my line of work, I dealt with the ugliness in life—including the dark side of bad relationships. My personal life was pristine compared to many, but my youth hadn't been happy and carefree. Barnaby and Birdie Knight's drama was enough to keep me and my siblings out of the spotlight.

Eliot and Austen weren't married. Aggie and Cody were finally each in the type of happy relationship we should've witnessed growing up. I'd seen enough shitty relationships, did the paperwork on them to know what they had wasn't the standard. It was the dream.

Dreams evaporated when you opened your eyes. But some of them became real. How?

"Chambers, got a question for you."

"Shoot," he said and licked his fork.

"What would you say the secret to you and Roxie is?"

I expected him to make a joke about how Roxie couldn't get enough of him or she didn't have much choice in a town as small as ours, but he leveled a serious gaze on me. "Asking a bit late, aren't you, son?"

My lungs constricted. Yeah, I should've asked earlier. I should've listened to how unhappy Sutton was, but we'd been a pair. We went together. And then she was gone. "For future reference," I said roughly.

He shrugged like it didn't matter anyway. "A lot of people these days think it's love, but I think it's respect."

I scowled at him. I respected the hell out of Sutton.

He didn't seem to notice. "Love, sure. Trust, absolutely. Sacrifice, unfortunately. But the foundation that supports it all is respect. You respect their personality, their strengths, and their weaknesses. You respect who they are, what makes them tick, what makes them feel safe, what they fear. Respect is the concrete that goes deep into the ground. Love and trust are the walls and rafters. Put all of those together, and you have a home."

He shrugged again, set his fork and plate by the sink, and shuffled back to the office as if he hadn't just demolished everything I thought I'd been doing right in my marriage.

✻

Sutton

The Purple Petal was full for an early Saturday evening. People would continue to pile into the most popular restaurant in Crocus Valley for the night. Aggie and I stopped in after hitting several rummage sales and filling the back of her pickup.

"I don't think you'll need to buy Ro clothes or toys for the next five years."

She took a drink of lemonade. "I can't believe the cute stuff we found. I wasn't even looking for outfits for her." She winced and touched her boobs. "I need to pump soon."

"We can call it for the day, too, if you just want to go home to feed her." I enjoyed my afternoon with Aggie. My mind hadn't had time to spin since I left Wilder shut in my bedroom, and that was fine with me.

Part of me begged to return home, dive between my covers, and inhale deeply. Would the bedding still smell like him?

"It's our time out," she insisted.

"It's okay." A yawn snuck out. "I didn't get much rest last night."

"The new medicine kicking your butt?"

"No." I frowned, hating how a little fib led to a constant string of lying. The meds weren't exactly new. "I still feel good." Physically, I was amazing. Mentally, there was a lightness that wasn't there before Wilder broke into my dance. The panic of the morning didn't drown out the anticipation of Wilder's next visit.

"Cravings and all that gone?"

I turned my attention to Aggie. I was already being a crappy friend. "Mostly."

I had polycystic ovary syndrome. Four years ago, I'd gone off birth control, thinking Wilder and I had needed to get to making kids if we were going to do it. I'd been over thirty and had already tackled my vet school loans.

We'd been in a good place financially to start a family. As a couple, we'd been okay.

The kids hadn't come, and periods had gotten irregular, sometimes painfully heavy, cravings hit me hard, and the fucking acne drove me insane. I hadn't had a breakout for almost twenty years until I went off birth control.

My doctor thought it was just a post-birth-control adjustment, but the symptoms stayed, along with the infertility.

Aggie waited like she knew there was more.

I couldn't get away with one-word answers with her, and she deserved more for caring about me. "I feel a lot better. More regular, but still...off."

She nodded like she knew what I meant, and that was the refreshing part. She didn't, and she still understood.

When Wilder had first introduced me to Aggie, I thought she was a sweet, wild girl. Being around her reminded me of how precocious I had longed to be, but the way I'd grown up hadn't allowed it. I never would've guessed how close we'd become.

Aggie listened to what I said. She considered my feelings, and she empathized. I wasn't brushed off. My concerns weren't diminished, and she never told me, "It's not a big deal," like my parents had when I told them what bothered me as a kid.

I would've asked for a divorce earlier if I hadn't been so afraid of losing her friendship. She was why I ended up in Crocus Valley. I was no longer an in-law, but Ro was my niece, and Cody's kids were also family, just like Aggie and Cody.

"My periods are regular." She waggled her eyebrows. "But they may not be for much longer."

"Oh?" I said, excitement growing. I adored watching

my best friend grow her family and in turn, my family. "You're trying again?"

"Better to have them close together, right?"

"Probably." My sister was six years older than me, and we weren't close. My parents had doted on her and her competitive figure skating career. They'd all had their eyes on the Olympics. Their attention certainly hadn't been on me.

"I know there's almost ten years between me and Cody," she said, "and we're close, but I can't be having babies until I'm forty like him. Ansen and I figured we'd better get it done."

A few of my heartstrings tugged. Forty was on my horizon. A couple more years and I'd be having the milestone birthday. I was nowhere near where I thought I'd be ten years ago.

"Speaking of forty..." I wasn't switching topics to keep my mind off my diminishing ability to have kids and the lack of a partner I wanted to have them with living under my roof. Nor was I willingly turning the attention to Wilder, but curiosity and maybe a little worry had been gnawing at me.

"Wilder?" Aggie asked.

I nodded. "Are you guys planning anything? I wanted to make sure he's not alone for the big four oh."

"You have a kind heart, you know that?"

I had a thing for my ex. That was the issue. "I never quit caring about him." A tiny weight lifted off my chest. I could admit a part of the truth.

"I know." She gave me a small smile. "I've been so worried. At first, I wondered if you'd both be able to stand each other or if I'd have to take turns inviting each of you. But you and Wilder have been so good about it."

The conflict in her eyes told me everything. He was her brother. She couldn't fathom not including him. I was like a sister, but in the end, I wasn't her sister. Besides, I knew that being sisters didn't always mean two women were close.

If Aggie had to choose between me and her brother, I was afraid of the outcome. "I'd never want to put you in a hard spot like that."

"I'm still worried about him."

"Why?" He'd been extremely fine the last time I saw him...like when I woke up next to him, but I hated that she was concerned.

"He keeps to himself more than usual."

"I'm not nagging him to go anywhere."

She gave me a supportive smile. "You didn't nag, and we both know it. He's stubborn and single-minded, like our parents were. No, it's just...he's quieter. Sadder." She held her hand up. "I'm not blaming you."

But it was my fault. My fault he was sadder and quieter, and my fault his family was distressed. "Aggie, I'm sorry."

"No, Sutton. You had your reasons. He's just different than he was, and I'll give him more time, but that's also why I want to make sure we do something for his birthday. He needs to be reminded that there's more to life than that uniform."

"And you claim I have a kind heart." I was a sneaky bitch and not feeling so hot about myself right now. I was grateful for Aggie on so many levels, but her love for her family topped the list today. Whether I confessed to Wilder or not, I didn't want him to be alone on his birthday. He wouldn't do a thing for himself, and while I'd been with him, no one else but me had either.

"Cody talked to Eliot, and we'll go down for the day. I think Wilder's on call, but we can bring some donuts to his house."

Wilder liked donuts more than cake. "I'm sure he'd love to see everyone."

"You think so?" Her question was serious.

I paused. Wilder was as expressive with his emotions as the rest of the guys in the family. Cody had opened up a lot since he met Tova, but his default was still serious. We all knew when Eliot was upset, but otherwise, he never talked about what he was feeling, and Austen was a guy who acted like he wanted nothing but a good time.

"He's never been able to live up to Cody." I fiddled with my straw wrapper. "Not being the oldest that everyone relied on bothered him. It's why he's so dedicated to the sheriff's office." I'd had to come to a lot of realizations, and those were what led to the decision of asking for a divorce. Wilder wasn't going to change. He was the way he was for a reason. "He loves being with his family. He might not admit he never gets enough time to spend with everyone. Because then he'd have to admit he's split himself into too many pieces."

"And that would be admitting that he wanted to do more and hated how everyone deferred to Cody when we were growing up."

I pointed at her. "And we have a winner."

Her mouth tipped up. "I can never tell which game show you get your sayings from. Except *Jeopardy!* That one's easy."

"That one's pretty general. I also can't say 'give me Dissecting the Ex's Personality for six hundred, Alex' anymore, since they have like two new hosts."

"Do you still watch them?"

God, no. I hadn't wanted to watch all the daytime and evening television I had in the first place. "I try not to. But back to Wilder." Anything but why I shed random game show phrases like nervous corgis leaving a trail of fur in my office. "Don't let him convince you he doesn't need anything. And if he gets called out, follow him," I joked.

She laughed. "Could you see us all rolling up behind him to, like, a traffic stop?"

He'd be irate that they put themselves in danger. "Make him celebrate."

She ran her teeth over her lower lip. "I'm really glad I can talk about him to you, but tell me if it's ever too much. Deal or no deal? Is that a saying?"

"Yes." I laughed. *Deal or No Deal* was after the bulk of my game show-watching days. If only she knew I'd had too much of her brother before she rang the doorbell this morning. "Deal."

"Is the tester vacation still on?"

Giddiness sent my stomach aflutter. My first real, albeit short, vacation since my honeymoon. "Still on. The Friday after Labor Day, I'll pack up the camper and do my test run for the weekend to Medora." Oreo would ride shotgun, and I would practice closing my clinic for long weekends that weren't just holidays. I wasn't working my life away, nor was I waiting on anyone anymore.

"And I will be on Berry and Sylvester duty. When's the big trip to the Black Hills again?"

"April, weather willing." Excitement traveled up my spine. I was getting away in April of all months. Since I didn't work with large animals as much as I used to in my practice, I didn't have to plan to be around for calving season. I was using Easter break to help fill in my days off so I wasn't closed for so many business days, but that'd be a real vacation. "Thank you for taking care of the pets. I couldn't go without your help."

"That's what friends are for." She took a long pull of her lemonade and scooted toward the edge of the booth. "Can you give me ten minutes? I don't want to cut the night short with you, but I need to get this pressure off."

"Go before something goes wrong. I work with animal mammary glands, not human."

She laughed and took her portable pump disguised as a cute tote with her. I scrolled through my phone. I had a few emails about appointments that I'd respond to tonight when I wasn't half distracted by my ex-husband hookup.

"Hey, Sutton."

I glanced up. Jennings was standing by the booth. Oh no. Would he bring up Wilder? My heart stopped and restarted when relief poured through me that Aggie was in the bathroom. If she learned I was lying to her, she'd be hurt. Then she might be upset I was messing around with Wilder. A double whammy to our friendship, yet I couldn't bring myself to cut things off with my ex. He'd raced to the street dance to cockblock me, and the over-looked kid inside me couldn't ignore his actions.

"You doing okay after last night?" Concern pinched his brows.

"I'm sorry, what?" I'd heard him clearly, but I needed to think of an answer. I was more than okay. I was still glowing from coming so hard.

"Last night. That guy?" Poor Jennings looked so concerned. Why couldn't I fall for him?

"Oh, yes. No, it's fine. We had some…talking…to do." A hard and fast and completely unplanned conversation.

Jennings's brows drew down. "I haven't seen him around. You knew him though? You talked like it, but I was afraid I was letting a stranger haul you off."

I suppressed a sigh. Crocus Valley was as nosy as Buffalo Gully. Why couldn't Jennings take my word for it? "He's my ex-husband. He can piss me off like no one else, but he wouldn't hurt me."

He also wouldn't listen. Couldn't understand what I wanted and needed when it differed from his wants and needs. He worked hard for everyone but his wife waiting for him at home. The man could emotionally devastate me, but I was physically safer with him than anyone else in the world.

"Oh." Jennings looked around the restaurant, his gaze dropping on Aggie's lemonade glass. "I guess I should leave you to it."

"No problem," I said brightly. "Aggie will be back any minute."

Surprise crossed his face. "Aggie? Oh, right. The hobby farm lady."

He must've thought I was here with my stranger. "Animal rescue."

"Her husband trains horses?"

"Ansen, yes." Many people in town knew who Aggie and I were already, and they knew we were friends, but I didn't spread the word that I had been married to her brother. I'd rather keep the speculation about why Wilder and I failed in Buffalo Gully.

"Oh, okay." As if he ran out of reasons to stay hovering over my booth, he knocked on the table top with a couple of fingers. "See you around. Next street dance?"

I didn't even know when it was. "We'll see." I willed

him to leave. Aggie breezed out of the bathroom, digging in her bag like she was triple-checking she'd grabbed everything.

Jennings smiled. "Promise me a dance?"

"We'll see," I said again, adding a touch of flirtation to get him to move his ass before Aggie got close. Then he'd want to small talk, and he might mention *that guy*.

He nodded and finally—finally—walked away. He passed Aggie, giving her a tip of his ball cap.

She slid into the booth. "Were you getting hit on while I was away?"

"I think so. He's nice, but he's not my type." Jennings had close-cropped hair, but it wasn't dark and thick with a hint of unruly curl. He wasn't sporting a five o'clock shadow when it was three p.m. His shoulders weren't as wide, his thighs didn't look nearly as powerful, and when he walked, he didn't stalk his prey. His swagger didn't make my pulse jump. I didn't get a steady throb between my thighs looking at him. He didn't look like he could swing me over his shoulder when I teased him about being a big, bad cop. He didn't appear half pissed off most of the time. And he probably didn't make the bed as soon as I got out of it or put the dishes away as soon as the dishwasher was done or fold laundry with military precision.

That was my type.

I needed to remember why I divorced Wilder, how I wanted him to be with me and how he wasn't, or I was going to nurse a raging crush on my ex-husband and fracture my already broken heart all over again.

WILDER

I needed to get out of town. I had to hit the road and get to Sutton's before she thought I'd canceled. But I was twenty miles out of Buffalo Gully, talking to my fellow deputy Kaplan. I'd assisted him and another deputy on a traffic stop that turned into a drug bust.

The deputy who had made the stop was off already, taking the guy to jail. I was left behind with Kaplan. He was older than me, and he'd been with the department almost as long as I had, having moved to Buffalo Gully from a county in western Montana.

"I'm almost done." I patted the top of my car. The sun was setting and bugs buzzed around us. I had plenty of the evening left, and I had so many plans for how to use it. "I'm gonna head back."

He followed me to the driver's door. "Hey, can you take call for me tonight? The wife made plans, and if she has to cancel because I get called out, all hell's going to break loose. She's still pissed about the Fourth of July."

The night of fireworks and grass fires. That'd been a long fucking weekend. "I can't tonight."

"Come on, Knight. Throw me a bone. Even a few hours?"

In a few hours, I'd be pulling into Sutton's garage. "I'm heading out of town."

"Oh, yeah? Where?" He shook his head like he knew the answer. "Crocus Valley?"

Shit. "Yeah." Kaplan wasn't buddies with Eliot, but the less I had to lie, the better. I knew how much the details could fuck up a good fib, only I was usually the one sussing out the truth. "Sorry, I can't help. Maybe it'll be slow."

"Knight," Kaplan groaned. "You've screwed me now. You never say that."

I opened my door, laughing. "Only if you're superstitious."

"I'm blaming you if I get called. Hey," he said before I climbed in. "Did you hear the boss is talking retirement?"

Ray hadn't talked any more about it since our phone conversation. His week had been busy, and he'd mentioned retirement before, and it'd gone nowhere. How'd Kaplan know?

"He's been meaning to retire for years," I joked.

Kaplan's smile was quick. "I suppose you'll be who they appoint for interim sheriff."

"Maybe." Was Kaplan interested? I could be made interim sheriff, but the election would be after the term. Whoever was in office would have a clear advantage. "Are you thinking of tossing your hat in the ring?"

He rolled his shoulders and looked into the distance,

his gaze skipping over the rocky hills and sparse green pastures. The sun was sinking lower. I still had a twenty-minute drive to town, and I had to change.

"No call. More control over the schedule." He cited the same reasons I wanted the job when I was married. I couldn't blame the guy.

"But there's the politics," I said. I was too much like Barns to get embroiled in politics. I didn't like to play games, but I also wanted to be a benefit to the place I lived and not a tyrant.

"Eh, I can handle the politics. Whatever. It's something to think about, right?" He gave me a measuring look, and I understood. We were two guys who weren't being completely truthful. Just like I was going out of town, but it wasn't to help my siblings like he assumed. And he wasn't taking as casual an attitude toward the sheriff's position as I was.

"Right. Have a good weekend, Kaplan." I got behind the wheel and drove away. I had somewhere else to be.

Kaplan's little revelation niggled at my brain. What would Ray think? He'd been grooming me for the office since I'd started with the department. I would be interim sheriff. We all knew it. I could win the election in a clean sweep. Unless...

Unless I was running against a family man who'd also been a part of the community for years. A candidate whose wife worked and volunteered and whose kids I high-fived in the halls of the school. Kaplan was a staple of Buffalo Gully. He'd be a worthy opponent. Running against Kaplan would be a challenge even if I was already interim sheriff.

I worked over the problem all the way to my house, but once I parked and was officially off duty, I tabled the worry. I had a night with Sutton. One night, and I'd have to leave in the morning. Everything else could wait for once.

✳

Sutton

It was finally Friday, and excitement coursed through me, kicking up my heart rate and getting me tingly in all the right places. I wanted to jump up and down like I won the grand prize and that big win was a night filled with Wilder's talented tongue and fingers and his magnificent dick.

All week, I'd been asking myself if I should cancel. Should I be the adult and do the right thing and tell Wilder we couldn't continue? Or should I do what I really wanted and shave everything and put on the shortest shorts that Wilder said made my legs look a mile long? I'd pair the shorts with a camisole top and no bra. Because he'd be stripping me down right away.

If I went with the latter decision, I wouldn't put on underwear either.

I tugged the shorts down and wandered through my house. Berry stared at me through slitted eyes. She was used to me being busy or doing paperwork on the couch. She wasn't used to my restless wandering. Neither was I, but I also wasn't accustomed to waiting for a booty call to arrive.

My phone buzzed, and my stomach dropped. Was that Wilder? Was he telling me he couldn't make it?

I should've known he was working late— Oh. Aggie's name was on the screen.

Are you busy tonight?

My heart thudded once. Twice. I didn't have to lie. I would tell her the truth.

I'm heading to bed. What's up?

Nothing.

The phone rang. I nearly dropped the damn thing.

I fumbled to answer. "Is everything all right?"

"Yeah." She sighed. "I don't know. I'm restless, that's all. Ro's sleeping, and Ansen's at his dad's with his brother."

"Is Allan all right?" Aggie's father-in-law lived in a trailer on their property.

"He's fine. They're having a guys' night."

"Did you ever think guys' night would be two brothers hanging out with their dad?"

She laughed, letting out a soft snort. "They're probably spoiling the cats he just adopted."

I'd checked both kittens and fixed them last fall. The two little fur bodies had been all of five months old and were probably dumped once the owner realized they had a male-female pair that were reaching sexual maturity. "Are you sure you're okay?"

"I'm fine. Really. I was just roaming the house, not quite tired, and realized it was Friday night. You work at the clinic tomorrow, don't you?"

"For part of the day. That's the plan anyway." I ended

up staying much of the day with walk-ins. I was glad for the work, but I also didn't want to open my own clinic only to be as tied to the job as my ex was to his. Besides, I had vacations planned. So, I limited my Saturdays to twice a month and narrowed my hours to the morning.

Closing the clinic for my short camping excursion was a test run. My clients would get used to me being out for the weekend, and I could assure myself that I wouldn't return to an empty schedule because everyone had abandoned me.

Dr. Jake was the other vet in town, and he wasn't the most well-liked by many people who'd been burned by his playboy ways or didn't appreciate his flirtations. Still, he was another vet in town. Clients had options. But I also wanted to travel and do all the things I'd waited on while waiting for other people.

Like I was waiting for one of those people now. In doing so, I was leaving Aggie alone. "I can come by tomorrow when I'm done."

"We're going to look at a horse. It's fine. I just saw you at dart night."

The rumble of the garage door came through the wall. I jumped. He was here.

Wilder was at my house. Again. And I was on the phone with his sister. Ugh.

"Dart night is different." I lived for my Thursday nights out with Aggie, Tova, and Vienne. Hanging out as a group was different than one-on-one. "You know people are trying to listen in at the bar."

"One hundred percent." She sighed. "I really want some wine and gossip. I can't have the wine while I'm nursing, but I thought I'd go for a good girl-talk sesh. I can try Tova and Vienne, but it's getting late."

The door opened, and Wilder stepped in. Flutters erupted in my belly. How did he look so right stepping into my kitchen? His dark hair was finger-combed after wearing his hat all day. He had on a tight green tee that hugged his biceps and his abs. The weathered blue jeans he wore were my favorite, and he knew it.

I mouthed *Aggie* and pointed to the phone at my ear. "Rain check? All the gossip and I'll drink your share of wine?"

"Yes. Get some rest."

"You too." We hung up.

Maybe tomorrow night. Now that Wilder was in my kitchen, leaning his long body against the counter with his arms crossed, ogling my legs with desire-darkened eyes, I was glad I didn't listen to reason. Good sense didn't get me laid by this man.

"How's my sister?" he asked.

"She asked me over."

Regret flickered in his eyes. "Sorry."

Neither of us liked sneaking around, but neither of us could deny the chemistry between us. We'd been ignoring it since I left, and it'd taken me years to separate good sex from the definition of a good marriage.

The marriage part was done. Now we were at just the good-sex stage. "How often are we going to do this?" I waved my hand. I had to be smart in order to be impulsively stupid. "I want to make sure we're on the same page."

He inhaled and braced his hands on the edges of the counter. He crossed one boot over the other. "As often as we fucking can, Sutton."

I scowled at him despite loving his answer. Heat flooded my body, and if my top didn't have a few ruffles,

Wilder would see how hard my nipples were. "No more than once a week."

"So tomorrow night's out?"

He said he had the weekend off. Tomorrow would've worked better. Had he said Friday because he couldn't wait?

I would've done the same. Which spelled trouble. "Yes, tomorrow's out."

The disappointment in his eyes echoed mine. "We don't tell anyone. We already sorted through that."

"Your family—"

"Is important to you. I know, Sutton. Chambers said he was worried about me, and I could see why you were concerned. All my siblings have been checking on me. They're so damn worried about me, and they might blame you if this doesn't work out." He clenched his teeth like the words left a bad aftertaste.

Neither of us wanted to think about the end. We didn't want to consider the odds of longevity in a relationship like the one we were embarking on. "So, once a week. You sneak in and sneak out?"

"I've got the garage code. I can feed Berry and Sylvester in the morning so you can get some extra sleep before work."

"What about when I don't work in the morning?"

"I'll still leave early—after I fuck you in the shower."

My legs trembled, and arousal pooled low in my belly. If I had underwear on, they'd be soaked. Planning this was too easy. Almost like Wilder and I coming back together was fate. I needed a splash of reality. "Until we meet someone else."

His gaze darkened. "Yes," he bit out, his voice rough as sandpaper.

"And this is just about sex?" I was too chicken to stress how we couldn't get back together. What if he got upset and left? What if he was cavalier and thought the idea of falling for me again was ridiculous?

"Yes, again." He tapped his fingers against the underside of the counter, his forearms flexing. "The clock is ticking, Sutton. You could be climaxing right now."

He didn't want to talk about the possibility of others. Turned out neither did I.

I lifted my chin. "Then why are you all the way over there?"

He prowled toward me. "I can see how hard your nipples are, Doc."

"I'd show you how wet my underwear is, but I'm not wearing any."

His growl reached me before he did. He grabbed my ass and massaged the globes of my ass cheeks. His forehead touched mine. "How many times did you get yourself off thinking about last weekend?"

"None." I ran my finger down his chest. "I wanted to save them up." To be extra naughty and give myself another heaping of common sense, I continued. "If you couldn't make it tonight, I would've done it all myself."

I thought he'd stiffen, but he only paused for half a second. Then he kissed the corner of my jaw. "I'm here now. All your orgasms are mine."

"Once a week. They're all yours, cowboy, starting now." I unzipped his jeans.

SUTTON

Wilder stayed the night last weekend, and he was coming for his night again tonight. I sat on the couch, phone to my ear, my legs folded with Berry in my lap. I bonded with Berry more while my mom and dad were on the phone. We were two girls who'd been skipped over for the more athletic sibling.

Mom had me on speaker with my dad for my once-a-month call. Dad joked that he set a reminder. Mom always giggled. They didn't realize it sounded like they would forget about me.

"Can you imagine? She refused to help her grand-daughter stay in lessons?" Mom asked, and yes, I could. I could imagine my parents' neighbors didn't want to bankrupt the household for skating lessons. I could also imagine that my parents didn't understand that a kid could enjoy a sport without wanting to dominate the industry. John and Kelly Grant would do what it took for their kid to succeed. Just not both kids. "Anyway. How are things with you?"

I was used to not being asked how I was doing until after I got the rundown on my sister Honey's accomplishments, then Petra's achievements, and then their own lives. And now their neighbors came first.

"It's been busy." I wouldn't tell my parents who was keeping me busy one night a week. They'd only get their hopes up about reconciliation. To them, I wouldn't be a failure because my marriage had ended if I got back together with Wilder. "Lots of kittens and puppies this time of year."

"Oh, that's sweet. So business is good?"

My parents took an inordinate amount of interest in Sutton's Animal Care. My growing upstart was a sign of my success, a symbol that I did more than deworm cats or stick my arm up cow rectums. Sutton's Animal Care was a safe topic.

Really, they were worried I'd crumple and a sports pep talk wouldn't do the trick.

Mom and Dad had helped propel my sister to the Olympic finals with positive thinking, visualization, good vibes, and every spare penny we had. They couldn't wrap their heads around why I divorced Wilder. To them, divorce was throwing in the towel. Divorce was the culmination of missed practices, of not spending hours on the ice, of not bringing my best to the competition. Divorce was proof of a lack of effort. *My* divorce was a failure, and they didn't know how to raise a failure.

I never told them how I felt. I never assured them that I knew they liked Wilder, everyone did, and that was part of the problem. He was a helpful guy. He gave to everyone but his spouse. I didn't tell them anything other than we were in different places in life.

I'll take "How to Avoid Conflict" for two hundred!

"Yes, things are good," I said. "I'm getting more clients, and a local rancher cold-called me for an emergency last week."

"More cows, huh?" Mom said in a tone that put my nerves on edge. The hazards of growing up with a competitive older sister.

The feeling that we were pitted against each other hadn't faded as much as it should have. "I like working with cows."

"Oh, I'm not saying you don't. But didn't you complain about them when you were working for Barnaby?"

My father-in-law had offered to let me get experience. The promise of doing large animal veterinary work for Knight's Arabians and Cattle Company, and how good it'd look on my résumé, won me over. Too soon, I'd learned there was nothing else in Buffalo Gully for me. The local vet clinic was family-owned, and Barnaby had scorched those bridges. By then, I was too in love with Wilder to consider leaving.

Barns had eventually put me permanently on the books, and I'd gone along with it so I could be with my husband. I was stuck until Barns died. Once Barnaby Knight was gone, I had assumed Wilder would cut the tether. That he'd listen to me when I said nothing would be different if and when his boss ever retired. Nothing had changed, and I was growing to hate the work I did. I'd left Eliot a little high and dry, but I had to take care of myself.

"I didn't like working with *only* cattle." Wilder and

Eliot had helped me stealthily treat their dogs and cats, and Cody had figured out how to compensate me for their treatment. Barns hadn't liked to waste resources on working animals he couldn't get a return from. "I also disliked the lack of flexibility and freedom."

"Oh, Mutton." I cringed at Dad's nickname for me. "It's the hard stuff that gets you the gains."

"I'm not going for gold in the Olympics of veterinary medicine, Dad."

"Did we tell you Melon took first in her master's competition?"

Melon was my sister, Honey. And yes, they'd told me as soon as I answered. "I heard."

"Oh," Mom said. "Did she call you?"

"No." Honey and I weren't close. Too many evenings and weekends apart on top of having little in common beyond our last name. I thought things would change after she got married. I babysat my niece while Honey was competing and her husband, Rolf, was supporting her. I couldn't babysit in veterinary school, but by then, Petra hit the ice, and they became one happy, figure skating family. Once they no longer needed a sitter, they also had no use for me.

"Rolf said he was cheering the loudest as usual," Mom continued excitedly. "John and I couldn't get there in time— Oh." She and Dad murmured, then Mom came back on. "We have to go. Petra's calling. She's at a special training camp—we can't miss her."

"Tell her hi," I said automatically. I missed Petra, but she'd long forgotten me in pursuit of skating greatness.

"Will do, Mutton. Love ya." The line went dead.

"Bye," I muttered. Sighing, I checked the time on my phone. Almost ten. Scant light filtered in from the blinds.

I'd already watered my flowers and the garden. Wilder was coming again tonight. He had to work tomorrow night, but he was on call starting at noon, so he could justify not going to the ranch.

This would be our third time hooking up. We were being intentional. We'd planned it. Like a workout. No feelings involved.

What was I doing?

My gleeful clit told me to shut up. My privates were yelling "Wilder Knight, come on down!"

Restless, I moved Berry to a cushion and started pacing. I hadn't bought a TV for my new place. Regret snaked a tiny tendril around my brain, but I shook it off. I'd spent enough of my life watching TV.

A half hour and a clean fridge later, headlights flashed through my window. Anticipation coursed down my spine. Wilder.

The garage door rattled open. My pickup sat outside. The equivalent of a sock on the doorknob if anyone knew what we were up to.

He came in, looking as hot and rugged as last time, only with a snug black shirt instead of green. He'd left his hat in the car. Since almost getting busted by Aggie, he'd made sure to continue limiting the spread of his belongings. I leaned against the kitchen counter.

"Hey," he said and shut the door behind him. His deep voice caressed my eardrums and worked its way lower. Wilder Knight would be coming on down.

"Hey."

He cocked his head. "What's wrong?"

I didn't think the annoyance remained written across my face. For a stubborn man, he could be perceptive. "It's that time of the month."

The corner of his mouth lifted. He knew what I meant. "How are your parents? Or should I say, how's Honey's skating career?"

My laugh was empty. Wilder had witnessed my moods after my parents' calls. I hated the childish feeling inside me, the kid who was jealous of her sister and wished her parents were around more. I stuffed it down, but Wilder was drawing those emotions back out.

The only thing between us was supposed to be divorce papers and sex. I talked to Aggie about what bothered me with my parents, but it was too late to bug Aggie. I couldn't exactly phone a friend when her brother was at my house for sex.

"Honey's getting gold. Petra's going to get gold. But they asked about the clinic to make sure I'm not a complete letdown."

His mouth turned down. "You've never been a failure."

"I've never been a winner like Melon." We'd said this back and forth plenty of times over the years, and I had needed to hear it again.

"You don't need blades and a medal to be a winner." I lifted a shoulder, and he propped a hand on his hip. "Do we need to go over it again?"

"No." I rolled my eyes and repeated the litany Wilder used to repeat every time I got upset with my family. "I put myself through college and vet school. I ran my own business—even though we both know it wasn't my own —your dad was a mob boss, and I had no choice." Wilder hadn't ever recited the last part.

His mouth quirked. "Believe me, I know the ways he tried to control people." He cupped a hand around his ear. "What's the success rate of getting into veterinary school again?"

I rolled my eyes, but my mood lifted. "Ten to fifteen percent."

"Mm. Sounds competitive. And you do run your own business now."

"Yeah. I just wish I grew out of wanting my parents' approval and attention." I shook my head and pushed my hair off my face. Wilder's gaze dropped to my boobs. I'd showered after messing around in the yard and hadn't put a bra on.

He lifted his gaze to mine.

I stuck my chest out farther. "I have some frustration to work off."

A sexy grin spread across his face. For the rest of the night, I didn't have to worry about dwelling on more than his strong body and talented touch.

＊

Wilder

As far as birthdays went, today could be worse. I wasn't using my one day of sex a week today because I was on call, but I wasn't at home hoping I'd get called out.

The hot sun beat down on me, but there was enough of a breeze coming off the little lake to keep me fishing later than I usually would. Ray was next to me, packing his tacklebox and fishing rod.

"Start planning," he said as he sorted his gear. I hadn't brought up his retirement. He had. "You'll get appointed, and then it'll be easier to get reelected." He'd mentioned that during his last term, but this time resonated differently. He sounded more serious than usual. More resolute.

"You're going to give me a complex about my ability to get elected."

"It's politics, Wilder. You never know how an opponent is going to come at you."

I reeled my line in to pack up with him. "What if my opponent is from the department?"

He straightened and adjusted the dark blue Murphy County Sheriff's Office ball cap on his head. "It's Kaplan, isn't it?" He shook his head. "He's not as concerned about the community. He's only interested in the time off."

Kaplan was a decent officer. We were all concerned about the time off as we took call and worked overtime each month, but I didn't argue.

"Your campaigning starts now, Wilder," Ray cautioned. "Every business you stop in, you act like you're on the campaign trail. Every connection, you make it count. Be seen. Be supportive. Listen to their complaints and make sure they know you care. And when the time comes, they'll turn out to vote for you."

Wasn't he listing everything I'd been doing on the job besides arresting people and confiscating drugs and stolen property?

"Not often we get to fish from the shore at this spot," I commented as I picked up my own tackle box and readied my rod to pack up. I had to head to town in a few minutes, and I'd heard what he'd had to say about campaigning for years. I'd like a pass on a birthday when I was on call and couldn't go far from work.

Eliot had called me a couple hours ago to ask if I

could give him a ride to town. His vehicle was in the shop, and he needed to pick it up around lunchtime.

"No," Ray grunted. "We could use rain, though. It gets so blasted hot this time of year."

Once we got some moisture, the shore would be too muddy, and I'd lose this spot that was close enough to town to fish, even when I might have to leave for a call. Without a nearby fishing hole, I'd be at home, mowing the lawn that didn't need it. Trimming bushes that didn't need it. Lurking around town to jump in when someone needed an extra set of hands or a strong back. What had been a way of giving back to a community that had been there for me during my toughest times was becoming a compulsion, a desperate way to pass time and keep from feeling like a failure.

My marriage had failed, not me, but I was having a tough time identifying the difference.

"Call me tomorrow if you're not busy," Ray said and started through the tall grass to the rough gravel parking lot.

I followed him. "Don't you have better things to do than entertain me?"

His dry laugh was the same as all the other times I asked him the same question. "It's always a pleasure killing time with you, Wilder. Even better when I don't have to chase you down."

The inside joke from when I was young and stupid never got old between us, but today the humor fell flat. Ray was divorced, and his kids were adults. He didn't have best friends. He had residents of the county he served and protected.

Today was the first time a question bobbed in my

head after his reply. *What will I have to look forward to when I'm his age?*

Shrugging off the yearning for an answer that wouldn't leave me wondering what the hell the point was, I waved goodbye and hopped in my pickup. On the drive to Eliot's, I nursed a minor case of heartburn. I needed to eat. No one wanted to feel like crap on their birthday.

No one wanted to be heartbroken on their big 4-0 either, but here I was.

I wove through the backroads I could drive in the dark with no headlights—had done so a few times before I straightened myself out. Pastures spread out on either side of the dirt road. The log house came into view with the peaks of the shops and barns behind it. Cattle filled one side of the road, and Arabians grazed on the other. I parked in front of the house. Eliot was out of the garage before I could kill the engine.

He hopped in, looking fresh in a clean pair of jeans and a T-shirt. Had he just showered? He was dressed nicer than me. "Happy Birthday, old man."

"Ha ha, jackass."

He grinned, but I couldn't summon my laughter. I used to wake up to *Happy Birthday, cowboy. Can I go for a ride?* I liked those birthday greetings better.

"Hey, can we stop at your house first? I need to borrow a ten-mil socket."

"You have a hundred of those."

"They're all lost."

"Fine." I'd argue that he could buy one in town, but he'd bicker for the fun of it, and I didn't have the energy.

My house came into view. I leaned closer to the steering wheel of my pickup. Dusty trucks lined my sidewalk like a country house party. "What the hell is this?"

Eliot was grinning his gotcha grin that looked more like Austen's. "Surprise."

I switched my glare from him to the house. The burn in my chest eased. A birthday party? I'd planned to either fish all day or hoped I'd get called out. This was a nicer option than either.

My porch was full of kids. A dormant part of my heart clenched. I liked the sight a lot. The house was big, and I didn't need more than a bedroom. The days when Sutton had Cody's kids over for sleepovers hadn't been that long ago.

Now, they were racing down the steps. Ansen had a baby to his chest and was talking to Cody. Aggie was on the porch swing I'd nearly smashed to pieces a few nights after Sutton walked out.

She'd bought it after the place was built, saying, *It's like that Tim McGraw song. We can face it west and enjoy the sunsets.* Not only had the porch not seen this level of family on its floorboards, but that swing had been empty for far longer than my marriage.

I scanned the small crowd. No Sutton. Not a surprise. She wouldn't return to Buffalo Gully and ignite stares and speculation. She also wouldn't want to cross the lines we'd set. Once a week. No sappy talk. A little bit of small talk and then nothing but getting each other off.

Austen wasn't there either, but everyone else was. Cody and Tova and the kids had made the trip, and so had Aggie and Ansen with Ro. They'd traveled with a baby for my goddamn birthday. And Eliot, the fucker. He'd made some bullshit excuse to run to town after I turned down his offer to take me out to eat. I knew he had a shit ton of ten-millimeter sockets.

I either had a raging case of acid reflux, or I wasn't

used to this level of attention from my family. "You planned a birthday party?"

"Aggie did," Eliot said with a grin. "I was a helpless bystander, doing what she told me to do."

My throat was growing thick. When Sutton gave me the divorce papers, I had blamed Aggie. And my sister, having been raised a Knight, had pushed right back, insisting I was the idiot who'd let my wife slip away. Sutton had been telling me she wasn't happy, and she wanted a change, yet I'd continued trucking along with life as usual.

Aggie was here. Throwing me a birthday party that was a poor disguise for a siblings' pity party. None of them wanted me to be alone for a milestone birthday so soon after the divorce was final.

Goddammit, I was grateful as hell not to be alone.

I parked in the garage. One of my siblings would give Eliot a ride home. My work car was in its normal spot.

When I got out, my nephew, Grayson, ran up to me. "Happy Birthday, Uncle Wilder." He threw his arms around me so hard I nearly staggered back. He'd gotten taller since I'd last seen him, and his hair was a little longer. Why did Grayson and Ivy seem like two people I had to get to know all over again each time I saw them?

"Thanks, big guy." I patted his back. "How's dance and football going?"

"You have to come to one of my games." He grinned. "I'll start dance in the winter again. Tova said she can still teach me with a baby."

If Cody had stayed in Buffalo Gully, Grayson would've been the most sullen football player in Buffalo Gully. As soon as the kid had found dance, he'd tapped into a well of athleticism that had surprised all of us.

Ivy skipped toward me. "Happy Birthday," she said in a singsong voice.

I squatted in front of her. "Dang, girl. You're going to be taller than me soon."

"I don't want to be that tall." She giggled and dipped into a curtsy, fluffing up the skirt of her swirly dress.

"Why not? You can reach the top of the cupboards." Sutton used to curse me for putting dishes we used regularly on the top shelf.

Ivy leaned in close, a conspiratorial glint in her eyes. "Then I'll have to clean them."

I barked out a laugh and ruffled her hair. "Always stay one step ahead of them."

She grinned, sporting a missing tooth she'd had when I last saw her, and skipped off.

When I rounded out of the garage, I spotted a platter of food and what looked like a cake tray by Ansen's feet. Aggie came down the stairs and gave me a rare hug. We weren't a touchy-feely family. Cody's kids were different, and their enthusiastic hugs were a breath of fresh air.

"Happy fortieth, Wilder," she said.

"You didn't have to do this."

"I know."

A worry gnawed at my mind. "I might get called out."

"Then we'll eat and leave when we need to leave," she said. "I knew you were on call when I planned it."

I had to clear my throat again. "I appreciate it."

"Good—now let's go in and get some food in case you have to leave."

I had everyone pile into the house.

Tova glanced around, her blue eyes wide. "I've never been in here— Oh, slow down."

I smiled at the thunder of the kids streaking down the

hall as they raced for the bathroom. Aggie started unpacking sandwiches, chips, fruit, and salad. "There's nothing in here they can ruin," I assured her. The place had furniture, and that was it.

Cody tied an "Over The Hill" helium balloon to a dining room chair.

"Just wait until you turn fifty," I grumbled, not caring a damn bit what my age was or how many balloons Cody attached to my chair.

"That's why I have to be obnoxious for all of your fortieth birthdays."

Aggie was in the kitchen, and I stood helpless as to what to do. I usually hated the feeling. The idea of Cody being in charge used to chafe, but today he could tie a million balloons to chairs in the house. They were better than being on my own with beer and watching old sports clips. Technically, today Aggie was the ringleader, and thanks to her, sounds that were rarely heard in my place filled the air. Dishes that hadn't been used for years were taken out of cupboards. Talking, laughter, and the occasional baby squawk filled the house.

Aggie handed Ro to Ansen and disappeared into the little-used kitchen. She came out with the dessert, which was actually a small cake surrounded by donuts. Tova dug out the candle.

My work phone rang and vibrated at my hip.

My stomach sank, and a groan slipped out. Ivy and Grayson jumped in to help with the candles. Aggie glanced at me, and Eliot and Cody eyed me.

"Excuse me." I went into the kitchen and answered. "Deputy Knight."

Brenda, the dispatcher who'd been with the department the longest, spoke. "A grass fire at the section line by

Thompson Road has gotten out of control. Help blocking off the road is requested."

A fucking fire. God knew how long it could burn during the driest part of summer. I didn't know when I'd return home, and I'd smell like a cross between a campfire and a stale blunt. I stepped into the dining room.

Cody saw me first, resignation in his eyes. "Gotta go?"

"Yeah," I said gruffly and bit back a sudden and intense hatred for my job. Where had that thought come from? I was being selfish. Wasn't that what Ray had accused me of when I'd gotten into trouble as a teen? What Cody had said when I wouldn't follow his directions immediately after Mama left? I was being selfish. The town needed me. I beelined for my bedroom, shut the door, and dressed. I had the task down to a science.

Out in the dining room, the candles were lit. The regret that I wore a badge was tough to beat back.

Aggie gave me an understanding smile. "Okay, really quick now and give Uncle Wilder hugs while you sing."

Aggie and Tova led the fastest rendition of "Happy Birthday" I'd ever heard. I got a quick hug from Grayson and Ivy.

I backed out of the dining room, waving to everyone, my gaze unfocused so I couldn't see disappointed expressions. "Thank you. This means a lot."

A chorus of "Happy Birthdays" followed me out the front door.

I trotted to my vehicle and got in. This was familiar. This was what I was meant to do.

Except my family had driven all the way out here. For me. When was the last time someone had done something for me?

Since before I faced divorce papers one life-changing afternoon.

Don't be selfish. I kicked the car into gear. I didn't need directions to the fire. The billowing smoke on the horizon was like a giant arrow. Thompson Road ran past the quarry. A nice swath of gravel and dirt mounds sat between town and the burn.

The next few hours were a whirlwind as I redirected traffic and gave directions to people unfamiliar with the county to find another route to their destination.

Ray stopped by to check on everyone and said, "Helluva Saturday, eh, Wilder?"

Hell of a birthday. Here was the call I thought I wanted. The irony would make me laugh if I wasn't so damn frustrated.

One of the neighbors who bordered Knight land stopped to ask if I could help him move hay bales in case the smolder wasn't crushed out. I couldn't leave Darren Mapmaker in the lurch. He'd been good to us despite Barns's prickly attitude. I initially told him I could. But then I'd gotten a text from Aggie that said everyone was leaving and locking my place back up. Regret was a dull burn in the back of my throat, just like the embers the rural fire department was continuing to slash. After I was cleared off the scene, I hauled bales with Darren for a couple of hours. By the time I was done and driving home, the sun had set. I opened the window to air out myself and the vehicle.

Once I was inside the house, I let the door shut behind me. One would never guess the place had been filled with seven people and a baby. The meal was cleaned up, and the chairs had been pushed back in around the table. The extra seats had been put away.

No one could tell my birthday had happened. How much time had I gotten with my family? An hour? Forty-five minutes?

All but Eliot had made a six-hour round trip.

Were they still in town?

I messaged Eliot to ask.

ELIOT

Since it was early, they went back.
Tova teaches her pole dancing class
on Sundays.

The fucker reminded me on purpose. Sutton was one of Tova's students, and I pictured her long legs wrapped around a silver pole far too often while I was showering and stroking off.

I did not need a boner right now. The anger I felt at myself burned too hot.

My stomach growled, saving me. It'd been hours since lunch, and I wanted some taste in my mouth that wasn't reminiscent of smoke.

In the kitchen, the light on the dishwasher said a load was done. I hardly had to use the damn thing. The cake was on the counter with half of the pieces cut out. The only letters left were H-A-P and B-I-R-T and part of the H. All the donuts remained. They should've taken it all home with them.

They shouldn't have bothered coming.

I could bring some cake to Ray. He was a sucker for office treats. I could eat a slice with him so I was actually celebrating with someone.

I rubbed the ache in my stomach. Hunger pains or guilt?

A message came through my phone.

SUTTON

Happy Birthday

I'd let my family down. Was this what it was like for Sutton? Only instead of coming home to an empty house, she'd had to stay here and wait. There'd been no other place for her to go.

Until there was. And she'd left.

Thanks.

I grabbed a donut, stuffed it in my mouth, and headed to the shower. This was the birthday I deserved.

Seven

SUTTON

After my pole dancing lesson, I stopped at Aggie's house to take care of a cyst on her Mangalitsa pig Skinny's leg.

She helped me pack my gear and load my kit into the pickup. "You didn't have to come today, but thank you."

"No problem." I had nothing else to do but worry about why I didn't get more than a thanks after I sent Wilder a happy birthday text. "I was surprised you were home already."

Indecision flickered in her expression. "We came back last night."

"Oh. Everything all right?" Had I been wrong, and Wilder hated the idea of celebrating his birthday?

"I think so. Wilder got called out. We deliberated on whether we should wait for cake, but after an hour, we broke and ate. Waited another hour and then took off." She worried her lower lip. "Maybe we should've stayed

96

with Eliot, but he said he was going to work all day Sunday anyway."

"And Wilder could get called out again." How disappointing. I should have righteous indignation coursing through me. Wilder's family traveled so far to see him, and his work interfered. But my heart hung heavy. That had to suck to miss out on their visit.

"That's what we thought. I could tell he felt bad enough as it was."

"Yeah." An old spark of anger flared and died. I had no reason to be upset anymore.

"Is that what it was like? Middle of a meal, and he had to go?"

I nodded. "I quit taking weekdays off because he'd have a meeting to go to even though he wasn't scheduled. Or he'd be in court. Have to meet with the lawyer. All those extra tasks never seemed to line up with when he was working, and they all happened on his time off."

"How often did he get called out?"

"At least once per day. They're so short-staffed, and you know how he is."

"I do." She folded her arms. "Are you happier now? I was so damn worried about both of you, but lately you seem to be lighter."

It was the orgasms. From her brother. The one I divorced and the one we were talking about, making me an awful friend. I bit the inside of my cheek until the bite of pain wiped out the building guilt. "I feel a lot better."

"Was it dancing with all the cowboys at the street dance?"

Just one cowboy. "It didn't hurt to feel wanted."

"They all had their eyes on you. Whenever you're ready to date again..."

When I pictured myself sitting in a restaurant across from a date, I saw a pair of dark brown eyes, ruffled hair that had been flattened and then had a hand run through it after a cowboy hat was taken off, and wide shoulders that were perfect to hang onto when he thrust into me.

Whew. I had to quit thinking of sex with Wilder, or I was going to blush furiously. Aggie would notice, and I'd have to lie again if she said anything.

"I'm in a good spot right now. I don't know about dating."

Was it relief that passed over her face? Was it weird for her to think of me and Wilder moving on with others?

Were she and Cody the reason why I dragged my feet when I was flirted with or asked out? Did I harbor a fear of going on a date and being seen by one of Wilder's relatives?

I could latch on to the possibility, but I knew the truth. I entertained a secret fantasy I was ashamed to acknowledge and that was hard to escape. A dream that Wilder would pound my door down, tell me I was the most important person in his life, and he'd been too clueless to realize it. He quit his job, and he was giving up law enforcement, and he would wait on me hand and foot while I worked. He would promise to be home whenever I got done with work, and it'd be the two of us forever.

He'd proclaim that he chose me.

Did all divorced people wish for this?

"Are we doing darts this week?" I asked to redirect my thoughts.

"Hell yeah. I mean, as long as Tova's not pushing out a baby, she's in." She grinned. "She and I have a bet going each week."

"About what?"

"How much you and Vienne are going to get hit on each night." She held two fingers up. "I bet two and two."

Laughter sputtered out of me. "I don't get hit on that much." She gave me a look. "Okay, there are a couple of guys who keep trying with me and Vienne."

"More than a couple."

"Vienne, maybe. She's a catch." On top of dressing better than me and not melting into the surroundings when she was out, Vienne was more aware when it came to guys. Sometimes she flirted, other times, she blew them off. The combination made her even more desirable to them.

I hadn't developed the social skills in high school because I'd been home so much, so I hadn't made friends. Taking my awkward people skills to college and pairing them with a frantic drive to study as much as possible and intern at any vet clinic that would take me, I hadn't been a social butterfly.

I'd been too focused on getting into vet school as a kid who didn't have much exposure to veterinarians or a variety of animals.

Wilder had barged through all those barriers. He'd called me Doc and kept hitting on me until I got it through my oblivious head that the tall, dark cowboy might be into me.

"Both of you are a catch," Aggie insisted, "but men are more intimidated by you. Vienne's been around longer, and she dated Theo, so they know she's open to going out. You're a mystery."

Unless I was at a street dance. And then Wilder had burst through the haze and rescued me.

Ugh. I had it bad. Good thing we had guidelines. Still,

I was worried about him. His birthday had ended with him alone. Presumably.

Carla Bosworth would've been happy to cheer him up.

What if he ran into her and needed consolation?

My gut churned. I shouldn't care. I believed that he hadn't been with anyone since the divorce. I didn't truly think he'd sought out Carla or anyone else, but the thought didn't shut that part of my mind up.

I left Aggie's place with a promise to see her at darts on Thursday. At home, I played fetch with Oreo and pulled some weeds before I went inside. I threw a plate of leftover meatloaf into the microwave and sat at my island to wait and glare at my phone.

I should leave it alone. We were only supposed to be sleeping together. Instead of thinking it served him right, I thought of him leaving in the middle of his birthday party and coming home to an empty house.

Huffing out a breath, I punched out a message to Wilder.

> Sorry to hear about your birthday party.

I pushed the phone far away. It vibrated on the table and continued to ring. The corner of my mouth ticked up. Wilder didn't carry on long text conversations. He didn't have the patience. When it came to me, he called rather than finding a reason to cut off the thread.

Warmth nestled around my heart when I answered. I was flirting with getting attached to my ex-husband again.

No. This was like checking on a friend. I was trying

hard not to be in love with Wilder, but love or not, I would always care about him.

"Hi," I answered just as the microwave dinged.

"Am I interrupting dinner?"

I briefly shut my eyes at the deep rumble going right into my eardrum and vibrating down to my groin. "I just heated up some meatloaf."

He groaned. Same effect on my body. "Did you make it?"

"Yes, but now it takes me three days to eat it for lunch and dinner before it's gone."

"You can make a half recipe, Sutton."

"I can't help it. I'm used to planning ahead with meals, since Mom and Dad usually forgot to leave me with new groceries."

He grunted. He'd heard the stories before. Some of them. I hadn't wanted to tell a guy who was surrounded by family and people who sought him out every day that I had been a forgotten kid. "Make it when I'm coming down, and I'll eat it for breakfast before I go—after I feast on you."

Desire lit my nerves like a winning bid on *The Price Is Right*. Yes, please. I fanned myself. Was this a hot flash? Most likely a Wilder flash. I didn't text him so I could get hopelessly turned on when he wasn't around to do a damn thing about it. "Aggie said you got called out right after they got there."

There was a beat of silence. "Did you tell them 'I told you so?'" he asked softly.

His family had been buffered from his schedule, and it wasn't that they didn't believe me. They might not have understood why his absence had bothered me so much, but each of Wilder's siblings knew how the ties to the family businesses messed with their own lives.

"No. There are no hard feelings from them."

"They're not going to divorce me for missing out?"

I clamped my teeth together. Ouch. His bitterness was undeniable.

"Shit," he said softly. "I didn't mean—I'm just irritated about yesterday."

"I get it."

"I know. The cake was good. I'll be eating donuts for three days for lunch and dinner."

I smiled, grateful we were on safer ground. I couldn't rehash the problems in our marriage and keep sleeping with him—and I wanted to keep sleeping with him. "Eliot would take some."

"I think he did, unless the kids ate a shitload of cake."

I laughed. "Eliot's got your back."

"My siblings are good for that." His tone sobered. "I'm glad Aggie has yours."

"She's a good friend." Aggie was my first real friend, and I didn't meet her until after I started dating Wilder, well into my midtwenties. I had been afraid I would lose her, but the divorce had brought us closer.

"You are, too, or she wouldn't be married to the love of her life and deliriously happy."

"That was the Fireball. Aggie and I were helpless bystanders." At least Aggie had the excuse of the alcohol when she'd reignited things with her ex. I'd been stone-cold sober when I'd decided to divorce Wilder. Maybe if I'd been drinking, my decision would be easier to regret. Aggie also hadn't had to worry about whether we'd have a falling out if she started seeing her ex again.

"Can I admit to being glad she has a baby so you two don't go out and make plans to lure in any other exes?"

The warmth cuddled around my heart cozied up harder. "Ansen could drive us home if we did."

A faint growl made it over the line. He hated even joking about the possibility of me finding someone else.

I poked the bear harder. "Besides, it'd be me and Vienne out this time, and I won't risk helping her get back at her ex in case she ends up with him again."

"Do you and Vienne go out together often?"

Why was he asking so innocently? Afraid Vienne would help me find the one I moved on from him with? What should be possible was more impossible than I feared. "Last night, actually. We hit the Fireball, and I offered you a bullshit job. Haven't you checked your email?"

He chuckled. "You'd have to do something different than what you and Aggie did to Ansen. I'd be too suspicious."

"I don't know. The job offer wasn't technically bull-shit, and I could use more hands at the clinic. I just hired a front desk clerk, but she can only work part-time and was aghast when I told her we all pitched in to clean."

"So if I get an email for a janitorial position at an up-and-coming veterinary clinic, I should be suspicious?"

"Maybe. Unless you're busy with Carla?" I winced. Why did I go there? We weren't supposed to be talking like this. Did "limited small talk" have to be included in our guidelines?

He made a choking noise. "What brought that up?"

I shrugged, more for myself than him since he couldn't see. "You never said you told her no. Only that you hadn't taken her up on her offer."

"Aren't they the same thing?"

"Nope. You're leaving the door open."

"You really thinking telling her no will get her to back off?"

"Have you tried?" *Don't you want to try?*

We were muddying our divorce. We were no longer together, and I didn't have a say on who he slept with. He'd said this arrangement was for as long as we didn't want to date others. What happened when he called me to say he'd had enough? He'd met someone? Or he thought he'd try being Carla's third husband?

"Sutton," he said, sounding resigned. "What's going on?"

"Nothing." I frowned at my meatloaf. I'd have to heat it up again. When I got out of the cringy conversation I'd started.

"I'm not fucking Carla, okay?"

"Sure."

"You and I made a deal, and I'm honoring it."

A deal. His words both made me feel better and tore at my heart. A version of *Deal or No Deal* where Wilder and I were the only contestants. "I don't like that woman."

"I know."

"She told me—" I locked my lower lip between my teeth. I hadn't told Aggie about my run-in with Carla either. Not this one. I had plenty. Everyone in Buffalo Gully had their history with Carla. The nature of small towns were those people—the ones you had to tolerate. But Carla had a sixth sense about where to target. "Never mind. It's nothing."

"She told our dispatcher, Brenda, she was such an inspiration because 'as we all know, older people have slower reaction times.' And then she went on to laugh about how computers weren't even a thing when Brenda was born, and now the county's safety is in her hands and a bunch of electronic equipment."

"Ouch. How'd Brenda take it?"

A low chuckle came over the line. "We thought she'd lob insults right back, but she gushed about how the kids these days talk about body counts, as in how many people you've slept with, but she tallies her body count with people she's helped save, and she's proud to be in the triple digits."

"Good for her." I licked my dry lips. He gave me the courage to continue, but Brenda's experience didn't prod at the weakness in our marriage. "Carla, uh, commented that her first husband was a cop in Bozeman, and that it takes a strong woman to stick by law enforcement, and she'd still be with him if he hadn't cheated."

"Was that before or after our divorce?"

"During." I was already caught in a tangle of self-recrimination because I'd stayed married longer than I was happy and hated myself for asking for a divorce. "I was in town to finish up some paperwork and ran across her at the bank." I'd been raw and second-guessing myself. Carla had beamed at me like she was brandishing her HIS SECOND WIFE: THE STRONG ONE card to be with Wilder next.

"You're a strong woman, Sutton," he said quietly. "Fuck her. Shit—not literally. You know what I meant, right?"

My smile was a relief. The last person I thought I'd tell about Carla's dig was Wilder, and he was the last person who should be making me feel better about it. "I know what you meant."

"You're picking up what I'm putting down?"

"And you think my game show lines are lame." I missed this lightness with Wilder.

"Never said that," he said almost defensively. "I was usually guessing what amount you were attaching to your *Jeopardy!* category."

"I'll take 'What's the Amount' for three hundred."

"See, now, I was thinking six hundred."

I smiled. "Close."

"I also never knew how to react to your sayings."

Frowning, I traced a line in the fake marbled surface of the island top. "What do you mean?"

"Remember when I got you the *Jeopardy!* board game for our first anniversary? I thought you were going to pass out and not from delight. Then you put it on the bookshelf, and by Christmas, it was gone."

"You noticed that?" I thought I'd been sneakier.

"I noticed you like to quote game shows, but you don't like to play them."

"I used to have nothing else to watch when my parents were with Honey at all her practices and shows and training camps. They didn't want to spend money on cable when they weren't home." I'd been home, but that hadn't seemed to matter. The antenna was punishment for not wanting to skate or watch skating. "You're lucky I'm not reciting *Days of Our Lives* storylines."

"Those soaps might be why you thought I'd go running to Carla."

Just like that, he took the heaviness out of the conversation. "If the soaps were the reason I was suspicious, I'd have accused you of sleeping with my twin sister while I had amnesia."

"You don't have a twin, and you never hit your head, and I don't like figure skating divas, so I'm in the clear."

"You are," I agreed, smiling.

"Tell me something crazy that happened at the clinic."

Nostalgia crashed over me. These phone conversations, minus the Carla aspect, were a lot like when we first started dating. He'd ask about work, and I'd tell him the uplifting or humorous stories. In person, I'd cry on his shoulder about the heartbreaking ones. "Me and River, my tech, worked for twenty minutes to get a cat out of its carrier. River started calling it the anti-gravity cat."

"Don't the carriers come apart?"

"This one didn't. It was a pain in the ass, and the cat wasn't having it." His deep chuckle was all I'd need to sleep well tonight. I didn't have any more stories. Eventless weeks were good in my field. Since he opened the door to personal conversation, I wanted to hear about him. He was home. "What are you doing tonight?"

"Watching ESPN."

Nothing new. I'd wait for him to get home so we could do something together, and he'd want to chill and watch TV. I'd had years to chill and watch TV.

"Ray's retiring."

"For real this time?"

Ray had planned to retire ten years ago, after Wilder had on-the-job experience and Ray's first grandkid was born. But no, he needed the health coverage. Valid.

He'd been about to retire again five years ago. But no, he'd be bored.

Then two years ago. But no, the population spurt in the county was causing growing pains, and his expertise was needed.

Figured he'd actually retire after the divorce. *If* he actually did this time.

"He's confident I'll get appointed interim sheriff," Wilder continued, "and then I'll run in the next election. He thinks there'll be no one to run against."

"I'm sure there'll be some takers."

"But would they be any good? Kaplan seemed interested, but he's in it for himself."

We'd also had this conversation before. Wilder was a lot like his brothers—no one else could do as good of a job as them. The difference in the next election would be that they weren't running against Ray. There might be a lot more interest than Ray or Wilder expected. "That's Ray's voice, since he groomed you and all."

There was a tsk on the other end. "You're making him sound like a pedo."

"You know what I mean." Ray had helped Wilder through some hard years after Birdie Knight walked out on her family, but he'd also targeted Wilder as a future deputy and sheriff and set about making it so. That Wilder wanted the end goal so badly had been kismet— for them. Death knell for us. "I guess we'll have to see if he actually submits any retirement paperwork."

"Yeah." A few moments of weighted silence passed. Did he think that becoming sheriff would change things? That he would have fewer hours, less court, and not fill any days off with meetings? But then, it didn't matter for him anymore.

I knew I should go. I should reheat my meatloaf and remember I was a divorced woman, and I was no longer invested in this argument.

"Hey, what's with the camper?" he asked.

I happily extracted myself from the subject of his job, also content to stay on the phone. "I'm going camping."

"Where are you going?" His curt question came off like I was being interrogated. If anyone else asked me the way he did, I'd be on defense. But I liked Wilder's interest. A lot.

"The Black Hills in April. I plan to do some sight-seeing and hiking and maybe even some shopping." Rapid City, South Dakota, wasn't a metropolis, but it'd be the biggest town I'd spent real time in since vet school. "But in September, I'm going to Medora. Kind of like a test run so I'm close to home if anything goes wrong with hauling the camper."

"Who's going with you?"

"No one."

Silence met my answer. "Sutton—"

"Don't give me the lecture. I'm tired of everyone being surprised a single woman can even back a camper into a spot." I wasn't expecting concern from Wilder. He was normally my champion.

"I've seen you back horse trailers a million times. It's you alone at night—hell, even during the day—in a remote spot, I'm worried about."

I should be defensive, but instead, warmth spread through me. "I'll have Oreo and bear spray."

"It's not the bears I'm worried about," he grumbled.

"There are no bears in Medora." Mountain lions, and I'd never see an attack coming. Oreo could sound an alarm. Maybe.

"How long are you going to be gone?"

"I'll return the next Monday."

"And in April."

"I'm leaving the sixteenth."

A grunt was my only response. "We still up for this Friday?"

My body tingled as an answer. "Yes."

"See you then, Sutton."

The low purr went right through the phone to the spot between my thighs. I hung up and went to the microwave above the stove to reheat my reheated meal. For two minutes while waiting, I let the fantasy of camping with Wilder play through my head.

If the camper's rocking, don't come a knocking.

I caught my smile in the microwave door. Then I watched it fade. A girl could dream, but my trip was only happening because I'd decided to quit waiting for a fantasy to become real.

Eight

WILDER

The din of the bar was as familiar as the house I'd grown up in. I'd spent many nights here as a single deputy on my nights off. Then I'd met Sutton, and occasionally, we'd go on dates here. Not often, which was likely my fault. Now that I was a single guy, I didn't come for the same reasons I did before I was a married man.

The bar pizza with a cold beer hit the spot better than what I could cook at home.

Eliot was with me. I was off for tonight, but Sutton had a girls' night on Thursdays. She was probably playing darts with my sister and Vienne and Tova. If she was getting hit on, I didn't want to know.

Yet my hand was fisted around my mug, worried my phone would ring, and she'd tell me she had a date and I shouldn't come tomorrow or ever again.

I took a drink, hoping to chase down the acid eating up my throat.

Eliot shamelessly snagged the last bite of pizza.

"You didn't even ask if I wanted any, jackass," I said after I swallowed.

He shrugged. "You're eye-fucking your beer. Thought you two needed a minute."

I was thinking of Sutton. Our phone conversation last weekend hadn't made things better. I'd gone to sleep that night, all cozy in the knowledge she was jealous of me and other women. If that made me an asshole, so be it. I got chewed apart from the inside out thinking of her with another dude.

If I listened to Ray, I'd be working on my campaign persona. I'd be chatting with the bartender, slapping palms with the other ranchers in the bar, and being the consummate politician I had planned to be. But Ray was still in office, and I had time. I had other things on my mind.

Eliot chomped off half the slice of pizza. We were tucked into a high-top along one of the walls of the bar. "What's on your mind anyway? You're not usually this quiet," he said around a mouthful.

I lifted a brow. Neither of us were talkers unless we were glossing over horse training regimens, feed requirements for whatever season we were in, or planning on when we were working or moving cattle or horses.

He rolled his eyes. "You know what I mean."

Eliot acted like he didn't care, but he'd keep bugging me. So I gave him part of the truth. "Did you know Sutton's going camping by herself soon?"

He swallowed and stared at me, his gaze contemplative. "No. How do *you* know?"

Shit. How would I have found out if Aggie didn't tell me? Did Cody know? I didn't know how I'd explain a conversation with Sutton when no one thought the two of us had crossed paths in months. I gambled on Eliot minding his own business and not asking follow-up questions of my siblings. "Aggie."

He narrowed his eyes for a heartbeat, then shrugged. "Sutton's smart. She'll be careful."

She would take all the precautions she could, but the what-ifs were killing me. What if she went for a hike, and no one heard from her again? What if some obsessed maniac stalked her back to the campground and broke into her camper? What if she met another lone tourist, and they hit it off and had a sex-filled weekend, and she took him to the Black Hills? She might come back engaged. Hell, married.

Acid washed back up my throat. When would I learn to quit eating bar pizza this late at night? Add in the beer, and I was in for hours of heartburn.

Right. Because it's the food, dipshit.

"Good for her," Eliot added when I did nothing but glower.

"You used to be my favorite brother."

He didn't smirk like I thought he would. Instead, he turned serious. "The time to do something about Sutton has passed. Unless things have changed?"

Everything had changed when she'd let me inside her one more time, from the second she let me take off her panties and stuff them in my pocket. The pair was washed and neatly folded in my underwear drawer. Her drawer was empty, and I hadn't been able to set one lone pair inside. So I tucked the white lace next to my Hanes.

"Nothing's changed," I said roughly. My trysts with my ex-wife were a secret. I didn't care to hear about how my siblings would think me being back in Sutton's life was a bad idea. They'd ask me if I hadn't fucked up with her enough already, and I'd have to figure out why doing a job that was important to me was messed up.

He slid his gaze away and took a long drink. I couldn't tell what he was thinking, and that was likely his goal. He set the mug down and smacked his lips. "Jodi Harbour is back in town."

I followed the direction of his gaze to a woman with mahogany hair swirling around her face. Jodi was between my age and Eliot's. Jodi and I had dated for a year in high school, we'd lost touch in college, and whenever she came home, she was easy to talk to, to slip back into that old familiarity with, but there'd been nothing but friendship between us.

As if she heard Eliot, she spotted us and waved. With a smile, she wove through the tables. Her legs were long in blue jeans, and she had on a camisole tank top. The bar's AC was set on max, but I was sure some nice guy in this place would love to offer to help her get warm.

"Wilder, Eliot. I was hoping I saw someone I knew tonight." She stood by the extra stool at our table, but didn't sit, like she was waiting to be invited. Eliot's gaze bored into me, but I ignored him.

"Hey, Jodi." I didn't offer her a seat.

"How's it going, Jodi?" Eliot asked, ripping his perplexed look away from me.

The conversation with Sutton about Carla played through my mind. I had been determined to keep my dick out of anyone in Buffalo Gully, but I hadn't encountered someone I thought I could have a real future with.

Jodi and I had history. We got along. She'd been divorced for years, from what I could recall. We'd been friends for years. Overall, she'd be a solid choice to seriously chase and move on with from my own divorce.

The burn in the back of my throat strengthened, and my stomach joined in, twisting and roiling.

"And I heard there might be a change in command?" Jodi asked, her smile warm. Was there an invite in her expression, or was I overthinking? "Dad said Sheriff Dahlen might finally be retiring?"

"We'll see." Others were making comments, and Ray's exit was more of a sure thing, but I didn't care to spend the night discussing my aspirations.

She tapped my wrist with her warm fingers. "I'm sure everyone's looking forward to seeing you take the position."

Eliot's gaze followed her move, and he started smirking. I ignored him.

"I'm ready for it." It was assumed I'd be appointed in his absence.

"Oh, I know you are," she gushed. "I always get stories from Mom about you at the school. Let's see, you do reading time with the kindergarten, then you're on duty for most games, and you even swing by the track meets."

I nodded, and she grinned, her eyes twinkling. Dimly, I was aware she was flirting. I also wasn't sure what to do about it. Did I want to be flirted with?

"Yeah. I like kids." I chugged my beer. Clarity was hard to swallow. I didn't want to pursue Jodi, and her flirtatiousness sent panic streaming through my blood vessels. Feelings that didn't bode well. Was I going to be lovesick, waiting for scraps from Sutton until she quit throwing them?

What was Sutton feeling?

Jodi and Eliot chatted. Eliot nudged me with his boot. "Did you hear? Jodi's in Sidney now."

"I can work remotely, and I needed to be closer to my parents." She was positioned slightly closer to me than to my brother, and when she spoke to me, her proximity bordered on intimate. Stupid small tables.

"That's nice." I went to lift my mug but noticed it was empty. Damn. I limited myself to one drink when I went out so I wouldn't tempt disaster—with people or cars.

Eliot scowled at me when Jodi glanced behind her. "Oh, Heather's here. I haven't seen her in years." She gave me an unsure look. A tendril of guilt curled around my tongue at the confusion in her eyes. "Nice to talk to you. Maybe see you at one of the football games? Dad loves going to those."

"Maybe," I said, nailing down the bordering-on-rude vibe I was giving off.

When she was across the bar, Eliot kicked me, landing the toe of his boot just below my kneecap.

"Ow. Asshole," I said, rubbing my leg.

"I'm not the asshole," he hissed. "What was that about?"

"I like Jodi," I whispered. "I'm not looking to fuck her."

"Why not?"

I snapped my mouth shut. The answer would get me in a lot of trouble. He'd lecture me, then he'd tell my brothers, and they'd be in my business. Aggie might get upset with Sutton.

No. No one could know.

Eliot blinked, then adjusted the brim of his ball cap.

"One of these days, you're going to have to get over Sutton."

"What if I don't?" I couldn't take the words back. They were out there.

He didn't laugh me off. I started to squirm the longer he seriously considered my question.

"I know the divorce was my fault." I needed to shut my damn mouth, but I wasn't used to Eliot judging my choices. "I know I can't change the trust, and my job is important, and she wanted more. But dammit—I didn't marry her because I thought that a decade later, I would want to do it all over again."

He shoved his mug to the side and leaned his forearms on the table. "You did fuck up, and I'm not saying that because it's been hell getting good vet care out at the ranch. You can be a deputy anywhere."

Barns hadn't trashed the Knight name anywhere else. No other county had a gruff sheriff who'd yanked a drunk teen Wilder out of a ditch and told him he could do more with his life. "The ranch?"

"Cody found a way around the trust. You can too."

"What about you?"

He scoffed. "When do you guys care about my circumstances?"

"You're right, I don't." I wasn't tied to the ranch as much as him, but he was my brother. I wasn't leaving him with more to do because I wasn't holding up my end.

"Asshole. Anyway, you might feel like you're always out at the ranch because you are—on your time off. But I'm out there nearly twenty-four-seven. Trust me, your contribution isn't making or breaking the place." He sat back. "Look, we have Chambers. Lorenzo can look into the parameters and see what leeway you have, like some of your inheritance goes to hiring some help. But…" He spread his hands. "You might have to take the pay cut. As for the deputy part, well, that's your choice."

"I can't be sheriff just anywhere."

"Can't? Or won't?"

I scowled at him. "Of all people, I shouldn't have to explain it to you."

"You don't have to explain shit to me, dickweed. You want to be married to your job, keep doing what you're doing. You want to turn down the Jodis of the world and sleep alone, go ahead. But when you're the one retiring, who's going to be there for you?"

Not Sutton. My reflux from earlier returned. "What's that supposed to mean? Ray has family."

"An ex-wife and the kids who never visit?"

I clenched my teeth together, angry at Eliot and myself for being on the same wavelength.

He picked up his beer mug, the inch of amber liquid left sloshing against the sides. He didn't drink it. Instead, he studied me, his gaze assessing. "Jodi would probably forgive your earlier moodiness."

She would. She'd always been understanding like that. But she didn't lean on me when we danced together, completely trusting me to whisk her away. She didn't call when she knew I missed company on my birthday. And Jodi's dark hair wasn't what I pictured spread over my abdomen while paler lips than hers were wrapped around my cock.

So. I had it bad for Sutton. Which was why I was just fine with our arrangement.

Eliot polished his beer off. "I guess it'll be me and you in thirty years, two old fucking bachelors complaining about the weather."

Finally, the focus was off me. "Why haven't you seriously tried to find someone?"

"Unlike you, I know my circumstances won't change, and no woman wants this life."

"Just because Mama didn't doesn't mean no one will."

He twisted his lips. "Mama. Aggie. Sutton. We know Meg would've left Cody eventually."

Yeah, she would've.

"Maybe I'll never retire," I said as if it solved all my problems.

✷

A buzzing woke me up. I squinted at the window, needing a moment to register I was in Sutton's house.

Light filtered around the shades. Early morning. Less than eight hours ago, I'd arrived after sundown to park in her garage and headed straight to bed. Neither of us had gotten much sleep. This was only our fourth time hooking up, but I was quickly becoming dependent, watching the calendar and the clock, waiting for the moment I could hit the button on the garage remote she'd let me use.

The conversation with Eliot in the bar the other night hadn't eased the urgency, only made it worse, as if I'd find my answers waking up in her bed.

"Hello?" she croaked. The sound hadn't been an alarm but was her phone. A moment later, she sat straight up. "No, I can be there in a few minutes. How far out are you again? Okay. Send me your address, and I'll plug it into my GPS. Okay—bye."

She scooted out of bed. I rolled over and watched her

scurry around, getting shadowed glimpses of her lush hips and breasts. "Another emergency?"

"Yes." She bounced on one foot to drag her jeans onto the other leg. "He's got a bloated cow. I've done some work for this rancher, and he's as intuitive as Eliot."

Our family's ranch had only survived Barns's last years because Eliot could spot an issue a mile away, and when he couldn't deal with something himself, Sutton had swooped in for the save.

She tugged a shirt over her head. "River is at her mom's for the weekend, but I think this guy's son is going to meet us."

She'd be alone with two guys she didn't really know? "You trust this guy?" I hated the idea of her going to ranchers' places by herself. Most of her ranching clients were men or couples and most were decent, but I wasn't the law here. I didn't have an excuse to be patrolling by, and I hadn't been born and raised in Crocus Valley. I knew no one, and Sutton hadn't lived in town long. She wouldn't know who to stay away from yet.

"Want me to go with?" I rolled up and got out of bed. It wasn't that small of a world. No one would know who I was, and they likely wouldn't be familiar with my family.

"No, it's fine. He has a good reputation."

"They all do until they don't."

"Wilder."

"Sutton, I wasn't asking."

"But—"

"Your safety is more important than secrecy. If anyone finds out we were together for a call, we'll make something up. Like..." We'd been sneaking around for weeks, and I hadn't thought of possible excuses. "Like, you packed some of my equipment when you moved out, and I needed it before shift today."

She stared at me. "Seriously? You think anyone will buy that? What equipment?"

I threw my hands up. I hadn't had time to grab clothing, and my dick jiggled with the movement. "I don't know. A backup vest?"

She arched a brow, then rolled her eyes. "Fine. I'm leaving in two minutes."

I was dressed, had pissed, and was by the door in a minute and forty-five seconds.

She swept past me and out the front door. Her pickup was outside. Mine was hiding in her garage. Sutton had to live in the community. People liked to talk, and a gorgeous, single woman like her seen with a guy's truck in front of her house would draw attention. Those fucknuts at the street dance had circled her like three bulls in a pen with one cow. Living a few miles out of town wouldn't matter. People would notice. They'd talk. We'd be busted.

I slid into the passenger seat, and she punched the pickup in reverse. The sun was up enough that everything was visible. Light blues and purples painted the horizon. She took the highway to the other side of Crocus Valley and then turned on a gravel road to the west in the opposite direction from where Aggie and Cody lived.

"What do you know about this guy?" I asked.

She didn't look at me, just kept her eyes on the road. The dust cloud kicking up behind us hung over the road. No wind. "He's older, pays on time, and hates Dr. Jake."

She pulled into a yard with a long, beige modular home. A garage had been built on the end of the house. A small chicken coop was in the backyard, and chickens were already pecking around in the grass. A large, white Great Pyrenees was lying in the damp grass, looking like a giant dirty sweater had been discarded. He popped his head up when we coasted down the drive toward the barn.

Sutton parked and hopped out. She greeted an older rancher scurrying toward us in all his bowlegged glory. Suspenders held his jeans up, but the legs pooled into a set of worn cowboy boots.

"Hey, Sutton," he said in a voice as rough as the washboard gravel we'd just been on. "Thanks for coming. My son came by. We've got her in the barn." He was turned and heading toward the barn before he finished his sentence.

For an old man, he could out-walk a racehorse. Sutton grabbed her kit out of the back of the pickup, and we jogged to catch up to him.

A man a few years older and a lot shorter than me met the old rancher. He nodded toward us, his questioning gaze darting from me to Sutton. "I thought for a moment you had Dr. Jake with you."

I'd heard about the player, Dr. Jake. He'd gone after Aggie as if she'd had eyes for anyone other than Ansen. Aggie didn't have to tell me the other vet was sniffing around Sutton, offering a helping hand, assuring her there was enough work for both of them. He'd even offered her a job—I'd managed to get that tidbit out of Ansen, who wasn't as tight-lipped about Sutton. My brother-in-law was probably getting back at me for running him off when he and Aggie were first engaged.

He'd deserved it. But then, so did I.

"Nope," Sutton said, her expert gaze stroking over the red Angus cow. "This is…Wilder."

She left off my last name. These guys might think I was her brother or her husband, and they'd be wrong on both accounts. Any questions, and we'd have some explaining to do. People talked, and I didn't want Sutton stressing about ending up on Aggie's bad side.

I shook their hands. Rough, solid grips from the both of them.

"I'm Sheldon," the younger one said. "This is my dad, Ryan. I do the bulk of the work, and he refuses to retire."

A rancher's creed. *Won't quit 'til you make me.*

"Well," Sutton said brightly, not-so-obviously moving on from the introductions, "can I take a look?"

"I'll go in with you," Sheldon said.

Ryan draped his hands over the pen rails and kicked his boot up. "I wish this could've waited. I hate calling her so early."

"She doesn't mind." Sutton worked half days on Fridays to make up for unexpected hours. Something I was glad to see her doing after Barns had her going at all hours every day of the week. Now that she was the owner and main vet at her clinic, she needed to make sure she got time off. Especially since she insisted on being available to get called out. She had freedom now that she'd never had working for my father.

"I know it," he said. "I could tell as soon as I met her she knows what she's doing." He blinked at me. One eye was cloudier than the other, but his gaze was no less sharp. "You a vet too?"

"No, just a guy who refused to let her come out here all alone."

He grunted. "Not a bad idea. You never know about people these days." He rubbed his face. His calloused hands audibly scraped over his gray scruff. "Dr. Jake used to date my granddaughter. Although dating's a strong word," he grumbled.

Sutton and Sheldon were talking back and forth, discussing how best to handle the cow. She was using hand gestures I'd seen her do before when she and Eliot were bent over a cow. I would've been attracted to her anyway, but seeing her work had made me determined to approach her for the first time at a horse sale. A horse had whacked its head against a trailer, nearly costing the poor animal its eye. She had waded into the fray, intent to do what it took to help the creature, cautious of the other horses but unafraid of their often picky owners.

"I imagine Dr. Jake has a lot of those stories." If I got dirt on Dr. Jake from this guy, it'd be a bonus beyond making sure Sutton was safe.

He peered at me. "You from around here?"

"Nope." I left it at that.

"That man's reputation preceded him." He shook his head. "He's nice enough—when he's not breaking your loved one's heart. But I'd rather give my business to a young girl getting her start."

I smiled. Sutton wasn't a fresh pony out for her first horse show, but she was a good thirty-five years younger than Ryan. "She appreciates it."

"Heard she's divorced."

Of course people discussed the pretty new vet, including her marital status. A prickly sense that old Ryan knew more than we thought tickled the back of my neck. "Yup."

"I did a little research on her before I hired her. She used to work for Knight's Arabians in Montana."

"Sure did." Of all people, this old guy was going to rat me out? Was he one of the guys who sat at the booths in the grocery store or gas station and chatted some mornings? He'd tell his buddies about Sutton, and news would eventually get back to Cody via the small-town hotline. I'd be cockblocked by one of Sutton's customers.

"Her ex is one of Barnaby Knight's sons." His words were pointed. He was a nosy guy who paid attention, and he'd figured out who I was. How much would he tell people? Would word spread that Sutton was bringing men who didn't work for her to calls at all hours? Would the info be held against her, and she'd lose business like Dr. Jake with his reputation?

I couldn't fuck up her career more than being married to me had, but lying would only dig a deeper hole. "Barns had me to thank for dragging her to Buffalo Gully to work for him." Sutton had me to blame.

He made a non-committal noise. "Wilder *Knight*, eh?"

My department could use his detective skills. "At your service."

His attention was off Sutton and the cow and solely on me. "You moving to Crocus Valley too?"

"No. I'm a deputy, and I still work for the family ranch." He could read into the rest. Figure out his own answer to why I was with Sutton this early in the day.

His unnerving stare was back on me. "My wife died five years ago."

The change of subject was unexpected, but I gladly clutched the lifeline. "I'm sorry to hear that."

He nodded and turned his focus back to Sutton. He was quiet a moment. "She was a city girl. Followed me out here. This was my dad's land, and he got it from his parents. You know how it goes."

"I know it." In my family, my father had gotten a

windfall from my mama's inheritance. Land that had oil and a working ranch. The outcome had been the same. Barns had been the country boy, and Mama had gotten the fuck out of Dodge.

"We were separated for a while."

"How'd you work it out?" I faced him. Suddenly, his answer was everything I needed to hear.

"She gave up her career." His smile was dry. "I wouldn't recommend that route."

I'd never asked Sutton to give up hers. Wouldn't consider it. I knew the siren call of working on something that was more your identity than your job. She'd never asked me to give up mine either. She knew how important being a deputy was to me.

Repeating that thought didn't make me feel better like it used to.

"Her roots are here now." The clinic was her baby. She wouldn't leave it.

"Yup. In this kind of life, someone's gotta sacrifice."

Hadn't Chambers said the same thing to me when I'd asked about the success of his marriage? We'd sacrificed each other. "Too little too late for us."

"You're here, ain'tcha?"

I wasn't getting into the disintegration of my marriage with Ryan. "I'm here. But I have a whole county counting on me."

He scoffed. "We got police here."

"I'm going to be sheriff." My reply came out like a proud fifth grader telling me what he wanted to be when he grew up.

"We got a sheriff too. It'd be nice to have a different one," he grumped.

"I also still help my brother ranch." For now, but I

felt like I needed a stronger excuse for Ryan. It shouldn't be hard to justify why I wasn't leaving a career I'd worked so hard for.

His grunt was more disgruntled. "That's the thing about sacrifice. One of you's gotta do it, or it's not going to work."

"We already came to that conclusion." I swallowed a dull burn down my throat. "I'd appreciate it if you kept seeing me to yourself. I don't want her reputation to get flagged."

He grunted. "Don't worry. Not everyone is as observant as me. Wife called it nosy. But I won't say a thing if it keeps her getting business over Dr. Jake."

My relief was acute, and my mind turned to what he'd said earlier. When Sutton had told me she wanted a divorce, I'd been stunned. Confused. Hurt and angry. We'd seen each other every day, yet she complained about how we weren't together. We didn't take fun vacations. Or do weekend getaways. And maybe because of my shift work, sometimes she was sleeping while I was awake, or I was sleeping during the day because I'd had a night shift.

So we'd sacrificed some quality time together, that shouldn't make or break a marriage, but we *were* giving up things to be together.

She'd hit me with, *If I'm going to live like a single woman, I might as well be one.*

As I watched Sutton bend and move over the calf with a hovering Sheldon at her side, I couldn't convince myself that equally sacrificing had been a good balance.

Nine

SUTTON

Tova lobbed a dart. The bar was dim, and the music wasn't as loud as usual. Our Thursday night girls' night hangout wasn't as busy as normal.

She spread her palms over her belly and grimaced. "Can I blame my wonky center of balance for my bad aim tonight?"

Aggie stepped up to the line of white tape. "Might as well. You're running out of time to use that excuse."

Tova wiggled onto a tall chair. "I'm going to die of nerves. Cody's been talking me down for days, and I get motherhood is supposed to be natural, but is it supposed to be scary?"

I could only listen sympathetically in these conversations. I knew about animal pregnancies, but human ones had evaded me.

"It can be, and then you do it anyway. And sometimes you want to do it again." Vienne tipped the pitcher of beer to top off her mug. "I had a C-section with Catherine after twenty hours of labor, and I would've had a second kid, but my ex announced he was done before my maternity leave was over."

Jennings walked by and tipped his hat toward me. I gave him a tight smile. I didn't intend to invite him over, but he veered toward the table. "How's it going tonight, ladies?"

Aggie and Tova murmured hellos and exchanged amused glances. Vienne swatted him on the shoulder. "We're talking babies, Jennings. Labor, specifically."

His good-natured laugh echoed through the bar. "I can't join in, I'm afraid, but my mom would happily tell you about her experience with me and my brother. We were each eleven pounds."

"That would've been like two Catherines at the same time." Vienne shuddered. "What a woman."

Jennings focused on me. The hair on the back of my neck prickled. Was it the slight concern in his gaze? "Missed you at the street dance last Friday. I thought about giving you a call."

"Oh." Shit. I'd had darts with the girls Thursday and had stayed home to shower and shave all the good parts for Wilder's arrival. "I was all danced out."

The corner of his mouth tipped up. "You danced for hours straight last time. Hey, I talked to Ryan Kranz yesterday."

My heart stuttered, and I coughed on my next breath. *Stop talking.*

"He said you were out last weekend."

"Yes. How's his cow?" I had checked in on Monday. The cow was fine.

"Good. He said—"

"I really like working with him. I appreciate him and his business. How about you? Working cattle soon?" We had to get off the topic of me at the Kranzes'. Wilder told me Ryan had figured out who he was. Had Ryan and Sheldon told many people Dr. Sutton showed up at the crack of dawn with her ex?

Jennings rattled off details about working cattle and how his brother and his family came out to help. His teenage nieces loved dressing up and being cowgirls for the weekend.

He dropped his gaze at the end of the story, almost shy. "Mind if I grab you for a minute, Sutton?"

Dread pooled in my stomach. I stuffed the paranoia that he knew about Wilder away and nodded. "Be right back."

Aggie's small smile was supportive. I might be looking too hard and seeing a glint of sadness. Tova toasted me with her can of ginger ale. Vienne took a huge pull of beer, but I caught the grin she was fighting off.

With leaden feet, I followed him toward the entry to the bar. Fewer patrons sat by the door, and the noise didn't echo as bad.

"What's up?" I asked brightly. *Please have a question about vaccines or the best brand of mineral.* Anything but the guy I was with at the Kranzes'.

He shifted from boot to boot. "I was just, uh, wondering if you'd like to meet up sometime. We could come here or find out where a band's playing."

I did not want to dance with Jennings again. Wilder ruined the dance floor experience for me. "I meant it, Jennings. I'm danced out for now."

"We don't need to find a band. We can just go...out."

Oh. *Oh.* He was asking me on a date. He didn't want a sure-thing partner on the dance floor who wouldn't get stolen from him. "I'm busy, you know, with work." I defaulted to my standard rejection that was never really the truth. "I'm still getting established, and my schedule's heavier until I bring on more help."

He ducked his head. "Sure, sure. Another time maybe?"

"Maybe." I smiled to take the edge off. My life would be so much easier if I was attracted to him instead of figuring out how to let him down easy.

"Nice to see you tonight, Sutton." His smile had a touch of regret. He paused, opening the door. "Another time."

He slipped out, and I watched the door close.

Another time.

He was going to try again. Not many new single women came through Crocus Valley, and Jennings had set his sights on me.

Jennings was my Carla. A less insulting version. I had confronted Wilder about not firmly shutting down Carla, yet I'd done the same because it was easier, and I planned to keep saying no until he figured out there'd never be yes.

I pushed out the door. Jennings was opening his dusty pickup door. "Jennings?"

He glanced in my direction, hope lighting up his face.

Ugh, this sucked. "Hey, I wanted to clear the air. You're a really nice guy—"

He barked out a laugh and took his ball cap off. "No need to say more."

Guilt left an acrid taste in my mouth. "Will the 'it's not you, it's me' line be better? Because it's true."

His chuckle lacked humor. "I'm the common denominator when girls say that. Don't worry. Ain't nothing I haven't heard before."

"You're a good guy, and I really hope you find someone who sees it."

The corners of his eyes crinkled. "That makes two of us. See ya around, Sutton."

He swung into his pickup, and I walked away so I didn't stand there watching his taillights fade in the setting sun. I'd look lovelorn when I was really inspecting why I was content with living alone and having stealthy sex with Wilder.

Inside, the girls waited for me. Aggie wore the same supportive but pinched expression. Tova shifted in her chair, but that was likely due to her belly pressing on her bladder.

Vienne's eyes danced with questions. "So?" she asked in a singsong voice. "What was that about?"

"Nosy?" I said and slid into my chair. I had to drive home, or I'd chug the rest of the pitcher to get my mind back to a blank state.

"Yes. So?" she prompted again.

"I told him he's nice and all—"

The girls all groaned.

"Oh no, you gave it to him hard but in all the wrong ways." Tova lifted her ginger ale. "Here's to not stringing him along."

"Was it just Jennings?" Aggie asked. "Or are you not ready?"

Many divorced women would've been dating by now. I might not be stringing Jennings along, but I'd have to lead my friends in a different direction to keep them from asking deeper questions. "I'm not attracted to him."

I wasn't, but I had a fierce attraction to one other man.

"If that's the case, I have a proposition for you." Vienne picked up the pitcher of beer and topped off my barely touched mug. "I've been too nervous to ask, but since you didn't say you weren't ready..." The dread was back, eating a hole through my stomach lining. "Jake asked me out, and he thought—"

"*Doctor* Jake?" Aggie asked, aghast. "You're not thinking of going out with him."

Vienne ticked a finger up. "Going out, not dating. A girl has her needs. But he has a brother, and he asked if I'd want to get Sutton, and we'd all go out."

My lungs crystallized into an ice cube. "Like a double date?"

Vienne gave a firm nod. "Yes."

"Just the saucy goodness this pregnant lady needs," Tova said.

Aggie glanced away. Her expression was neutral, like she wanted to make sure she didn't influence my decision.

I opened my mouth. Shut it again.

"I know." Vienne held her hands up. "It's Dr. Jake. But I know what he's like, and from what I've heard, his brother's really nice. Hot, too. It'll be fun."

Fun wasn't the word I'd use. I grew up watching daytime soaps on TV. Why did it feel like I was living one?

*

Wilder

. . .

I parked in front of my house and logged off for the night. I was on call, but I couldn't wait to get inside and change and veg in front of the TV. After the late night and early wake-up last weekend, I'd helped Eliot until I went back to work on Monday. Then it'd been shifts and on-call time and disrupted sleep. I got called out for Guy's not-missing pickup again and a bar fight between college students who were old enough to know better and who needed to go the hell back to college. Which they would, after they posted bail.

I stepped out of my patrol vehicle just as a small red convertible was driving by. Carla waved a hand with nails the same color as her classic Cadillac. "Yoo-hoo, Deputy. You off for a while?"

"I'm on call." Despite being evening, the end of August was still summer, and the sun was high in the sky, but relief I had a valid excuse cooled me off.

She pouted. "That's too bad. I'd love to take you for a ride." Her purr told me she wasn't talking about the car.

"Thanks for the offer. I'll have to pass."

Tapping red lacquered nails on the steering wheel, she didn't drive away. "You're hungry though? I can cook you a good meal."

What Sutton said came back to me. I was also tired of sidestepping Carla, and after two-stepping and a whole lot more with Sutton, I didn't have the energy to be evasive. A six-hour round trip each week for a booty call shouldn't wear on me, but leaving Sutton's bed was getting harder each time.

"I'm not interested," I said with a tone of finality she was likely to recognize.

The sultry pout was back. "Are you sure? I make the best—"

"Carla." She blinked but quit talking. "I'm sorry. I'm not interested." I held her gaze so she would know I wasn't talking about her Cadillac or her culinary skills or small talk.

Sincere disappointment filled her eyes. "It's been a year and a half, Wilder," she said quietly.

"I know." The year and a half had been obliterated in the back of my pickup. "I'm not ready, and honestly, I don't care to complicate my life with anyone in town." The God's honest truth right there. If Sutton had left me but stayed in city limits, life would be hell. Life was hell with her three hours away—two and a half if I drove straight through and pushed the speed limit seven over. "Barns showed me what a mess that can be."

After Mama left, he'd dated several women. Strung them along, had his lawyer summon them to the reading of the will, then humiliated them for doing nothing but tolerating him.

Her lips curved up. "Your daddy had a way of juggling it all. Nothing was complicated until he passed away and shamed them."

I didn't want to remember the night of the will reading. So much was fucked up about that night.

She let out a gusty sigh. "Well, can't blame a woman for trying to land a Knight. I'm not going to be the one giving up on you." She drove off with a finger wave before I could reply.

I didn't return the wave. That'd been a clear Sutton-diss if I'd ever heard one.

I soaked up the AC and got out of my uniform. I hung my bulky vest on its hook. Locked up my sidearm. I'd grown up with rifles and shotguns propped against various walls of the house, but I maintained good habits in my own home. Kids or not, I didn't want my work piece lying around.

My utility belt got draped over my desk, and then I undressed and hung my brown uniform shirt and pants up. All my shit was in place, ready to dive into if I had to go. A couple more nights, and then I was off. I was supposed to see Sutton Sunday night. I told Eliot I'd work all day Sunday. I had Monday and Tuesday off—I didn't tell him that. Sutton would be working, but school had started already, and my nephew, Grayson, had a football game Tuesday evening. Then I'd go home after.

I wanted to see my nephew play since I'd missed the dance performance. I'd seen countless school football games and looked forward to cheering on a relative this time.

In the bedroom, I changed into a fresh white T-shirt and gray sweats. I dropped onto the couch and flipped on the TV just as the phone rang.

Dammit, was I getting called out already?

No, it was my personal phone. Sutton's name was on the screen. I answered before it rang again. "What's up?"

"Hey, Wilder..."

I sat up at the hesitancy in her voice. "Something wrong?" Was she breaking it off?

"Vienne asked me to go on a double date with her," she rushed out.

My teeth clenched together. "You said no, right?"

A moment of silence amped up my blood pressure. "I'm supposed to be the perfect person for her to ask to go on a double date, Wilder."

She wasn't. She was *mine*. "So this is it?" I kept my voice measured. My world couldn't be crumpling around my ears once again. "You're going to start dating?"

"No," she said quickly. "But I didn't know what to tell her. Jennings had just asked me out, and I turned him down…"

The space between my ears echoed with my heartbeat. Who the fuck was Jennings? I faintly recalled the name.

"…I think I can just go and be like a wingman for her. I can be nice to the guy and leave it as not interested."

"Except that you'll be on a date with the other guy's wingman." And what if she was interested? Irritation was a pile of gunpowder behind my eyes, ready to explode into anger. "Who is she going out with anyway?" As if I'd know him.

"Dr. Jake."

"No."

"Wilder." Her tone made it clear I had no say in her personal life. *Goddammit.* "She's only going on a date because she hasn't gone on a date in a long time, but she doesn't want him to think she's serious. She just wants a fun night. His brother's in town, and they invited us out."

"Have you met this brother?" Was the douche as slick as Dr. Jake? I didn't know either guy, but it didn't matter.

"No. I'm also not interested in dating, okay?"

Her words were reassuring but foreboding. We said we'd stop as soon as we met someone, but I wasn't prepared for it to actually happen. This scenario was too close to the real thing. Way too damn close. The pressure inside my head didn't abate. "When's this supposed to happen?" Where? What time? Who was picking who up?

"I guess we're going to dinner, and then—"

"You've already said yes?" My balls tied themselves in knots. She'd made her decision. The notification was nothing but a courtesy call.

"She took me by surprise. I couldn't exactly tell her that I'm having perfectly good sex with my ex-husband, so let me think about it."

"The sex is more than perfectly good."

"Wilder."

The corner of my mouth hitched up at the exasperation in her voice. "Sorry, but it's true."

"*Anyway*, dinner and a movie. Coal Haven has a movie theater. I don't know what the movie is."

Sutton hated going to the movies. I'd noticed her fidgetiness on our first time going out and hadn't taken her again, and she'd never asked. The flash of smugness chased away the growing panic in my chest. I knew her. Her not-a-date didn't. "When?"

"Saturday."

Fuck's sake. Saturday was supposed to be my night off to get a decent night's sleep after taking call for the week. I worked until evening, and then I'd come home to think about Sutton on a fucking date with Dr. Jake's dickweed brother. "Okay." I chewed on my words, but I had to be the bigger guy, or I'd chase her right into some unknown man's arms. "Have fun, but I hope he's an intolerable ass."

"This is so messed up," she said, resigned.

"I turned Carla down tonight, FYI." I told her in case the news helped keep Sutton's panties in place on Saturday. She wasn't the type to jump in some guy's bed—I wasn't some guy, and my pickup wasn't a bed—but I wasn't exactly thinking rationally.

"She hit on you again so soon?"

"I don't think she knows how not to hit on guys." I didn't tell her what Carla had said. The statement would only hurt Sutton and make her more defensive.

I hated that a part of me also felt like Sutton had given up on me. Like Mama. The weightlessness, like I was coasting through life being myself, and it not being enough for anyone was all too familiar.

Ten

WILDER

I tucked my pen into my uniform pocket. "That's all the information I need, Mr. McCormick. I'll keep an eye out for your vehicle, and you stay home by the phone in case I call."

I was in the McCormicks' house after working with Delilah. I needed to talk Guy back inside before he careened all over town and caused an accident looking for the pickup he'd sold years ago.

"Thank you, Wilder." Guy shuffled to the kitchen to wait by their landline. Delilah had kept the phone just for this reason. She'd said the more like the old days things were around the house, the easier it was for her to handle Guy when his mind dipped into the past.

Delilah pinched the bridge of her nose. "Can I talk to you outside?"

Her tone was different than normal. Usually, she walked me out, and we discussed how we'd handle the evening until Guy moved on from the pickup or went to bed, but we'd become old hands at the routine.

I stepped out and walked farther from the tidy little house they'd raised their kids in. "Everything okay?"

"No." She let out a shuddering sigh. "A room finally opened in Miles City at a nursing home. They have a memory care unit." Her eyes misted over. "Yeah. It's going to be so hard."

I had a lot of gear around my waist and strapped to my chest, but I pulled her in for the best hug I could. "I'm sorry, Delilah. Anything you need, let me know."

She sniffled and pulled back. "Thank you. I've worked on most of the details while he naps, but I have to tell you—we'd have never survived this long without you. The other deputies just aren't as good with him."

"It helps he's known me all my life."

"This town is lucky to have you. I was so happy to hear that you're going to be our new sheriff."

First Jodi and now Delilah. Word hadn't spread like this the last few times Ray said he was going to retire. I normally lived and breathed this type of statement. Everything I'd worked for since Ray asked me if I wanted to be a blemish on my family name or give back to society was happening.

I should have been thrilled Ray's retirement was getting more real each week. He hadn't told me a date, but if others were hearing about it, his plans must be concrete. However, today was Saturday. With the time difference, Sutton would be going on her date in a couple of hours. I wasn't excited about a damn thing.

"Glad to be of help," I said automatically. Was Sutton in the shower, getting ready? Would she put her hair in one of those braids she liked to wrap around her head? What would she wear?

If it was that fucking dress from the street dance... I knew how easy it was to get beyond that fabric.

"...hard not to compare."

I'd missed what Delilah was saying. "Compare?"

She waved her hand like she could brush the words away. "I know I shouldn't compare. We're not those two young kids anymore. Those kids didn't know they'd grow old. They'd struggle with bad knees and dementia." A soft laugh escaped her. "We were just babies. We didn't know one date would turn into forever."

Cold crashed over my head just as heat flushed around my neck like a slowly tightening collar. "A date turned into forever?"

"Can you believe a movie back then cost a little over two dollars?"

The collar cinched. "Let me guess—dinner and a movie?" I croaked.

Her smile was fond. "That's how it all started."

I gritted my teeth together. "Sweet memories."

She patted my shoulder. "Sometimes I feel like they're all I have of him."

Her words were a bucket of ice. This conversation wasn't about me. "Call me if you need anything. I'm on for another hour."

"Oh, Wilder. Go home and relax. You work so hard."

I got in my SUV and entered the data for my report. My mind was half on the task. The rest was stuck on Delilah and Guy's dating history. Her tales of dinner and a movie and wedded bliss rang through my head the entire rest of my shift.

I passed Carla on my way to the house. She was out

for another jog, but she only smiled in a way that said *I'm yours when you're ready* and kept running.

My phone was clear. No messages, not even from Ray. Sutton would be waiting at her house about now. Ready for her date. Or would she be at Vienne's? Had Jake and his goddamn brother picked her up early?

I told myself I'd be cool. Sutton assured me she was just going through the motions. She was basically going out tonight to hide the fact that she and I were sleeping together.

My increased blood pressure didn't know the difference.

We didn't know one date would turn into forever.

I glanced in my rearview mirror at the fading form of Carla and the quiet town.

If I had to sit in the house, I'd drink beer and watch ESPN. So the real question was—how did I distract myself tonight?

Sutton

Ethan Kraft was Jake's brother. Like Jake, he was around six feet tall. Where Jake had deep brown hair, Ethan's was coppery brown, and he had a close-trimmed beard. His clothing screamed corporate, and apparently, he was in the C-suite of the coal mine outside of town, and he lived in Beulah.

The hardest part about tonight should've been getting used to saying Jake and not Dr. Jake. Instead, all of tonight was hard.

The difficulty originated with Ethan himself. He was handsome, charming but not in a way that fired up alarm bells, and easygoing with a sense of humor that had kept us all laughing.

Ethan was a catch.

But I was having sex with my ex-husband. I wanted the night to be over, so then it'd be tomorrow, and I'd spend the day knowing Wilder would swagger through my door and take me right to bed to get between my legs.

The thought alone had my body humming. A steady beat pulsed between my thighs, and like at the street dance, I was struck with something akin to vertigo. A disconnect between what my body was feeling and my surroundings. *Who* I was with.

I wasn't supposed to be turned on, sitting in a booth with Vienne, a man I'd just met across from me, and his brother who was trying to fuck my friend next to him.

I thought I left the uncomfortable dating days behind in Colorado after I met Wilder at a horse show.

Ethan leaned across the table and lightly touched his warm fingertips to the back of my hand. "You with us?" A smile danced around his lips. He really was good-looking, but my sex drive down-shifted and began to ebb.

Because Wilder wasn't swinging in tonight to get me off.

"Yes." I had my fork poised over my creamy herb chicken. Since the movie theater was in Coal Haven, we were eating at the popular bar, Rattler's, not far from it. The chefs had opened the place years ago, and folks drove from all over to eat here.

The food was good, and I almost commented that I'd have to tell Wilder we should eat here sometime. I stabbed a hunk of chicken and stuffed it into my mouth.

Vienne slid a concerned gaze my way, but I flashed her a closed-mouth smile. Everything was fine.

Just fucking delightful.

I'll take "Inappropriate Reasons Why I Wish This Night Was Over" for a thousand!

Would Wilder have guessed a thousand?

"The food here is sooo good," Vienne moaned over her steak bites. She eyed Jake's steak, already gone with only a few chunks of fat left behind. "How was yours? I almost ordered that."

Her high energy cut right through the moment, taking everyone's focus off me. She was a damn good friend. I hoped she'd find someone who made her happy. I'd met her ex-fiancé a few times. A complete dud. The way she talked about her ex-husband came off as frustrated and fed up, but I worried she was still hung up on him. He'd done some emotional damage she didn't talk about. Jake wasn't her happily ever after. He was known for saying he was allergic to relationships. I didn't think he'd make a good happy-for-now either. He was the type to see Vienne as a notch in his belt.

Maybe she'd be interested in Ethan?

Setting my friend up with my date wasn't the best sign I was moving on. Neither was having sex with Wilder, but I wasn't as lonely and miserable when I was expecting his visits. My brain knew he was gone. He didn't live with me. So when he did show, he came because he wanted to. A huge difference from when we were married, one I doubted he'd ever understand. Which was why we'd stay divorced.

I managed idle chatter as we ate. I had ridden with Vienne to the restaurant, but when we finished at Rattler's, we hopped in with the guys to go to the theater.

Vienne sat in the front with Jake. I was in the back of Jake's Dodge pickup with Ethan.

I was in the back seat of a pickup with a man. My body fired up like I'd been hit with a live cattle prod. The disconnect was back. I wasn't in the back seat with Wilder.

"The movie doesn't start for half an hour," Jake said. "Let's drive around for a while."

I stifled a groan and swallowed bile. My clothes were on, and we weren't alone. At no time in my life did I spontaneously have sex with a guy I picked up one night in the back seat of a pickup.

The incident with Wilder notwithstanding.

I swallowed my nerves and smiled when Ethan asked about my work and how it was different from Jake's business.

"I'm concentrating more on small animals, but I will pick up large-animal clients."

"The ones who don't like me," Jake said from the front.

I chuckled, but he was right. Wilder had told me why Ryan and Sheldon wouldn't use Dr. Jake if they could help it.

"Do you work with exotic animals?" He leaned closer when he said it.

I smiled and fought my inclination to press into the door. "You won't find me working at the zoo, no."

He leaned back. "I'd love to see you in action sometime. I get a kick out of catching Jake at work. All I can see is the little kid who dragged our cat around playing doctor."

Everyone laughed. Ethan was so damn congenial, so easy to be around, yet I was ready to crawl out of my skin.

After driving to Hazen Bay by Lake Sakakawea and stretching our legs, where Ethan acted like a shadow the whole time, Jake drove to the theater. The smell of popcorn and butter enveloped me as soon as we walked in. I wasn't hungry, but a salt craving hit me hard. That time of the month was coming soon. I needed something to do anyway before Ethan got the bright idea I wanted to hold hands like I was twelve again.

The theater was one huge swath of seats twelve chairs wide. An aisle ran down either side and exited to the main area that led to the bathrooms. We settled into our seats. I waited for Jake and Vienne to shuffle in. Ethan gestured for me to sit by Vienne.

I hugged my popcorn. "I like the end seat." I could lean into the aisle and not be crunched against him.

"What the lady wants." He sat, and I perched next to him. As the opening credits rolled, I relaxed and munched on my popcorn. For almost two hours, I wouldn't have to worry about saying something that could be taken as suggestive or worry that my expression said I was thinking about my ex.

Then Ethan snaked his hand into the popcorn and grabbed a handful. "You don't mind, do you?" he murmured.

"No," I croaked. A kernel of popcorn caught in my throat, and I coughed. There were only a few other people in the seats behind us and two more up front, but I shoved the straw in my mouth to quiet myself.

Cold lemonade washed down the tickle, but my dismay remained. He'd fondled my popcorn. That felt somehow...intimate.

"You okay?" he asked quietly and took my drink from me. "May I? I should've gotten my own."

"Sure?" I squeaked.

He took a pull from the straw.

Fuck's sake. Borrowing one of the Knights' favorite swear words was fitting in this case.

How was I supposed to drink now? I was used to getting peed on, drooled on, spit on, and having various body fluids splashed on me including the emptying of anal glands. That smell could make a strong stomach weak. But I wasn't prepared to swap spit via third party with Ethan.

"I'm fine." I took my lemonade back and put it on the other side of the armrest.

The corner of his mouth lifted, giving him a more debonair air with the lights of the screen playing over his strong features. "Good."

He propped an arm on the seat behind my head. Wasn't that uncomfortable? It should be.

I glowered at the movie, not seeing what was playing. The gorgeous movie stars with the brilliant white teeth couldn't keep my anger from simmering. I wasn't supposed to be in this position. I wasn't supposed to be ready to date. I wasn't supposed to have a sex life to hide from a date.

My popcorn was almost gone when he snuck another handful, crowding my personal space even more.

I gave him a tight smile. "I have to go to the bathroom," I whispered and shoved the popcorn bucket at him. He juggled it with his free hand but had to remove his arm from the seat to keep it from tipping to the floor.

I scurried up the aisle, my mind a mess. I kept my gaze riveted to the floor, hoping the other few attendees didn't think I was running for my life. I glanced over. The older couple was cutely cuddled together, their focus on the screen. A guy was by himself on the far side, and that was it except for another lone man at the very back with his head resting in his hand, his fingers splayed over his face. How was he even seeing the screen?

I rounded the corner into the dark vestibule when what I just saw dawned on me. That man alone in the far back had nice wide shoulders. Hair squashed from wearing a hat. Like what a Montana deputy wore all day.

He *didn't*.

I backed up until I faced him. The movie was nothing but a drone in the background as I went cold and then hot.

There was my ex-husband. Spying on me. He looked up. Whatever scene was playing cast his expression in shadows, but his chagrined features were visible.

I opened my mouth to demand to know what the hell he thought he was doing showing up at the movies I was on a date at, but I slammed my lips shut. I couldn't call attention to us. Vienne would recognize him. Wilder at the movies in Coal Haven would be tough to explain.

I slammed across his knees to get to the seat on the other side. His groan was barely audible. That was what he got for having impossibly long muscular legs. I plopped into the seat, the chair making a thunk as it unfolded all the way. We both froze and watched the group of three from my double date.

When they didn't move, I faced Wilder. "What are you doing?" I mouthed.

He leaned in close. "Did I interrupt your snack with your new boyfriend?" His hot breath wafted over my earlobe and feathered its way down my neck. I shivered, and all the longing and throbbing from earlier turned to high.

"I didn't offer. He took."

"You let him."

The older lady looked back at us. I sank against the seat. It would be too hard to talk without drawing attention. Before I could tell Wilder to go out so we could whisper-argue by the bathrooms, he twisted in his seat, his warm hand landing on my knee. The hem of the dress moved farther up my thigh with his touch. His gaze dropped. He noticed.

He put his mouth right on my ear. "Did you like when he touched your things?"

I mouthed "no" and glared at him. His hand inched up my thigh, his fingers deftly flicking the skirt of my dress up until his fingers were under my dress.

My butt was rooted into place. I couldn't move. What I'd been wanting and waiting for was here. I should be anywhere other than where I was right now, but I stayed.

His fingers went higher.

We were in a movie theater! I had to put a stop to this. I didn't.

His mouth remained at my ear. "Christ, you need the release, don't you?" He talked like he was calming a wild mare. And it worked, dammit.

I relaxed more. My thighs eased open. His hand got closer to where I needed it.

"Wilder," I breathed.

"Shh. Just be a good girl and stay quiet."

My mind went blank. I followed his orders. He traced the hem of my underwear with his fingers, and I kept my attention on the party of three I was supposed to be sitting with. Instead, I was getting off in the back row.

By the next breath, he was slicking a finger through my pussy and going straight to my clit.

I bit my lower lip. I could not make a sound.

"You're so fucking wet." His voice in my ear. His finger tracing my needy nub. I gripped the armrests and widened my legs even more. What we were doing was wrong, but I couldn't deny him. When he was around, there were no mixed signals. He was the one I wanted.

He slid two fingers inside me, going straight for what he knew worked—being full of him with his touch between my legs.

"Were you wet for me when you were with him?"

My teeth dug into my lip, and I shook from the effort of holding still. I'd make too much noise if I rocked against his hand. If we got busted, everything would be ruined. This arrangement. My friendships. My reputation. I nodded.

"You were thinking about me?"

I squeezed my eyes shut and nodded, then opened them again. I had to be on the lookout. I would dive to the floor fast if one of the group twitched.

"I'm going to finger fuck you, and then you're going to finish your date knowing I'm waiting at home in your bed with my cock in my hand so you can crawl on top and ride me."

Trembles racked my body. I was so damn close. I needed to catapult myself over the edge and not draw this out, but the pleasure was exquisite. The extra danger only amped up my already wired hormones.

"And if he tries to kiss you, you're going to give him your cheek because those lips are going to be wrapped around my dick tonight."

I shattered. Clasping my fingers over my mouth, I

shook into his hand, keeping as silent as possible. The effort only drew out the orgasm longer. My eyelids fluttered, and his gaze riveted on my reaction made my body soar higher.

Would the girl who's in so much trouble come on down!

He withdrew his fingers and put them in his mouth and slowly drew them back out. "He can keep his fingers out of your popcorn bucket. You're all mine."

SUTTON

Random tingles spread throughout my body for the rest of the movie. I'd try to sit in one position, but my leg would quiver. So I shifted to another. Ethan, to his credit, didn't try to share my lemonade or put an arm around me again.

When the guys dropped me off at Vienne's car at Rattler's, I gave Ethan a wave. A clear, platonic sign. "It was nice to meet you. Thanks for the movie."

Jake's gaze jumped between me and Vienne. "It's early to call it a night, isn't it?"

"I'm beat," I said immediately. "It was a long week." It was a long damn movie. My body had wanted to find Wilder and take him home instead of sitting with Ethan. Guilt had stretched each second out to minutes. I was a crappy friend to yet another person.

I had three friends! How would I betray Tova?

"I should get home." Vienne ran a hand through her

hair, somehow keeping her many bracelets from tangling in her long strands. "I have some work to do in the morning, and I promised Catherine we'd do some shopping."

Jake's shoulders drooped. Ethan had an amused smile, like he knew what Jake was after. Gah! He was a nice guy. Why didn't I go for the nice guy? I bet he was home every night and would spend the weekends with his wife instead of working.

I bet a guy like Ethan wouldn't give up his passion because of his dad.

I bet a guy like Ethan wouldn't let his wife walk out before trying everything.

The more time that passed since my orgasm in the middle of a dark theater, the more my common sense returned. How dare he spy on me? How dare he touch me?

Just in general—how dare he?

On a wave of growing frustration and anger, I stomped to Vienne's car. She got behind the wheel of her red SUV, and when we were closed in, she started it and stared out the window. She kept the vehicle in park.

I was content to mentally froth over Wilder's audacity.

"Is there anything you want to talk about?" she asked lightly, almost deceptively.

Oh, no. Did she see anything? "No?"

She tapped her chin. "That's not a confident answer."

I picked at my nails. Almost a month of sneaking around, and I had thought I could handle it. Wilder crossed a line tonight. But the fact was that I knew it, and I still let him get me off when I was on a date. "I'm not ready to talk about it. It's...private."

"Mm-hmm." She narrowed her eyes while looking

out. "Mm-hmm. So when I thought I saw a guy who looked like Wilder pull into the parking lot while we were getting concessions, I probably wasn't imagining things?"

My stomach clenched into a tight ball. A cold flush of horror wrapped itself around my head and neck. "Uh... Um... What?" My voice pitched up.

She was giving me the mom-stare. She didn't believe I was innocent of anything to do with Wilder right now.

I covered my face in my hands. "I'm sleeping with him."

Her silence prompted me to peek through my hands. Her stunned gaze was on me, her mouth hanging open.

I plopped my hands on my lap. "It's as bad as it sounds, isn't it?"

"I...don't know? Sleeping with your ex?" She shook her head and chewed the inside of her cheek. "I did it. Once." She grimaced.

"That bad?"

"Sex with him was always..." She wrinkled her nose. "Dry. But I was madly in love with him, and he was the one to end things, so yeah. I hopped between the sheets again." Her lips thinned. "Anyway, it was just another one of his games. It was wrong. My hopes that he'd man up officially died after that. I don't get the impression Wilder is a game player."

"No." I rested my head against the headrest. My secret was out, and I didn't realize how much the secret had bothered me. "He's not. But I'm not his priority. I wasn't when we were married, and I'm still not. Yet he showed up at the street dance and we just... I wasn't having sex with anyone else, so why not?"

Her brows drew together. "The street dance?"

I told her what happened, to include the steamy

pickup session in the pouring rain. "And yep. We're having great sex, and we aren't telling anyone because what if Aggie thinks I'm a horrible person? She's been worried about him. The guys were too. They didn't tell me, but I could see it when they mentioned him. They were afraid he wasn't moving on." He hadn't moved on. Neither had I.

Understanding filled her eyes. "They won't think you're horrible."

"What if I lose them? What if they think I'm toying with him, and they decide to just...move on?"

"They love you, Sutton. People don't just move on from people they love."

They did, though. My parents loved me, but I wasn't their preferred child. Wilder loved me, but I didn't offer the sense of service his job did. And I loved Wilder. But I had needed someone who wouldn't leave me while living under the same roof. I'd had enough of that growing up.

"He must not have been happy about the date," Vienne said. "Why did you agree to it?"

"To keep from being asked why I wasn't interested in dating after you all saw me turn down Jennings." I chewed the inside of my cheek. "And then tonight happened." Heat flushed my cheeks, fueled both by anger and the memory of his fingers inside me.

Her direct gaze was narrowed on me again. "He was in the theater, and when I was worried that you got food poisoning or were secretly panicking in the bathroom, and I'd pushed you too far too soon to go on a double date, you were talking to him?"

I rolled my lips in. Not only was I a questionable friend, I was a bad date. "Talking. Yes."

A brow arched. "Oh." She blinked. "*Oh*." A frustrated noise escaped her. "Theater sex. Gah, I miss good sex. I had some, you know. Good sex in college. Married sex let me down. Then I met Theo and thought he'd get better. And, argh! Maybe I will sleep with Jake."

"Vienne!" Sympathy and despair pushed through me. I knew the position she was in. An empty bed when you were used to having someone sucked. "We didn't have sex. He just— Never mind. I'm so sorry. I'm sorry I wasn't honest with you, and I'm sorry I snuck around behind you." Literally.

"No, you were in a tough position." She snorted. "A *hard* spot?"

I snickered through my relief. She wasn't upset. I didn't deserve her.

"I can't believe he crashed your date," she said. "You know what that means, right?"

I closed my eyes. He'd been jealous. Territorial. Intrusive. Too many emotions in a sex arrangement. "Yeah. We need to stop."

"You need to stop—or work out what this thing is between you."

"He won't ever pick me." Tears pricked the back of my eyes. "I gave him so many chances, and now he's going to be sheriff. We're in different places, and that's where we're going to stay."

"I'm sorry." She put her hand on my arm. The AC in her car was kicking in, and her hand was on the cool side, comforting. Clarifying. "For what it's worth, I won't tell anyone. I understand how complicated it would be if his family found out."

"Thank you." I gave her a small smile. "You should've gone out with Ethan. He seems like a nice guy."

She grimaced. "Definitely not. I'm looking for a good

time, not a long time. I've been let down enough by men, and I'm kind of over their opinions."

"Theo had a lot of them."

She rolled her eyes. "So many for a guy who couldn't find a clitoris if I painted a target on it."

"No wonder he hated darts."

Laughing, she drove off. The next stop was home, where my ex-husband waited for me.

✳

Wilder

I sat in Sutton's living room for a full hour before the cat ventured out. The sun had set, and it was nearly dark out. I hadn't turned on any lights.

Staying a secret and all that for when Vienne dropped Sutton off.

I also wasn't in the bed with my dick in my hands. Something didn't feel right. The air between us was off when she left me to go to the bathroom and told me I should leave before I was seen.

What I did was fucking wrong. I shouldn't have come. I should've trusted her. Left it alone. But I hadn't, and I wasn't sure if I regretted my actions or not.

My phone rang. Berry was on my lap, and she lifted her head to blink at me. I didn't want to be on a call when Sutton arrived, but I had no clue when that'd be.

She was on a goddamn date. With a guy who sucked from her straw. Jealousy burned in my blood. I might've gotten her off, but he was the one she'd stayed with.

Ray was calling. Goddammit. I had to answer, or he'd

stop over at the house. If he saw me gone, he might ask Eliot where I was since I was usually at the ranch if I wasn't working.

"Knight," I answered.

"There's a going away party for the mayor's son tonight before he leaves for college. We should make an appearance before they shut it down."

"Isn't it late?" I didn't want to go. The mayor's son was a good kid. Could sink free throws like no one's business, but crashing a party I wasn't invited to wasn't my idea of a Saturday night.

"They were at the mayor's house, but they opened the community center for midnight basketball. I can pick you up in ten."

My heart rate jumped. "I'm out of town."

"What? You were just on the clock."

He didn't have to sound so surprised I had a life. "Yeah, I was." I didn't elaborate.

Berry picked that moment to meow and bump her head against my free hand.

Ray was silent for a moment. "I'll let you go, then, but the football team is having a scrimmage tomorrow. You should make an appearance if you're not going tonight."

"I'll be gone for a few days. I traded shifts."

More silence. "Football season is a good time to be seen and talk to everyone."

"I've been out and about, Ray. I talked to the bank president yesterday and listened to him bitch about the kids who speed down his road."

"It's a good start, but you gotta do more than get groceries and run errands. Think of it as pre-campaigning."

My patience was wearing thin. He'd talked to me already, and I was doing what he asked. I should be able to leave town. "I'm keeping it in mind."

"You do that," he said in the low growl that meant he was displeased.

When I hung up, the flash of headlights turning into the driveway penetrated the night. The cat darted off my lap when Sutton opened the front door. Vienne was already driving off when Sutton flipped on the lights.

Damn, she looked good. Each time I saw her, I drank her in. I hadn't thought I took her for granted, but not seeing her every day made moments like these shinier than any badge. Her skirt brushed her thighs as she stepped out of her boots.

"So," she said.

One word formed an ominous cloud in the air between us. *So*. "Why don't you have a TV?" I hadn't had shit to do while waiting.

Same with working in the house. I was acutely aware this place wasn't mine, nor was anyone expecting me to be here. While waiting, I planted myself on the couch, got bored scrolling through my phone, tried to crack the password on her Wi-Fi, and settled with petting the damn cat. The more disgruntled I got, the more the cat reveled in the attention.

I was so sick of sitting around with only my thoughts and a strange cat as company, I would've happily cleaned Sylvester's cage, and I wasn't a reptile guy. Had Sutton taken a page from my book and started working all the time?

Why didn't that sit well with me?

Then there was the camping.

Sutton's expression blanked. "I had enough TV growing up."

She hadn't gone into depth about her childhood. I had pressed, and she'd answered with generalities. When we traded stories while we'd dated, she'd said she had pets that were her best friends and that her parents were gone a lot for her sister's practices and performances. But a niggling started at the base of my brain. I would've noticed if she shut down talking about her past, right?

"How was your date?" I asked innocently.

She put a hand on her hip. "Vienne saw you."

Shit. "How?"

"It's a small town, and you drive a big pickup."

"So does every other guy in the state."

She threw her hands up. "You can't do that, Wilder. We're not supposed to be—you and I—" She let her arms drop, her expression lost. "We're over."

The hell we were. I stood and ran my suddenly clammy hands down my jeans. "We're not over. The way you respond to me isn't a fluke. You weren't enjoying your date, admit it."

She waited a heartbeat before she answered, but I died a slow death from the contemplative way she stared at me. "I can admit it. You know why? You were supposed to be my last first date, Wilder."

My gut clenched like she'd punched me in the stomach.

I hadn't been her last first date. Regret washed up the back of my throat. She'd have another first date. Maybe another. She'd find a man who'd be her real last date.

"You were supposed to be the last time I had to make small talk with a man I just met wondering if I found *the* guy I could be with forever. It was supposed to be *you* on the other side of the table at Rattler's I could gush to about how amazing the food was. You, Wilder. You were supposed to be the *first* and *last* of everything in my love life. But you never put me first. Always last."

Her deluge washed over me, but the last sentence yanked me into the present. "How can you say that? I asked you out at that horse show. I dated you. I asked you to marry me. What else did you want?"

"I wanted you to be around."

We'd had this argument before, but I dove right in. The base of my skull prickled, warning me to let up. "I was around. I never left town, Sutton. I went to work, and I went home to you. I told you it'd get better, and you didn't wait."

"How long should I have postponed my life? All those trips you never took time off for? I was living the same life I swore as a kid I'd never live again. You came home to sleep and eat and fuck." She waved her arm around the house. "And I guess that's all we're doing here."

"What are you saying? You really want this to be over?" Fatigue crowded through my brain, pressing out into my temples. It'd been a long fucking year of adjusting to the divorce. Of being around my family and dying to hear what they knew about Sutton but acting like I had my shit together. As I was leaving town tonight, my coworker called. I'd made excuses to him about why I couldn't take his call for the weekend. Then I flew here, acid eating through my guts at the thought of what I might see—or not see, which was worse. And now we were wading back into the scraps of our marriage, and I still didn't fucking understand what else I could've done for her.

She shook her head. "I'm saying that maybe what we're doing is making everything harder. I can't move on, and..." Her expression turned stricken. "Neither can you."

"You want me to move on, Sutton? The whole reason I ended up at your house was because you didn't like the idea of me moving on."

"With Carla," she snapped.

"What about Stella Dobson? Or Hannah Ruiz?" Our family lawyer's daughter had gotten engaged last month, but Sutton wouldn't know that. "Or—or Cora Wang?"

I'd had to meet with the three of them about planning for an all-school reunion last year. I had made sure I was busy on the ranch the day of the reunion and was on patrol the rest of the time. Telling the women planning the event I was getting divorced had been like chewing busted glass. I wasn't going to explain my life to the rest of our high school class. But during the interaction, each of them had let me know who was single.

"Yeah," she said, sarcasm dripping from her tongue. "And I'll show up in the back of the bar, so I can suck you off between beers."

I didn't know what I expected when I had come here tonight. My motivation had been so pathetically obvious I didn't care to inspect it. I had needed to know what was happening on the date more than I needed to draw air into my lungs. I could blame the date for fucking up what Sutton and I had going, but the blame rested squarely on my shoulders, right next to the fault behind the divorce.

A pressure twined around my pants legs. The cat. Disbelief crossed Sutton's face. I stooped and gave Berry a few scratches around her ears and earned a contented mewl in return.

"Maybe I should get a cat," I said, knowing damn well I was going for a low blow. "Then I can have one female on this planet who hasn't walked out on me."

Sutton slid her gaze away, her jaw working.

I carefully stepped away from Berry and went to the door between the kitchen and the garage. I stepped into my boots, sensing her in the entry of the kitchen behind me. "Grayson's game is Tuesday night. Cody's grilling for everyone beforehand. Fair warning, I'm gonna be there."

"I'll just go to the game, then. I'll give you time with your family without me making it awkward."

Air leaked out of me. She sounded way too fucking calm. She was leaning against the wall, her face drawn, her eyes shining. I wanted nothing more in this world than to take her into my arms and carry her to bed. Kiss the tears away and fill her with pleasure. Ease the knots around my heart in the process.

But that was how we ended up rehashing the arguments that led to the divorce. So it was best to go. I'd work my shift and be back Tuesday. For my family only.

Twelve

SUTTON

The weather was perfect for an early September evening. With the sun still high in the sky and the garage on Cody and Tova's house blocking the wind, I should've been salivating for the good food lining the picnic table.

I might've been facing Aggie and Vienne, but my focus was on a certain pair of broad shoulders standing next to Cody and Ansen at the grill.

I wasn't supposed to be here. I told him I would stay away so he could enjoy his night with his family. Yet I was parked next to his sister, with his youngest niece propped against my shoulder, her little puffs of air ruffling the strands of hair hanging out of my ponytail.

The dress I almost wore was tucked safely in my closet. With that time of the month making my abdomen achy, I was more comfortable with the counter pressure of my Wranglers. I also didn't want to appear like I was trying to capture Wilder's attention.

We both knew what happened the last two times I'd worn that dress.

"Whenever you're tired of being a bed, I can take her," Aggie said.

Vienne grinned at me. "Auntie Sutton isn't letting go of Ro anytime soon."

"It's been a while since I've had baby time." I wasn't close to my sister, but I'd babysat for Petra when Honey would leave for competitions. Honey's husband would go with her, our parents too, and I'd be on auntie duty for an entire week.

I'd been in college, but I'd study ahead so I could have uninterrupted time with Petra. Those weeks had been both harrowing and reaffirming. Stressful days with a baby when I had no prior kid experience and busy when she started to walk and open drawers and doors. The dreams I'd had after those days... I'd meet the perfect man, we'd have a tiny, cute baby with teeny, little fingers and a round button nose. We'd be a perfect little family who stayed together. The three of us. Maybe the four of us. Five? I wasn't sure what the future would bring.

When I got into vet school in Colorado Springs, my babysitting weeks were over, and Petra had started her own lessons by then. Soon, I was the forgotten aunt. But then I'd met Wilder, and he'd offered me everything.

My PCOS and I couldn't fulfill the baby part of the bargain. Wilder couldn't fulfill the present-husband part. So here I was, holding a niece who was actually my ex-husband's relative. Single and plagued with painful cramps that reminded me why I couldn't make babies.

Fucking PCOS.

Were my OTC pain meds wearing off already?

The dull ache in my gut was growing stronger with

each heartbeat. If I didn't get on top of the pain, I was going to get nauseous.

Periods like this almost made me wish for the days before I started on my new medicine when my periods weren't so regular or heinous.

No. That time of whatever month my body chose would still be heinous. I had to see what else I had on hand for pain relief. "I hate to hand off a sleeping baby—"

Vienne held her hands out, her fingers wiggling. "Me, me, me!"

"I love you guys," Aggie said. "I never thought I'd have so much help with kids."

Because her mom had walked out, and Cody had been left with mama duties. She hadn't grown up seeing family pitch in to help family.

My heart twisted, causing my breath to shudder. Wilder's words from the other night rang through my head. The way his mama walked out had left an ugly print on him. He was that hurt kid inside who couldn't see beyond my leaving to what my real reason had been.

I hadn't met Birdie Knight, but I'd heard a lot about her from Aggie, and I had known and worked for Barnaby Knight for years. How much had Birdie tried to make her life better, to enjoy her children, but Barns had pushed back harder to keep her in the role he thought she should fill?

Wilder didn't have the attitude, and he respected me more, but I was his wife and therefore I should stay no matter what because he was the Knight and his priorities were more pertinent.

I dug in my purse. Did I bring some ibuprofen? *Come on, big money.*

Tova wiggled into a seat next to Vienne. "How are my two favorite pole dancing students and my favorite neighbor?"

"I'm your only neighbor," Aggie said, adjusting her shoulders like the pressure in her boobs was growing. "But they aren't your only students."

"A gal can have her favorites." Tova shook her head, the dark pile of hair on her head bouncing. The girl could toss on a tarp and put a rubber band around her head, and she'd look more like a Disney princess than if she wore a costume. Whenever she wore a blue dress, my niece Ivy called her Snow White. "I got two more students signed up." She took a drink of her sparkling juice and rubbed her round baby belly. "A married couple. They booked private lessons, though, and are willing to wait until the first of the year when I'm done with maternity leave."

"I might have to miss Thursday." I brandished a packet of ibuprofen. *Sutton Knight, you are the next big winner!*

Aggie's gaze dipped to the meds and sympathy crossed her face. "Is it bad?"

"Getting there. The first days are the worst, but I don't want to be painting the town red during class."

Empathy shone from Tova's blue eyes. This wasn't the first week I'd canceled. "We can always do a make-up session." She winked. "I only offer the option to my best students."

"I'm okay skipping." I wasn't going to make the heavily pregnant dance instructor work more.

"You need to get a pole for your house," Tova said.

I shook my head. "Uh-uh. I don't need to fall and

break something and not be able to get to the phone. Berry would lie on me, and that'd be all the help I got."

She grinned. "We'd come looking for you before Berry started nibbling your toes."

"Doubt she'd wait that long." The cat had a food obsession.

And a Wilder obsession. She rarely came out when the girls were over. Cody's kids knew not to go looking for her, or she'd hide better. But Wilder? She was twining around his legs like she was going to trip him so he'd break something and have to stay.

"Grub's ready," Cody announced, bringing a plate of hamburgers and hot dogs to the table.

Catherine and the kids stopped the line dance they were doing and ran to the table. Cody and Tova's new black Lab mix, Buster, stuck with them, his tail going wild.

I waited for everyone to line up for the food. Vienne was by her daughter. Cody and Tova were helping oversee their kids. Ansen had Ro so Aggie could dish up. I ended up right by Wilder. No one was paying attention to us, but the tension was going to cut off the air supply to my brain.

"Sorry about being here," I said quietly to him. "Tova invited me."

"It's alright, Sutton. I don't dictate what you do."

His granite jaw suggested it wasn't all right. He was facing the back of the line, the planes of his face hard and his expression carefully neutral. The scruff on his jaw was more than a couple days old. We shuffled forward.

The skin between my legs tingled, but my gut wrenched. My lower abdomen muscles were a dishcloth getting wrung out. I grimaced and pressed my hand to my abdomen.

Wilder's gaze dipped down, then lifted to meet mine. "Cramps?"

I nodded. He knew the drill. "It's been better since I moved here. I go to a doctor in Coal Haven. She listens a lot better than Dr. Beemer ever did."

He grunted. "Dr. Beemer needs to retire."

I had gone to a physician in Sidney, but I should've made the drive to an obstetrician in Billings. I would've been better earlier.

"Got your Midol?" he asked like he couldn't help himself.

"And I took ibuprofen." But it'd be an uncomfortable night on the bleachers. I wouldn't let a rough period ruin my good time. I also hadn't wanted Wilder to think I was purposely avoiding him.

We reached the table. Wilder grabbed a paper plate and handed me one. He took two buns out of the bag and dropped one on my plate. I preferred hamburgers over hot dogs. We were slipping into old habits.

I met his gaze, letting my dismay show. I couldn't handle how much he cared about me right now and not ask him to just hold me.

A furrow formed between his brows. "Right," he said and moved down the line.

The awful truth was I liked how he took care of me. I missed it. And I wished I kept my mouth shut last weekend so he hadn't left.

In case I hadn't cried enough over the weekend, I could cry again tonight, but it'd have to wait until I was in bed with a heating pad on my belly.

✱

Wilder

The game was over. I got to see Grayson make a few passes, twirl his way out of a hard sack, and I high-fived him when his team won. I even went back to Cody's house with him. The kids had gone to bed an hour earlier, and Tova had claimed she wanted a long soak, but she probably was giving me space to talk to Cody in private.

He updated me on all things Knight's Oil Wells, and he confirmed Chambers was doing an adequate job as a bookkeeper. Bonus was that he was a bookkeeper who could put up with Eliot.

I slapped my knees. "I should let you go."

"You work early tomorrow?"

"Noon," I answered, staying right where I was. My plans of camping out with him or Aggie the last two nights had been shot when I drove home Saturday night. I took call Sunday, went to the football scrimmage, and worked for Eliot on my normal days off. I cost myself time with my family by being a jealous dumbass.

"You'll get to sleep in."

"If Eliot found out, he'd give me shit. I don't know. Maybe I'll go help with chores."

A wistful smile crossed his face. I wasn't used to how easily he smiled these days. "When the kids get older, I might get a few head of cattle. Start growing a little ranch operation. Once the shop is built, I'm getting some haying equipment."

"You're going to do your own thing?" I stuffed the envy down. I was doing what I wanted.

He shrugged. "I've got KOW and the kids. But maybe? Ivy's asking about 4H. She's talking goats."

I chuckled. "Look at you. Opening the door to two cats, then a dog, and now goats. You're going to have a hobby farm, not a ranch."

He rolled his eyes. "Tell me about it." But he was grinning. His late wife had hated animals. She'd disliked living in Buffalo Gully, and ranch life hadn't been for her.

This life fit him better.

He'd moved to get it.

The thud in my temples returned. Cody was a financial guy. He wasn't the deputy Ray was relying on to be sheriff.

"I should get going." This time I stood up. "Thanks for the invite."

"Anytime." He rose.

I couldn't just let tonight go. I was happy for him, and I needed him to know it—without admitting to how much I wished I could have what he did. "Crocus Valley looks good on you."

"I can't argue. It's better for the kids and"—his fond gaze traveled in the direction of the bedroom where Tova was pampering herself—"for me. But they miss you and Eliot."

"I'll put a bug in Eliot's ear. He's gotta get off that ranch more."

"Just him?"

"I get out of the house plenty." The air between us threatened to grow heavy again. I couldn't withstand more scrutiny of my life. I didn't need to hear that Sutton was right, and I was an idiot. That I should've channeled my dad and played dirty to make Sutton stay.

His stare turned contemplative. "I never thought you wanted to be a deputy."

"There's nothing else I wanted to do."

"Did you even have time to consider, or did Ray tell you that you wanted to be a deputy, and that was it?"

Defensiveness heated the back of my neck. My brothers talked shit about Ray, as if they hadn't been in the same house I lived in, getting treated like dirt by Barns. "He was the first one to think I could be something."

"More than a rancher?" he asked, his eyes full of challenge, as if he was asking if I thought I was too good to work the land.

"Barns let me go to college, but we both know it wasn't to do anything I wanted."

Cody lifted a shoulder. "He didn't fight you on being a deputy because it'd keep you close by. I don't think any of us realized how committed you'd become."

I worked for the county for more reasons than because it was one of the few careers Barns wouldn't give me shit about. He'd probably thought I'd give up and go back to ranching. Ray's confidence in me meant everything. He thought I could be more than the second oldest in a family of five. "Law enforcement is serious work. You can't half-ass it, or you end up one of the bad guys."

His stare turned assessing. "The badge isn't branded into your chest."

That was where he was wrong. "No, I wear it with pride." I left, grateful to be done with the conversation, but wishing it'd have gone differently. Cody had a way of pursuing what he thought were important discussions or insights. Usually, he hit on fucking finances, not my personal life.

The imaginary imprint in my skin burned the whole way to my pickup. I got in and took the gravel road to the highway. At the highway, I needed to take a right to head toward Montana. Going left would take me in the direction of Sutton's.

I had no business going to her house. No reason.

The way she'd put her hand on her stomach was emblazoned in my brain. I knew how much pain she was in. She'd have gone home after the game, taken a long bath, doped herself as much as medically possible, and laid in bed with a hot pad. There was one other thing that helped her a lot, but she'd have learned to take care of herself without me.

I turned.

✳

Sutton

I was in bed when I heard the garage door rise and then lower. Frowning, I stared at the dark wall across from where I was curled on my side with my arms pressed across my middle. My back was to the door of my bedroom, but I didn't move. The door to the kitchen clicked open, then closed.

The only person who knew the code to the garage and could get into the house—and wouldn't leave Oreo barking his head off—was Wilder.

He might've left the remote behind, but I hadn't

changed the code. I could use the excuse that I didn't have time.

I'd had time.

The recognizable cadence of his footsteps down the hallway made it hard to breathe.

"Wilder?"

He didn't stop to undress, but pulled the covers up and crawled in. "Yeah."

The question was obvious. "What are you doing here?"

"I know what you need."

His strong arm banded around me and pulled me flush into him. My back was pressed into his front. A wall of heat. Counter pressure.

My eyelids fluttered shut, and I moaned.

"Just let me take care of you."

Tears squeezed past my closed eyes. The sweet results of all my pain relief attempts came together, and my muscles began to unknot themselves. The sharp ache ebbed, remaining dull but manageable. I could actually fall asleep and not be a zombie veterinarian in the morning.

All because Wilder knew what I needed.

These moments were why I had stayed married to him so long. He was a good guy. A fantastic lover. But in the morning, he'd be gone. And I didn't know if he was coming back.

I didn't bother to stop the tears. Crying turned to sobbing, and Wilder just held me. He stayed until I drifted off, and when my alarm rang in the morning, I was alone in bed.

Thirteen

SUTTON

A week and a half after being held while I broke down in the dark with terrible cramps, I was in my Sunday pole dancing class. A very pregnant Tova circled me and Vienne. Her belly looked like it needed its own kickstand when she stood in place, but nothing about it made her a less active teacher.

Vienne sagged against her pole. One of the back rooms of the old theater in Crocus Valley had been converted into a workout room. My red and sweaty face was painfully clear in the wall of mirrors Cody and Ansen had installed.

The other three students who practiced with us had already left, but Vienne and I always stayed later to shoot the shit with Tova and help her clean up.

"I can't feel my arms," Vienne panted. She fanned herself. "How do strippers not sweat all over the stage?"

"Some guys are into it." Tova made a motion for

Vienne to keep stretching. "Besides, they don't notice much beyond the boobies."

I snorted and folded into a deep bend.

"I'll be right back," Tova said. "I've got to pee. Again."

Once she disappeared, Vienne straightened. "And then what?"

I laughed and pushed the hair out of my face. I had parked at Vienne's house five blocks away and told her about Wilder's visit, but Tova had been unlocking her studio, and I'd clammed up. "That's it. I fell asleep, and he was gone when I woke up."

Vienne flattened her lips. "He really cares about you."

He did. "Not enough." Not in a way I fundamentally needed.

"I wish I had something magical to say to make it better." She went to the little cabinet in the corner and took out the disinfectant. She withdrew two rags and tossed me one. Tova wasn't cleaning a thing tonight.

"Me too."

We finished the wipe down before Tova waddled back into the room. "You guys are the best. My back is killing me, and my bladder is tired of being a trampoline."

We walked out with Tova. Crocus Valley was safe, but neither I nor Vienne let Tova lock up alone. When Tova drove off, I walked Vienne home. The wind blowing through town was still warm this time of year, and the sun sank lower in the sky.

Once Vienne disappeared into her house, I got into my pickup and drove home. In the garage, I scrolled through my phone. I needed a shower and a good night's sleep. A morning of spays and neuters waited for me, along with a new admin person to train in.

I continued killing time on my phone. Was tonight when I admitted I had a hard time being in the house by myself when I knew what it was like when Wilder was there?

We hadn't talked or messaged since that night. He held me and blew out of town before dawn.

How had his week been?

I tsked. We had talked more than I cared to admit when he'd been sneaking into my house.

I shut off my brain and texted him.

> Thank you. For the other night.

My message made it sound like he'd been here a couple days ago. I huffed out a breath and got out, hoping to leave my embarrassment inside.

By the time I got in the house, I had a message waiting.

WILDER

Anytime.

Shit.

You know what I mean.

I pressed my fingers into my cheeks. I was grinning.

Continuing to text him would be a bad idea, but I did it anyway.

> What are we going to do with ourselves?

Have sex and not worry about it?

Didn't I wish?

We tried.

WILDER

Have sex, not worry about it, and don't go on double dates?

To clarify—no dates.

I giggled.

I'll be hiking with Oreo next weekend, so no dates planned, double or otherwise.

Still smiling, I went into the bedroom and undressed. I carried the phone into the bathroom, knowing damn well I should leave our conversation where it was.

WILDER

Practice camping trip is still on?

Yes. Are you working?

Was he off? And still alone even though I'd ended things? More likely he was on call. He never spent this much time texting. But he did it for me. My body warmed, and it wasn't from the water.

WILDER

McCormicks' truck got stolen again.

Poor Wilder. It was hard for him to deal with Guy.

That sucks. I'm sorry.

I flipped on the water for the bath.

WILDER

Hey, guess who I busted with a meth
lab in their barn?

Hmm… I'll take Hansen Was Making
Meth for two hundred.

Ding-ding.

I sank into the water. My fingers twitched to send
another message, but at some point, I had to leave my ex-
husband alone. I had to learn to live life without him but
also with him in my life as the brother of my friends.

WILDER

I miss your game show references.

Instead of shutting our conversation down, his open-
ness made me want to do the same.

I had a lot of research hours put in
while Melon was at practice.

Honeydew gets what she wants,
Mutton.

I will drive there and puncture your
tires if you call me that again.

Sutton-mutton.

Cowboy, you're on thin ice.

A few minutes went by. I waited for his witty reply,

enjoying the humor he brought to my night. Emptiness yawned in my chest. He probably got a call he had to go on.

My phone buzzed again.

A selfie of Wilder with a foot kicked out behind him like he was going to do a flip jump. He was in the middle of a road outside of town, dressed in his uniform, round hat and all.

I laughed.

Smart-ass.

Mischievousness welled inside me. I held my phone in front of me and took a selfie, making sure no boob shots made it into the frame. The ends of my hair were obviously wet and the tile of the tub surround was behind my head. There was no mistaking where I was.

I sent it without a word.

Several minutes ticked by.

My phone rang. A grin spread across my face.

I answered with "Isn't it late, Deputy Knight?"

"I can't have an erection and pull people over, Doc."

His nickname always got to me. Was it simple and predictable? Maybe, but it was mine, and he gave it to me. And it wasn't Mutton.

"Why, cowboy, I have no idea what you're talking about."

"Listen—I know this is wrong; we both can admit it. But I want you to slide a finger into that pretty little pussy of yours and let me hear you come."

I sucked in a breath. My hand was on my belly before I knew it. Water sloshed up my chest. My legs were bent, my knees above the water. I wouldn't need much to get me off.

"It is wrong," I said, stroking my fingers lower. "So why do I want to do it so badly?"

"I'm having a hard time caring right now. Can we question this later? I need to hear you, baby. It's been too long."

"Are you parked?"

"In the trees by our place."

The house was no longer ours, but his slip made the warm glow inside me hotter. He was parked at a popular speed trap tucked into the deepest part of a curve in the road. If he shut his lights off, no one knew he was there.

"Sutton."

Not a question. Not a plea. More of an *"are you with me?"* check.

My fingertips landed on my clit, and I groaned.

"That's my girl," he purred into my ear, and I was his for the rest of the night.

✷

Wilder

I parked my patrol SUV outside the sheriff's office, a wide brick building in downtown Buffalo Gully. The city offices shared the same space, along with all the county offices.

Ray wanted to meet with me and talk about his retirement. My thoughts should have been centered on adjusting to the job and what I could change to increase my chances of winning the vote in the next election, but my mind preferred to center on Sutton. Over a week had passed since we had started a torrid texting affair that was often followed by phone sex. We'd made it a whole week and a half from ending our sex arrangement before launching a phone-sex relationship, but neither of us could help ourselves.

Hearing her fall apart on the other end of the line while I was fisting my dick paled in comparison to holding her. I hadn't ventured bringing up the topic of going to see her again, but I planned to tonight, or she'd go on vacation, gain clarity, and write me off.

Each call, each text, I worried she'd come to her senses and realize we had to stop falling down the same rabbit hole that led to a dead end.

Would she let me go see her again?

The days she would be gone were like a gaping hole in my future. Before she left, phone sex. After she left... What?

I dug out my phone to stare at her message from last night for the eighteenth time. I'd unsubtly asked her about her practice-run camping trip, like I did every time she called.

> **SUTTON**
>
> I think I can leave early. Maybe noon or one?

She'd be off, hauling her Coachmen behind her with Oreo in the pickup. He'd always liked road trips.

Noon or one. With the time difference, that was about four hours from now. She'd likely leave closer to noon. Her house might be cluttered, but her mind wasn't. She'd be ready and leave as soon as she locked up the clinic.

Delilah and Guy were shuffling to the front door. Delilah was in a blouse with cotton pants and mismatched sandals like she'd rushed after Guy before he could leave alone. Guy was in plaid pajama pants and a stained white T-shirt. Shit. Had he woken up confused?

I got out and jogged toward them. "Hey, Mr. McCormick. What can I help you with?"

Relief crossed Delilah's tired face, and I was glad to be in the right place at the right time.

Guy's white brows crashed together. "My pickup got stolen."

I nodded and pulled a small notepad out of my pocket. "What's the pickup's description?"

Guy blustered through, giving the exact description he always did.

"All right, sir," I said, tucking the pen and notepad into my pocket. "The best thing you can do is go home and wait by the phone. I'll be in touch when we get news."

The pinch of his brows eased, and he nodded. "Thank you, Wilder." He turned to shuffle back to their car parked in the lot by the courthouse.

Delilah shot me a grateful smile. I returned it and followed them to the car.

"I'd like to drive, Guy," she said when he veered to get into the driver's seat.

"Of course, dear," he uttered and got into the passenger side with Delilah's help.

She put a hand on my elbow when the door was shut. "Did I tell you we're moving next week?"

The move was quicker than I expected, but Guy was deteriorating. I walked her around the front of the car. "Need any help?"

"No, but thank you for offering. You've done so much for us. I'm moving, too, and selling the house." We stopped by the driver's door, but she made no move to open it.

I knew she'd found a place for Guy, but I didn't realize she was also leaving. "You're moving to Miles City?"

"Where he goes, I go." Her smile was sad. "It's not leaving I'm concerned about. I would've moved years ago, but I worried about Guy's transition into long-term care. The church, the quilting circle, all that?" She waved her hand. "They'll find someone new, or they won't." She shrugged like either option was fine. "Dillon's taking a month off work to help me sort through everything."

Her oldest son was about ten years older than me. "That's nice he can take so long off."

"Well, like he said, sometimes you don't have a choice. Work will always put work first. It's our job to put family first." She opened the door. "Thank you, Deputy Knight."

Delilah's life was here. She was as much of a fixture of Buffalo Gully as our family ranch and oil wells. And she was leaving.

I thought about what town would be like without them. A new family would move into their house. Maybe they'd have kids I'd see at the school when I was at games or giving safety presentations. They'd be gone, but the town would be the same.

People came and went from Buffalo Gully all through the year. It was the same in all the small towns of the county. A house I might've responded to domestic assault calls in for years would suddenly have new owners. Land would get parceled and sold. New houses would be built.

Ray talked about the changes constantly, along with how to keep up with them.

He'd been at every game while Barns had purposely missed every one. If it wasn't ranching, we shouldn't have been doing it. My brothers and I had covered for each other. Aggie had tried, and we'd hardly let her do a thing, too worried about hiding our own transgressions from Barns. We couldn't have him on her case too—more than he had been.

The oddness of having Guy and Delilah pull up stakes so suddenly stuck with me as I wove through various city departments to Ray's office. I waved to Brenda as she chatted in the hallway with Uma from accounting.

Ray was behind his desk. His brown sheriff's uniform was stretched over his vest and both were waging a silent war against his buttons. His thinning gray hair matched the shade of his neatly trimmed mustache. He looked like a lot of sheriffs I'd met throughout the years. But Ray was always ready to head to the field, and he might not look like it, but he could still run down a teen who thought he could escape a minor in possession at a pasture party in the middle of the night.

He'd done it to me, and I'd since seen him do the same to countless kids out drinking with friends. None had gone on to become deputies. He hadn't worked with them like he had with me.

"Hey, Ray."

He glanced up, his gaze sharp as ever. "Wilder, come on in."

"You been here a while?" I was just ending my shift. He'd tacked on the meeting in the morning to keep from interfering with my schedule.

If I was still married, I would've missed Sutton going to work. I'd stuffed down the annoyance then, wrote the occurrence off as part of the job, but residual irritation threatened to rise. I'd missed a lot with Sutton.

"I came in early. Couldn't sleep." He shuffled through some papers. "I'd like to go over some of the budget details with you since we're nearing a new fiscal year. It'd be good for you to see what rolls over and what doesn't." He glanced up, his mouth tight. "That way you can see the fine print of why I've made the decisions I have."

Ray had never liked getting questioned. As I got more experience, my inquiries were less about curiosity and more of a challenge.

My gaze drifted to the clock on the wall. Less than four hours, Sutton would be leaving.

"We can also talk about your thoughts for a campaign." He licked a finger and leafed through some papers. "It's never too early to start."

"I thought you said I was a shoo-in."

"You should be, but politics can be dirty business, and it's still a sheriff position. Lots of officers want the promotion." His chuckle was dry. "I took office when you were in college. I keep thinking you were right there with me."

He'd kept me informed, calling about college and to check in. He'd mentioned campaigning against the current sheriff in office. A significant experience for a kid who'd been little more than a ranch hand to his dad.

"Right." I glanced at the printed spreadsheets he pushed in front of me. Rows of numbers swam in front of me, but all I could focus on was the tick of the clock. *Pay attention.* This was an important meeting. Ray was trying to set me up for a successful start as interim sheriff. "Have you set an end date yet?"

"April fifteen. That'll give us almost seven months to work together." He leaned forward and dropped his voice. "Look, the county board is going to vote to appoint you as my replacement. You've always had their full support. After that, you'll need to win over the residents of Murphy County to nail the election. I'll work with you on that until April too."

He was done the fifteenth of April? Sutton was leaving the day after for her trip. A heavy sense of loss draped over my shoulders, like we'd be definitively going our separate ways.

I ran my thumb and forefinger over my lower lip. The numbers on the spreadsheet blurred together.

In addition to my normal shifts and helping Eliot, I'd also be working with Ray to get trained in. I could talk to the family lawyer about hiring someone else. I'd get a pay bump as sheriff. My ranch pay could go to someone else while I went to Crocus Valley when I could.

How long could I realistically expect to have phone sex with my ex-wife? Would we be able to strike up the same arrangement we had before but be more official?

I wanted more than real sex. To hear about her work and forget the stress of my job. I'd like to see her leave for work even if it meant rushing out right after her so I wouldn't get busted at her place.

He tapped on his keyboard. "We can comb through budget topics all weekend and talk fundraising for your campaign next year."

All weekend?

His chair squeaked as he turned from his computer screen to face me.

Did we have to discuss the job this early?

"Wilder? You seem distracted."

I pushed a hand through my hair. "Yeah, sorry. Just… thinking."

"Can't believe it's real?" He grinned, pride radiating in his smile. "You're going to be sheriff."

"Right." I rubbed my eyes. I'd worked the night shift, but I wasn't ready to drop. I just wasn't ready to deal with a day full of numbers, and the proud-papa look he was giving me wasn't boosting me like it normally did. "It's really happening."

"Tell me about it. Every time I think about retirement, I panic." He shrugged and dropped his gaze to the top of his desk. "But I'll still be around. I'll probably be counting down the days until I can leave the office."

I glanced at the clock again.

"Late for a very important date?" he asked lightly. He must've noticed my furtive time checks.

"No," I said quickly. "No." I wouldn't be surprised if he hated that I hadn't told him why I'd come home early when I wasn't sharing information about why I was out of town. I didn't want my siblings on my back about Sutton, but Ray would be more disapproving. He'd think she was a detriment and not an asset to my career goals. He'd think she was a distraction.

He might be right, but I wasn't planning to stop whatever I had going on with her.

He sat forward and put his elbows on the corner of the desk. "When's the last time you took a whole weekend off? Didn't you take call for Kaplan when you were supposed to have those days off?"

"Plans changed. Figured I might as well work."

He lifted his chin for the door. "Go. I got your call covered through the weekend."

Shock made me question my hearing. Ray filled in when there were openings, but he rarely kicked us off the schedule to do it himself. "Sheriff—"

"Go." He smiled, delight entering his eyes like the thought invigorated him. "I'll cover it. Weekends always make me antsy anyway. I can only mow my lawn once. Go on. Got yourself a three-day weekend if you don't sleep all day."

I was scheduled on a night shift on Monday that I'd swapped with Kaplan so he could get to an appointment Tuesday morning. I'd get almost four days off. That was enough time. "Thanks. I owe you."

"Leaving this office knowing you'll be the one in the seat next is all the payment I need."

Another mason block piled onto my shoulders, weighing more than the rest. "Absolutely."

Fourteen

SUTTON

Oreo was loaded into the back seat. The RV was hooked to the back of my pickup. I ran through a mental checklist.

Flutters zinged through my stomach. How could a camping trip loom so monumental in front of me? I would only be gone until Monday. The campground was two hours from Crocus Valley. The camper was smaller than some stock trailers I'd hauled.

I'd been on my own before, towing well into the six figures of horse flesh behind me. The horse trailer itself had cost a pretty penny—but they hadn't been my coins. Nor had they been my horses.

The pickup was mine. The camper. My time. All alone.

I shook my head and got into the driver's seat. Being alone didn't bother me. Getting over the fantasies I'd had as a young married girl about all the adventures I'd go on with my husband were hard to shed.

I slid on sunglasses, checked my mirrors, and pulled away.

I lumbered to the edge of the driveway and slowed to check the highway for traffic. I was not crashing out of this vacation before I left my property.

A pickup barreled down the road. A honk made me frown.

Was that...Wilder?

My stomach flipped, and I wanted to celebrate. I got to see his handsome face in person and not on a phone screen.

I watched Wilder approach, his window rolled down. He screeched off the pavement and skidded to a stop next to me.

I gawked at him.

"Roll down the window," he called, and I jerked, still not believing he was here.

He'd been bugging me about the vacation, obviously worried I was going alone. I expected him to call each day I was gone. I had been looking forward to it.

I rolled the window down. "What are you—"

"I'm going with you."

"What?" Shock stole the rest of my brain cells. I didn't hear him correctly.

But he was here.

"I'll park in the garage."

"It's the entire weekend, Wilder. Aren't you on call?"

"Ray took it for me."

Dismay cinched around my throat. "Ray knows about us?" Wilder's boss was a decent guy and a good sheriff, but I'd always thought he was subtly manipulative with Wilder. Like an overbearing dad who expected things to be done his way. I would've thought growing up under Barnaby Knight, Wilder would be sensitive to those tactics. Instead, his childhood had made him think Ray only had his best interests at heart.

I had disagreed. I still did.

"No. He noticed I haven't had a long weekend in a while. I'll be right back." Wilder pulled away.

Stunned, I watched through the rearview mirror as he pulled into the garage. He was coming with me? The swirls started in my belly, but I was afraid to get my hopes up. So many questions about how feasible this would be ran through my head.

He appeared again with a duffel in his hand and closed the garage door. He jogged toward the pickup.

My mouth went dry at his long-legged lope in his worn jeans with his wide shoulders and the way his hand closed around the straps of his duffel. His cowboy hat was tucked low on his head, shadowing his face.

He disappeared behind the RV and appeared again at the back passenger door and put his duffel on the floor and set his hat on top.

Oreo let out an excited bark, and Wilder's chuckle made the day even more surreal. He was laughing and petting the dog like we were a family. And we were going camping together, just like I'd dreamed of.

He jumped into the passenger seat, and his smoky-whiskey-and-vanilla scent surrounded me.

"Wilder." I put the pickup in park. My brain was coming back online, but I was as confused as ever. "What's going on?"

He ran a hand through his hair after wearing his hat

for the short jaunt down the driveway. "I don't know. I just know I want to be with you."

Heat wicked through my body. Orgasms with his voice in my ear weren't the same when he wasn't next to me. "So we sneak away and camp together? What if Ray wants you to return?"

"I can't if I have no vehicle, and I'm riding with you."

That was a change. He used to arrange his time off around what Ray might want. "And when we get back? Then what?"

His expression was as lost as I felt. "Can we have a fun few days where we don't have to worry about seeing people we know?"

"And then what?" I enunciated. An entire long weekend with Wilder would definitely keep me from moving on.

Did I want to?

We still had his family—my surrogate family—to consider.

"Then we take it day by day? Week by week?" He got a defeated look in his eyes. "Hell, month by month? It's going to be winter soon, and then travel will be unpredictable. But I'm not going anywhere when it comes to you. Maybe we do some long-distance stuff?"

"Like phone sex?" My cheeks warmed. I wasn't against what he was saying. Looking forward to seeing his name on my phone was better than not seeing it at all.

His gaze swept down my torso and back up. "Yes. And the real thing as often as we can."

God, I liked the sound of that too much. "A long-distance relationship? What do we tell your family?"

"Do you want to tell them we're dating?" He said it like he'd support whatever I wanted.

The urge to keep him secret stayed close to my chest. I didn't know if we'd work. I'd asked for a divorce, and then I ended our arrangement, and while his siblings didn't know that part, it might all come out if we attempted dating and failed to keep it a secret. Keeping our long-distance arrangement to ourselves would involve more lying.

God, I hated this. But I also missed Wilder. Twice we'd tried to be done, and here we were for a third time, talking about trying again.

How would it work anyway? "Dating seems like a stretch from fucking like rabbits when we have overlapping windows of time and are in the same zip code."

He twisted in his seat and put his elbow on the console. "Just so happens, we're both free and in the same zip code."

I laughed, but a steady beat began between my thighs. I hadn't driven away yet. We could run into the house—

No. I was camping. I'd missed over ten years of traveling because I'd been waiting on him. Would a long-distance relationship work, or were we destined to fail no matter what we did?

Was there anything wrong with trying? My heart had been broken and hadn't healed. Maybe I was just prolonging the pain, stretching it out until I knew for certain we were done, over, that *we* weren't possible. And if that was the case, I'd rather spare our loved ones the pain of seeing us part all over again.

"No, let's keep this between ourselves. We don't even know if it's possible."

His Adam's apple worked, but he nodded. "I agree. Just between us. Again."

We shared a smile. The absurdity. Long distance? Who were we kidding?

But I couldn't not try.

I wasn't sure I could fall out of love with this man.

Wilder

"Good thing you didn't get a gooseneck," I said as Sutton pulled up to her camping spot. Leafy trees clustered around each camping section. Some sections had tents and SUVs, others had campers like Sutton's, and there were a few camper/trailer combos.

"Will you never let that go?"

"I paid about as much for the window as I paid Guy McCormick for the one I broke when I was ten." I had told Barns I was the one who broke the rear window on the ranch pickup by jackknifing the gooseneck while backing up to load horses.

She tossed me an amused look. "I already thanked you for taking the blame."

She'd thanked me good and hard. I'd been born backing trailers, and that day had been one of Sutton's first times. Barns had probably known it wasn't me, but he'd made me pay for the deductible and oversee getting it fixed and then dumped extra work on me for months until I out-stubborned him and refused to admit Sutton had broken the window.

Since then, Sutton had backed trailers hundreds of times, and she was as good as me and my siblings. But watching her expertly steer and maneuver the camper into its spot nestled in a cluster of trees still got me hard, not gonna lie.

On the drive, she'd asked about Ray's retirement. I had said I had to figure out all the campaign bull-shit and left it at that. Best to prevent having old arguments this early in our third attempt to be together.

She stopped and put the pickup in park. "Home sweet home," she smiled. "For the next three nights."

I liked the sound of those words coming from her lips, aimed at me. Home sweet home.

She directed me through finishing the set up for our stay. When we were done, she propped her hands on her hips, and we faced the camper.

"Is now the time to tell you the bed is only a double?" She bit her lip, her eyes dancing.

I curled my hands around her waist and murmured in her ear, "You think you're funny."

She giggled. "You're right, I'm kidding. It's a queen bed with a wall on either end."

I groaned and buried my nose in her hair, relishing that I was holding her instead of poring over spreadsheets. "I'm going to be curled into a ball all night?"

"Yup," she said cheerfully and went to the door. "Come on, Oreo."

We crowded inside, and she set up the area where Oreo would sleep. The interior was spacious for a small, tow-behind trailer. Perfect for Sutton and a dog. A little crowded for the two of us. I slid my gaze to the bathroom. I'd be crunched in half to fit under the shower, but it'd do the job.

I was with my girl and my dog. That was all that mattered.

When we returned, I'd be busy figuring out where the hell my life was going.

Sheriff. My dream job.

Stress threatened to tighten my shoulders, but I shrugged it off. I needed these days off.

She rose from where she tucked a fluffy dog bed under the table she'd unlatched from the wall. Her gaze stroked across me and the rest of the camper. Her gray eyes settled on me. "It's weird seeing you in here."

"Because you bought it thinking I wouldn't be around." She'd shopped for the camper. Planned to use it. Arranged to be gone. And I hadn't been anywhere in the picture.

"Technically, you're still not supposed to be around, but we've already acknowledged our self-destructive ways."

I crowded closer to her, questioning my intentions for dumping myself on her holiday weekend. "I'd never want you to self-destruct."

"Oh, Wilder." She cupped my face. We hadn't touched until now. I closed my eyes and turned my face into her warm hands. "I know you'd never want to hurt me."

I opened my eyes. I had hurt her. And I would do it again if I wasn't careful.

"Enough of that." She abruptly pulled her hands away. "It's gorgeous out, and the weather is supposed to be the same all weekend. No heavy conversations allowed."

Meaning, no rehashing the past or why we didn't work. We'd accept our circumstances for now and figure the rest out later. If there was anything to figure out.

The rumble of her stomach punctuated her declaration. She wanted camping and hiking and sightseeing. I wanted to keep her on her back, naked in this camper. We could strike a nice balance.

"Whatcha got planned for meals in this tin can?"

"Sandwiches and some stuff that includes cooking, but I figured I'd want a treat after driving and getting settled."

We were eating out, then. I'd interfered enough. "Got a plan of where to go?"

She shook her head. "No, I was going to find what looked good and stop in."

"All right." I slipped my fingers into her jeans pocket and withdrew her keys. "Load up, passenger princess, and let's find somewhere to eat. Then, when we get back"—I let my gaze wander down her long body—"I'm having dessert."

Sutton

We found an open table in the throng of people at a restaurant on the main road through town. Wilder had never been to Medora either, and while I'd planned the trip, I'd left my days open to explore and do what I felt.

"The zipline?" Wilder asked after we ordered. He was forming an itinerary, and I was happy to be in his capable hands.

I shuddered. "No heights for me."

He frowned. "You're afraid of heights? How didn't I know that?"

"I wasn't going to announce to a husband who faces

danger with each shift that I hate ladders and make it a personal goal to never have to go on a roof."

"No wonder I had to change all the lightbulbs," he mused.

"Didn't you notice the ceilings are lower in my house?"

He smirked. "I noticed it was an older house. Well kept up."

"Well kept with no arched ceilings that have recessed lighting. I couldn't call Aggie every time I had to replace a bulb. The rest I can hire out for."

"So, no zipline." He studied the tourist magazine he'd picked up from a stand outside the restaurant. "The musical?"

"Absolutely." I took a drink of water.

He blanched. "You're afraid of ladders. I'm afraid of singing cowboys."

I choked on my water as laughter mixed with my mouthful. I scrambled for a napkin, and Wilder's eyes sparkled. When I recovered without making a scene, I scowled at him. "Eliot sings."

"Exactly. He's singing, and you think his mood can't be that bad. Then he's cussing out the weather and half his help and getting me to agree to more work."

"Only half his help?"

Wilder smirked. "There are a couple guys even he's afraid of scaring away. They'd be too hard to replace."

I thought Eliot secretly liked being a boss. A lot of his family had left, but his workers were with him day in and day out. "How's his intern doing?"

"Moved on already. Found a ranch in Texas to work on. Said he'd take the heat over the winters." Wilder turned a page. "I'll still go to the musical if you promise to hold my hand."

The easiest promise I'd ever make. "Deal."

"Cowboy museum?"

I shook my head. "I've never been a museum girl."

"When you've already been with the best cowboy, the rest just can't compare."

Good thing I wasn't drinking water again. This was the charming Wilder I'd met who didn't get his head stuck mulling over work issues. "I want to drive through the park and hike tomorrow. Pack food and water and do the picnic thing."

"Sounds fun."

For me, maybe. I was prepared for a day hike. "You're wearing cowboy boots, Wilder."

His gaze dropped to my collarbone. "I packed other shoes, Doc."

His tell. He was lying, but I wasn't going to call him out. He'd have to keep up, or I'd leave him behind. "Good, because I want to hike on Sunday too."

"Hike away. I'm ready." He leaned forward. "Just know that you might be a little stiff in the morning."

Yes, please! rang through my head. I'd been trying not to think about tonight since he'd hopped into my pickup. If I let myself go there, we'd never leave the camper. I'd be naked and under him already.

"You think so, cowboy?" I asked innocently.

"Challenge accepted."

Our food arrived. I was almost done when I got a message from Aggie.

> Are you okay, or do I need to call for a
> search?

"Oh, crap. I forgot to tell Aggie I arrived." I punched out a quick message.

> Sorry! I'm here and polishing off a burger basket. Thanks for checking in.

"Ansen owes you for moving near them and becoming their vet. Dr. Jake would've driven him crazy."

I grinned. "Aggie wasn't interested, but Ansen said he'd pay double or triple if I ever thought of leaving."

"Doc Sutton?" a vaguely familiar female voice said.

Adrenaline flooded my veins. Who would know me in Medora? I found one of my customers waving at her family to continue following the hostess. "I'll catch up," she said to them.

Walter the Maine coon's owner. What was her na— Got it. "Monica. Hi. Getting away for the weekend?"

"Definitely. We always come to Medora before the season's over. A little back-to-school, goodbye-summer trip." Her gaze jumped to Wilder and returned to me, brown eyes full of interest. I purposely didn't introduce him.

Monica might be closer to fifty, but she could still appreciate Wilder's rugged appearance with the stubble shadowing his cheeks and jaw and the way his dark eyes made you want to confess all your crimes. His ruffled hair from wearing his cowboy hat earlier softened the edges of his face. But I doubted attraction was why she kept looking at him.

"Are you going to the musical?" I was asking for my own recon. Where did I have to avoid so I didn't have to explain Wilder?

"Tonight." Her gaze swirled to Wilder again.

My smile was turning forced. "Well, enjoy."

"You too." She inspected Wilder one last time, then wove through the tables in the direction her family had gone.

I faced Wilder. "Sorry. I didn't want to—"

"You don't need to explain."

I felt like I did. Not acknowledging the guy I was going to have sex with all weekend seemed more than a little disrespectful. "Her cat is gorgeous and one of my patients."

"I could tell you like her and her cat. You lit up in a way you never did at the ranch. Tell me more about your patients."

If he wasn't bothered, I wouldn't be. I did enjoy getting to know the people and pets who came into my office. Each new client was a testament that perhaps I hadn't made the wrong choice. Some days, I needed the confirmation more than others.

I launched into stories about the cats and dogs I cared for, the occasional chicken and duck, and of course, Aggie's pigs. When we finished our meal, we left but stopped on the sidewalk outside the restaurant.

"Did you see they have an ice cream shop?" Wilder asked.

"Really?" I looked around.

He grabbed my hand, and we started in the direction of where the ice cream shop must be.

"Have you committed the town's layout to memory already?"

"It's only as big as Buffalo Gully."

He acted like it wasn't a big deal, but pleasure wound through me, leaving warm, glowing trails. He'd studied Medora while we ate. He was putting in the effort.

I couldn't dwell on what his attention meant. I didn't want to ruin my vacation by reminding myself this was temporary.

We found the place, went inside, and ordered. We carried our cones outside to the sitting area next to the shop. He took a bench seat and patted the spot next to him.

I sat and crossed one leg over the other, angling myself toward him. I swiped my tongue across the chocolate ice cream. Creamy sweetness burst across my tongue. "Ohmigosh," I groaned. "This is so good."

"You're killing me, Doc." He chomped a bite off his mint chocolate chip.

I deliberately licked along the top of my ice cream and held his gaze.

"You're playing with fire, Sutton."

Giggling, I kept it up but mostly out of necessity. How else was I supposed to eat an ice cream cone? But I loved the way his eyes focused on my tongue and how I swallowed.

I was close to the cone and got some chocolate on my upper lip. "Oops."

I had a napkin halfway to my mouth when he growled, "Don't touch it."

He leaned in and put his mouth on mine, then licked across my lips and gently sucked until I melted more than my ice cream. When he pulled away, the intense promise in his eyes took my breath away. "Remember, this still isn't my dessert."

The tingle ignited between my thighs. I couldn't wait until he indulged. "We can finish the rest while we walk back to the pickup."

❋

Wilder

Once Oreo was hooked up outside, and I had Sutton to myself in the camper for a couple hours, I pulled her into my arms for nothing more than a long embrace. I couldn't wait to get inside her, but I needed to hold her more. I needed to know she was not a voice on the other end of the phone.

"Wilder." She put her hands on mine. I stilled, anxiety rising. Was this too much? She'd been flirty with the ice cream, but I'd also invited myself as her camping buddy. Was she second-guessing our new attempt at a sex arrangement?

"Yeah?"

"I'm going to have to be quiet. I can't walk out tomorrow morning and have everyone know I'm a screamer."

I barked out a laugh, my relief acute. "I've got you, baby." I wrapped my arms around her waist and picked her up, lifting her only enough to get her boots off the floor. "I want you in that small-ass bed."

Her laugh cut to a desire-filled gasp as I set her down and flicked open the clasp of her jeans. She sucked her stomach in on another inhale as I dragged her jeans and underwear over her ass and down her legs. I shed them, taking her boots off at the same time.

She was splayed before me, only her bra on. Lust punched me hard, low in the gut. I'd made the right decision to race to Crocus Valley and catch her before she left.

I reached behind her. While I was snapping her bra

open, I caught her lips and kissed her until her back was flat on the comforter. I dropped the bra behind me with the rest of her clothing. I knelt and spread her legs open. She was bare to me. Everything. I got all of her. No matter how many times I'd had Sutton, I'd never quit craving her. She was the only one I wanted.

She was mine.

For now.

My erection pounded at my zipper, but I was more concerned with getting the flavor of Sutton back on my tongue. "You're so fucking wet, I can't wait to drink you up."

She arched her back off the covers. "My finger has been a poor substitute for your tongue, cowboy."

Damn right it was. I'd show her how nothing and no one could compare to me.

I delved between her folds, licking her pussy from entrance to clit. I meant to go slow, be sweet and ease her toward an earth-shattering peak, but I was a starved man. A few nights with her in the last year and a half weren't enough to satiate me. I'd spend eternity trying to catch up.

"Wilder!" She rolled her hips into me, but I held her tight. My lips were clamped around her clit, and I devoured her. "Oh my god. Oh. My. God."

I barely remembered her earlier comment. I pulled away only to grab her shirt and wad it up. "Gotta keep this between us, baby. I can't have everyone hearing how you sound when you come."

She snatched the shirt out of my hand and stuffed the garment in her mouth.

"That's my girl." I tugged her ass closer and relentlessly attacked her clit. Her muffled cries were still loud.

"Aw, baby. You're fucking soaked, and I'm not even close to done."

She lifted her head enough to peer at me between the globes of her breasts. Those pretty pink nipples were going to get their share of attention too. "Again?"

"I'm severely behind on your orgasms. Better get that shirt back in your mouth—you're coming again."

"Wild—" Her groan cut her off.

I was back at her swollen nub, licking her and threading a finger inside of her. She whimpered but wiggled her hips for more. She was so fucking responsive, but it was for me. I hadn't been with anyone because I knew it wouldn't be like this. I made sure she was the same.

With one hand I shoved her leg higher, opening her up more. I would die of need if I didn't bury myself in her, but having her at my mercy was the best drug in the world. "I won't ever get enough of you."

She answered me with a moan. Her second climax came quicker than expected.

I didn't bother undressing. My blood pounded through my dick, and my jeans were going to cut off the flow. I ripped my pants open, shoved them down enough to stay out of my way, and pushed her other leg open wide.

"You know what it's like being inside you?" I pushed in. Her eyelids fluttered back.

Her body was a furnace. Wet and smoldering, she was branding every square inch of my skin. Lust made it hard to keep from pounding away to seek my own release.

"I know what it's like with you inside me," she said breathlessly. "I can never get enough."

I stroked out and thrust back in. Her walls fluttered

over me. I was over-sensitized, every ripple a fist around my cock. A ragged groan left me, followed by a grunt. "It's heaven. Warm and wet and all fucking mine." I gritted my teeth, pulled out, and rammed into her again.

She gripped my shoulders and hung on. The shirt slipped off her face, but she shoved it back in, clenching her teeth down on the material, addicting sounds coming from her throat. Soft mewls, needy moans, and high keens.

The sound of our bodies slapping, our heavy breathing, filled the air. If the camper was rocking, I couldn't help it. I wasn't even sure I could keep from roaring into the night and drawing security to our door. If Oreo wasn't used to hearing us fuck through the walls, he'd be barking.

And wasn't that the thought that rocketed me to my peak? This was us. We did this, and it wasn't unusual. Being together wasn't something we should hide. We belonged together.

Sutton Knight was my wife.

I tossed my head back, my teeth clenched, a growl ripping from my throat. Sutton's body was a vise around my cock as I emptied inside of her, milking every last drop from me. I was all hers.

I collapsed on top of her, my chest heaving. I yanked the shirt from her to make sure she wasn't getting smothered.

She wrapped her arms around me. "That was something," she murmured into my neck.

"It was. And also, I'm not done."

She giggled. "Have I told you how much I love your stamina?"

I grinned and rolled us to our sides. I was looking

forward to a weekend of sex in this closed-in bed. But I couldn't wait to wake up tomorrow and spend the day with Sutton. To watch her get excited about the souvenir shops and study a new menu. The way she deliberated over entrees she'd never tried before. How excited would she be at the musical?

We might've been married for ten years, but this weekend I was getting to know Sutton Knight all over again.

Fifteen

WILDER

The sounds of the campground filtered into the camper, along with copious amounts of light the thin camper curtains had no chance against. I angled to my side to straighten my legs.

Sutton shifted next to me. The number of times we'd had sex last night didn't matter. Blood redirected to my dick. The novelty of waking up to her and not having to leave was something I'd treasure.

"You don't have to go anywhere," she said, sleep heavy in her voice. She'd read my mind.

"You're not kicking me out."

Her chuckle shook the bed. "Not after last night."

"I'm ready to go again."

A dog's whine sounded on the other side of the pocket door.

"Oreo needs to go out," she said in a way that told me I was the one who was taking Oreo out.

"I'll take 'What The Lady Wants' for a thousand."

She giggled and rolled over. I swung my legs down and craned my neck from side to side. The bed was nothing like mine at home, but I'd had the best night of sleep in a long time. My quality slumber wasn't from all the activity before bed, but who I got to sleep with and why I wasn't rushing off.

After a pit stop in the bathroom, I got Oreo's leash. I'd walk him around since he wasn't used to being cooped up as much as he was for vacation.

Outside, I nodded and said "good morning" to people as I passed. The atmosphere was relaxed, and the temperature was already warm.

My phone went off. Goddamn phone. One weekend. Was that too much to ask to be left alone?

Oh. It was Eliot. My frustration crept back to its dark corner.

> You're not at home or at work. You
> doing okay?

Aw, hell. I didn't tell him I was leaving town. I didn't tell anyone.

> Had to get away for a while. Figured
> you weren't counting on me.

> I never plan on you.

I frowned, staring at his message. The words lacked context. Was he kidding? Was he being serious? On call or not, I had gotten called away a lot when I helped him.

> You good?

If only he knew how good I was.

I'm fine. Doing some hiking before winter hits.

When the hell do you hike?

When I'm hiking to kick your ass.

I run faster than you, but I'd win anyway.

Would not.

Would too.

I rolled my eyes. Fucking Eliot. Oreo whined at a bird in a tree.

Are you getting a dog to hike with?

My pulse jumped. Then I realized Eliot couldn't have heard. So why the question?

People with dogs are everywhere on these trails.

You should get a cat instead.

Why?

So you can say you got some pussy.

Cocksucker. I exchanged a glance with Oreo as if he was in on the conversation. "Brothers, am I right?"

I couldn't resist.

I got some last night.

No ducking way.

*fucking

Duck yeah.

That wasn't a typo.

Where'd you go? I struck out last night.

Shit. I'd gotten cocky. I'd never been one to kiss and tell, and Sutton was a whole different level of privacy. She always had been.

A gentleman never tells.

You didn't get any. You're lying.

I saw my out and took it.

You got me.

My phone buzzed, and I nearly dropped it. Eliot's name flashed across the screen.

I looked around as if my family was lurking behind the prickly bushes behind the trees. I answered with a "What?"

"You did get laid."

"You said I was lying."

"And you didn't argue," he said smugly. "So you

really did, and you want me to drop it."

"What do you care?" I ground into the phone. Campers and vehicle doors were shutting, and voices were ringing across the campground.

"Because I've been worried about you, and then I find out you left for a weekend—which you never do—without telling anyone but Ray." Another way to tell those of us who grew up with Ray. He was only Sheriff Dahlen if you worked under him or were in trouble. Otherwise, he was Ray. "I worried you were going off the deep end. And then after our talk at the bar about how celibate you are, you announce you laid pipe."

"Grow up."

"Ah—deflection. Who is it?" He didn't sound like he wanted gossip. His tone didn't come off as me having random sex was a good thing in his opinion. Had that been part of their worry after the divorce? I'd be a hermit or a man-whore? Neither one was me, but either one should be fine.

Okay, maybe I'd been the hermit. "Stay out of it, Eliot."

"Does anyone know where you're at? Ray was surprised to hear you weren't at home."

Figured they'd run into each other the one time I did not want my location speculated about. "No. I'm fine."

"Safety first, Deputy. Where are you?"

I could hang up, but then he'd call incessantly. Worse, he'd call Cody, and I'd have more siblings in my business. "I'm camping, and that's all you're getting."

"Camping," he echoed.

"Yeah, and I've gotta get ready for a hike or—"

"I talked to Aggie yesterday. She mentioned taking

care of Sutton's animals all weekend. Because, you know, she's camping."

My stomach sank like a stone. I'd ruined everything by being a terrible liar. "Eliot, leave off."

"You son of a bitch!" I had to hold the phone away from my ear. "You're with Sutton!"

"Goddammit, Eliot."

"Are you two getting back together? I can't see her moving. She has that clinic. If you're going to be sheriff, you'll still have long hours. Then there's—"

"No, all right? We don't know. We're figuring it out."

He went quiet again. I stuffed the tip of my boot into the gravel. The only footwear I'd brought. Oreo tugged me to go sniff at a tree.

"You sure this is a good idea?" he finally asked.

He wasn't upset at Sutton, so that was a good sign, but the information was only just sinking in.

"No, but we can't help it." I told him about the street dance and our first arrangement, how I'd fucked that up, and then when we started calling again. I skipped the phone sex part. "So we know it's a bad idea. She's terrified you, Cody, and Aggie will be upset with her if we don't work again." Probably Austen, too, but he only visited a couple times a year. "They live in the same town, and you all are family to her."

"*If* you don't work out, Wilder?" he said flatly.

"It's a long-distance thing. And that's just how it's going to be until... Until we can't anymore. Okay?"

After a moment, he finally said, "Okay. I wish nothing more than that you two would work out. But..."

"I know. My future's been decided."

He snorted. "You and me both. So, the sheriff thing?"

"What about it?" I had the support of the community, but Eliot made it sound like I didn't have his vote, like he didn't want to see me with the title.

"You really want that job?"

"You know I do." Not the resounding yes I should've said, but I was mad at myself for revealing the deal between me and Sutton.

His scoff was as loud as a gust of wind. "I used to get so jealous of you."

"Why me?" Wouldn't he be envious of Cody? The oldest, who had more freedom to do what he wanted. He hadn't taken it, strapped down with obligations like the rest of us. Or Austen? He'd fled entirely and was doing meaningful things with his life. We could all be jealous of Aggie's complete freedom from anything Knight.

"You were old enough to remember Mama better than me, then you had Ray Dahlen. The guy was always asking me why I wasn't more like you."

"The same Ray Dahlen who ran me down at a party and made me do a breathalyzer when I was fifteen?"

"The same Ray Dahlen who gives me a ticket if I'm even two miles over the speed limit." Ray's hobby was irritating some of the big ranchers in the area, Eliot included. "So anyway, you got a second dad, and I was stuck with my one and only." I didn't realize Eliot had felt like that. It wasn't our habit to talk about feelings. "I honestly wasn't surprised when you chose him over Sutton."

"The fuck I did." My anger was instant. The sun beat down on me, and even Oreo stopped his sniffing of the ground to look at me. "You're telling me if you were married, and your wife hated the ranch, you would abandon the place in a heartbeat?"

"I get it," he said, sounding tired. "Forget I said

anything." I couldn't. Sutton had said something similar. I had no idea how to prove them wrong, but it wouldn't help. "Enjoy your camping trip, and I'm here if you need me."

"I won't need you."

"None of you ever do. Anyway, tell Sutton I said hi and that she has shitty taste."

"Will do and fuck off."

He snickered through his goodbye. We disconnected. My stomach bottomed out again when I realized I forgot to clear up a few things with him.

Keep this between us?

Your sex exchange is safe with me. It'll last as long as you do in bed.

I sent him a middle finger emoji.

He sent me back a set of lips.

...you chose him over Sutton.

What the fuck? I didn't choose Ray. I had a life plan, and Sutton had known it when we met. She knew it now. I was with her all weekend, so I'd forget what Eliot said and enjoy my time with the woman I wished was still my wife.

✷

Sutton

Rocks crunched under my athletic shoes and Wilder's boots. The trails weren't technical, lucky for him and those cowboy boots. He was dressed in worn jeans, his hat tipped low over his face, and a dark green T-shirt that made his dark eyes darker, like he was thinking about sex all the time, and also made the bulge of his biceps stand out. I was in moisture-wicking, capri-length leggings and a loose shirt. My hair was in its wraparound braid, and together we looked like Workout Barbie and Cowboy Ken were taking a hike.

I shifted the backpack I was carrying with my water bottle and snacks. He'd insisted on hauling my bag, but I made him buy his own, along with a water bottle. "You sure you're holding up okay?"

He lifted his hat like he was airing out his head and then set it back in place. "Quit worrying about me, Doc."

The day was hot, and not much wind was sneaking around the buttes the trails wound through.

"I can't when I know you're used to sitting in an air-conditioned vehicle for your entire shift." I couldn't resist teasing him. Some summer days, he'd comment that the AC wasn't strong enough for the battle against the heat, and the same with the heat in the winter. He was also out writing tickets, securing crash sites, investigating accidents, and rescuing people from all sorts of weather in his uniform and gear.

He adjusted his hat again, shooting me a mock glare. "I should be asking if you're okay, you know, since you play with kittens all day."

I laughed and continued in front of him. He'd insisted on letting me go first so he could watch my ass. We had done a couple of other trails, and the shock of hearing that Eliot knew about us had worn off. Wilder swore Eliot didn't trash me when they talked, and that he wouldn't spread the news.

Now I was fighting guilt not coming clean to Aggie.

To be fair, I didn't know I'd be camping with her brother all weekend. "There's supposed to be a picnic place at the turnaround point."

We walked for another quarter of a mile. The trail wasn't that long, but traffic going through the park was heavy, slowing down our spectating and cutting into hiking time, which was fine on a hot day like this. The paths would be open, with little shade, leaving the sun to beat down on us.

When we arrived at an opening with signs, surrounded by rocky areas, a family with small kids was milling around. The mom was strapping a baby into a carrier she wore on her back, and the dad was trying to wrangle a toddler and a school-aged boy.

"Brynn, no—" The dad caught the toddler by the arm. He lifted her to sit on his shoulders. "Come on, Roman."

The mom smiled at me when she passed. The dad was lucky he could see anything with the way the little girl clung to his head. A sweet family living had been my dream. Stuffing away the wistful tug at my heart, I took my backpack off at a little picnic table by one of the informational signs.

Wilder set his beside mine and put his hat down next to his pack. He ruffled his hair. "Brave family, doing these hikes with kids."

"Probably wears them out." I smiled. "Maybe wears the parents out more."

"No doubt." He helped me unload sandwiches. As we ate, quickly, because it was hot, another couple with kids swung through.

The dad grinned at us. "Finally a decent path for the young ones."

Wilder returned the smile and pointed toward the youngest kid climbing on the rocks. "I think she's getting away."

The dad's eyes widened, and he jumped away with a "thanks."

I traded a smile with Wilder. When they left, another woman hiked through. She was dressed like me, only her top was snug around her baby belly. She said hi, read the signs, and went right back down the trail.

"Lots of families this weekend," I said to make conversation more than anything else. We hadn't been alone like we were this weekend since we'd been hooking up.

Wilder packed his empty containers into his backpack. "Good place for it." He put his hat back on while I finished my grapes. "Can I ask…"

My chewing slowed. We weren't supposed to have heavy conversations this weekend. Anything he was hesitant to ask about would fit the description, yet I was helpless to refuse him. "Go ahead."

"Why didn't you want to meet with the infertility doctor?"

I popped another grape in my mouth to give myself time to think of how to answer. He'd never asked why when I canceled the consultation. He'd taken a shift, and I went to work. The time of the appointment had become a normal day.

"Were you scared?" he asked. "Were you afraid nothing could be done?"

"No." I wiped my mouth and carefully closed the baggie with the rest of the grapes. "Maybe all I would've needed was medication. Maybe we would've been facing shots and in vitro. In the end…" I didn't want to hurt

Wilder, but he had to hear this. If he was asking, he cared, and maybe if I'd told him at the time, he would've realized the depth of my frustration. But then I hadn't understood it myself until later.

"In the end, I knew I'd be alone at most of those appointments. If whatever we did was successful, then you'd be missing the prenatal stuff." He frowned, and I put my hand out. "I know you wouldn't mean to, but we both know how it would've gone. I didn't want to have a baby just to be a single parent. I didn't want..." This part was the hardest to admit. The decision to have a baby was both of ours. The decision to not have one had ultimately been mine.

"What didn't you want, Sutton?" His voice was quiet, rough.

I pushed past the tightness in my chest. I didn't want to hurt him, but transparency was necessary if we were going to survive even long distance. "I didn't want to just be having a baby to keep from being alone. That's a lot to put on a child, and the sad irony that it would be the polar opposite of how I grew up wasn't lost on me. I couldn't do it. So, I thought if it just happened, then we'd figure it out." And I'd feel less guilty.

His focus sharpened on me. "What was it like growing up?"

The band around my lungs got smaller. I shrugged and stuffed my empty sandwich container and fruit into my bag with more force than necessary. "I told you. My parents were gone with Honey a lot."

"Sutton." He hadn't moved.

I chugged from my water bottle, then capped it and shoved it into my pack. "We should go so we can hit up another trail. There are a ton of short ones in this section of the park."

He rose with me and tossed his backpack on. I thought he'd push more, but to my relief, he didn't, or I would've stopped breathing. He dropped behind me.

I sucked air in, and each lungful wasn't enough. The pressure on my chest would suffocate me if I didn't get some of this emotion out. I'd come this far with my story. I could go further.

I stopped and faced him. "I was alone. All the time."

He wasn't surprised. I'd made similar claims before. He knew how little my parents visited us. They barely made it to our wedding. But this was the first time he got a faraway look like he was processing the information and putting all the pieces together. "How old were you?"

I lifted a shoulder. A bead of sweat trickled from my hairline and down my neck. "They started leaving me home for the shorter practices when I was nine."

"Nine?"

I nodded. Now that he'd tapped the well, words flooded my brain. I turned and walked slower. The path was wide enough for us to walk staggered, not quite side by side, but the edges of the trail were level. "Just once or twice. Then I turned ten, and I don't know, it was legal or something. Honestly, I liked it better. I didn't have friends at the rink. My parents were glued to what Honey did. At least at home I had TV."

"Damn." Wilder kept off the sparse vegetation. "So you stayed home and watched game shows?"

"Game shows, soap operas, primetime. The news. Everything that I could get without cable. They were safety conscious in that they didn't want me telling anyone I was home all night most nights by myself. Then I was fifteen, and the weekend trips started."

His boots skidded to a stop. "They left you *alone* for the entire weekend?"

I nodded and kept walking. I didn't need to see his face to know how fucked up my childhood was. I also didn't want to see the pity for the girl whose own family hadn't wanted to be around. "Mom and Dad didn't think of it as neglect, but I can see that it was."

"Fuck, Sutton. I'm sorry."

I knew he would be. It wouldn't change how I had grown up. "I didn't have much of a social life, and I was cooped up. I couldn't really play outside in case I got hurt. Who'd know?"

"You had your cats?"

"A dog would need walks, and there was the safety issue. When I started being home all week and weekend, then Mom relented and got me the cats." They'd both been older rescues and had passed by the time I met Wilder. But they were the reason I wanted to be a vet. Those cats had been my companions.

"You know that's all kinds of fucked up, right?"

"I do. They don't."

"You think that's why they keep their distance? They feel guilty?"

I stopped again and faced him again. "Maybe? But I doubt it. They're too self-centered to realize how their actions hurt me."

He stepped closer, blocking out the worst of the sun. "Why didn't you tell me?"

I licked my dry lips and gathered my courage. So much for no heavy talks. "Because if I told you, and you still didn't change, the hurt would've been worse. And I didn't think you'd change."

I held my breath. Would he get defensive like he used to when we talked about his schedule? Would we reenact an old argument? Would he agree?

He furrowed his brow. Pain flashed in his eyes. "Sutton."

He'd *heard* me, and it hurt him. I put a hand on his warm shoulder, the bulge of the backpack strap under my palm. "You might've at first. Then the obligations and expectations would've gotten to you. That's the thing with being the independent kid. You know that when people realize how self-sufficient you are, they forget that you still need support."

"Goddammit, I want to believe I would've been better."

"I know, but ultimately, that's why this will only ever be a long-term, long-distance fling for me. I don't know if I'll ever get over you, Wilder. But now you know how I feel, and you understand why I can't risk more with you. I refuse to be dependent on anyone's timeline, which is probably why I'll never be interested in dating and getting married again. So this arrangement we have? It suits me. Does it suit you?"

Disbelief and sadness filled his eyes, and he gripped my hand.

Laughter and voices came from the parking area. In minutes, people would be rounding the curve around a short outcropping and see us.

I couldn't put this conversation in a time capsule and save it for later. It was done. "We should keep hiking."

✷

Wilder

After our talk yesterday, we'd settled into a comfortable routine where we didn't discuss the future as it pertained to us. We'd walked through the rest of town, dipped into more souvenir shops, hit up the ice cream place again, and generally got lost among the crowd of people roaming the small town until the musical started.

It was Sunday night. Tomorrow, Sutton wanted to pack up and leave mid-morning so she could clean and unpack and enjoy the afternoon. I had a campfire going. Oreo lay on the ground beside my chair, and Sutton was on my lap, her legs stretched out and cradled in mine. My ankles were crossed, and we watched the fire crackle.

In between our chatter about what we saw, the early Christmas gifts she bought Grayson, Ivy, and Ro, and a little onesie for Cody's new baby when it arrived, my thoughts turned to her revelations from yesterday.

Not only had what she said about the way she'd been neglected growing up shocked me, but the truth of her admission about why she'd kept quiet left a churning pit in my soul. A swirl of guilt and regret and the pathetic realization that she'd been right. I would've tried to change. And then I'd go to a Buffalo Gully football game or basketball game or some other school function, and I'd see myself in the kids. I'd remember how lost I'd felt. How worthless. And Ray had been my lifeline. He'd seen me, and for the second oldest of five siblings, I'd needed to be individualized. I'd needed to be set in a straight line and be told I was good for more than morning chores and cattle drives and horse hauling.

Sutton hadn't had that. She'd had two cats and two

parents who checked in on her. Now she had a family who included her. Who went out of their way to invite her. Was being with me—again—threatening her standing with them? Eliot had seemed more upset with me, but he wasn't Sutton's best friend.

Her phone buzzed. When she dug it out of her pocket, the screen said Mom.

"Their monthly alarm must've gone off," she murmured before she answered.

"Hey, Mutton," John said.

"Sutton," Kelly gushed. "I wasn't sure you were going to answer."

With her head on my shoulder, I could hear the conversation. They were both on speaker like usual. The call brought back memories, like the way her shoulders would tighten or how she'd always look a little lost and hurt after she hung up. How I'd try to cheer her up, oblivious that I was also part of the problem.

"I'm camping."

"That's nice." Her dad sounded mildly interested.

"This time of year?" her mom asked.

My blood pressure rose. Sutton told me about her camping trip, and I'd immediately thought of her safety. I'd wished I could go with her. I'd obsessed about it. Her parents were half distracted.

"And the clinic?" John's favorite topic, according to Sutton. "You had to close shop while you're away?"

"It's a weekend," Sutton explained.

"Aren't there emergencies?"

"There might be, but they'll just have to go to one of the bigger towns unless Dr. Jake is available."

"Hopefully, he doesn't poach your customers while you're kicking around the wilderness."

"We're more like colleagues than competition."

"Speaking of competition." Kelly's squeal was muted. "Guess which grandma and grandpa are making the trip to Poland for the Junior Grand Prix?"

"That'll be fun," Sutton said as if her parents traveling overseas was everyday news. They often made it to national events. Ice-skating only. Montana had been a black hole in their schedule.

"My passport's filling up because of that girl." Pride rang from John's voice. "Seeing her makes it all worthwhile."

I tensed, afraid of Sutton's defeated reaction. I ran through my usual pick-me-up lines like when we'd been in her kitchen, but she didn't twitch or flinch. "Give Petra my best, and tell Honey and Rolf hi."

"Oh, we will," Kelly reassured her. "Maybe we'll make a trip down before the end of the year— Oh, I don't know about Christmas. You know how winter season is."

Were they still using that line?

"I do. Enjoy your trip. Send me pictures of Petra."

She hung up and set the phone on my lap as if she didn't have the energy to put it away. A sigh slowly eked out of her.

I'd known what John and Kelly were like, but witnessing their dismissal of Sutton took on several more layers after learning how Sutton was raised. They weren't just perfectly nice people who came off as scatterbrained. Their lives weren't built to have Sutton in them.

When we'd been married, they'd visited Buffalo Gully twice. Once for our wedding, and once a few years later when our house was built.

I hugged my arms around her. Her phone slipped to

the ground. Oreo gave it a sniff, then ignored it. "Think if we put skates on the dog, they might actually visit?"

Her body shook with her laughter. The crackling fire lit her face. Her smile was there, but her eyes were sad. "If I said yes, would you be surprised?"

"Actually, I thought you'd say he had to get at least bronze before they figured out where Crocus Valley was on a map."

She laughed again and turned her face into me. "You know them so well for only having met them a few times. Didn't that seem weird to you? That they never came to see us?"

"I wasn't especially close to Barns. Cody was the oldest and most important to him. Then Eliot because he was taking over. If I moved, it wasn't like Barns would leave the ranch to visit me."

"He never did for Aggie?"

"Yup. Kinda sucks that absentee parents are our mutual experience."

"Agreed." She crossed her shoes on top of mine. "You know what I miss the most since the divorce?"

"My dick?"

She gave my hand a playful slap. "I've been seeing that a lot lately, so no—but also, yes. Which was why you got in my pants so easily."

"You weren't wearing any, Doc."

She wiggled her butt on me. "And I won't be wearing those underwear again because you still have them."

They were tucked in my drawer where they belonged. I pressed a kiss into her hair. "What'd you miss?"

"The grill-outs Eliot would have after we worked cattle and those times we helped move horses. Most everyone was there. You guys would throw the best parties."

"They weren't really parties." Those had been the times Barns didn't mind that we lay back and shot the shit with each other. Huge annual accomplishments that were a normal part of ranch life but were an excuse to let go, if only for a night. I loved them, too, but I also still got to do them.

"They were the closest thing I ever got to a party. I had to work overtime in college and do volunteer work at the animal shelters so I appeared familiar with animals on my vet school application. Your family was like a built-in friend group."

Goddamn, her college years were still as lonely, just busier. "I never thought of them like that. Some days, I feel like I only deal with the worst people. I guess without Eliot to bitch to, I'd feel like that's all there was."

"Maybe that's why you help other people out?"

I thought her words over. I was used to defending my work, but she wasn't being critical. "Maybe. I like being useful."

"Because you were in Cody's shadow."

I frowned. "I wasn't in Cody's shadow."

She patted my knee. "Sorry I said anything."

Cody and I led remarkably different lives. Growing up, he'd been the oldest, and everyone assumed he was the most responsible. He acted like it, yet it wasn't like I got a chance to help when Cody was there first. Until Ray made me see the light, I wasn't the guy who wanted more responsibility. Afterward, proving myself didn't happen at home. Cody was in charge, besides Barns. So, yeah, maybe I liked having a chance to show I was as good as Cody. "You really think that's why I want to be sheriff?"

"It makes me feel better to think that." She sat up and looked over her shoulder at me, a brow cocked. "We're getting deep again. We should go have sex."

My dick twitched to life, but I couldn't abandon the conversation. We'd gotten nowhere but divorced avoiding the heavy subjects. "You're going to drop that bomb on me and then ignore it?"

Her expression turned guarded. "Yes, Wilder, I am. I'd much rather have orgasms than talk about your job that I resented for so long."

She'd reached her limit. I'd much rather give her orgasms than talk about my job, but the conversation was important. I was finally getting deeper insight into what went wrong between us.

Or perhaps I was finally understanding it.

Sixteen

SUTTON

Returning to normal life was harder than I anticipated, and the problem stemmed from the Wilder-free part of my normal life. An entire weekend of pretending we were something had probably been worlds better than camping alone. Unfortunately, I now knew what being isolated in a camper with Wilder was like. Solo camping would be an adjustment. One I would have to make eventually. There was no way he would get two weeks off in April—if we were still doing what we were doing.

Thankfully, it was Thursday and dart night, and I didn't have to tie myself in mental knots trying to see the future of us. Country music pounded through the speakers of the bar. Dart league was over, but I stuck around to play a few games with the girls.

Tova took aim with her dart, one hand on her belly. She took her shot and let out a breath. "Oof, this is getting hard." She backed up to the high-top table and wiggled into her seat.

Vienne propped her chin in her hand. "Are you sure you don't want to go to the Purple Petal and sit at a short table?"

"They're closing soon." She gripped the table as she centered herself. "I like the challenge. Okay, Sutton. The camping trip. How was it?"

I'd returned only a few days ago and hadn't had a chance to talk to my friends. I'd messaged Aggie that I'd gotten home okay, but I'd also avoided her. Lying to her didn't come easy, and I'd have to keep what really happened from Tova and Vienne, too, since Vienne thought I broke things off. What would she think if she learned we were trying again?

"Good. We went to the musical and got lots of hiking in."

Aggie cocked her head. "We?"

Shit. "Sorry. I left Oreo in the camper with the AC while I went to the musical." I almost said he'd gone hiking with *us.* I couldn't get through one sentence without messing up. I wasn't cut out for sneaking around.

"I've been camping with the kids in the yard," Tova said, "but I've never been camping for real."

"The kids would love Medora," I said. "So many souvenir shops and short trails they can take."

"They still have some horse-friendly riding paths too," Aggie added. "We should plan a big family trip there." She grinned at me. "But not in April."

"Wouldn't it be fun if you all could meet me in the Black Hills?" I wistfully thought of sitting around the campfire and laughing and talking with my friends and family. The trip would be more fun with people.

Medora without Wilder would've been nice. I would've gotten some rest and maybe chatted with a few other campers. But it wouldn't have been a company-filled weekend.

Goddammit, I *liked* Wilder. A lot. The sex was amazing, but I also liked his sense of humor, the way he looked after Oreo and other animals, and the ease of talking with him. We'd touched on heavy topics, but we'd also laughed together. A lot.

"A big Black Hills trip would be fun," Vienne agreed. "Catherine's wanted to do s'mores. She refuses to use the microwave, but I don't do fire. I'd burn down the neighborhood."

"You can come out to our place," Aggie said. "Ansen will get the fire pit going. It's not the Black Hills, but maybe we can get us all out before the baby's born?"

We all looked at Tova. She smiled, sheepish. "You know if we plan any time in the next month, I'm going to drop as soon as you bring the marshmallows out." She shifted in her chair and winced. "I might actually ask you to pick a night so I can get this watermelon out."

"That'll help me plan when to be on auntie duty." I laughed. The plan was for me to stay at Cody and Tova's so the kids didn't have to get moved around. Aggie was across the road to help see the kids to school and take over football games when I was at the clinic Saturday mornings.

Aggie nodded. "Then let's do two weeks from this Friday night. Campfire and s'mores and maybe babies. Also, I'm pregnant."

A collective gasp erupted from the table. Elation

swept away the panic from my earlier "we" slip. We all hopped down to embrace her. She'd been drinking water and juices when we went out because she and Ansen were trying, but I'd almost forgotten until now.

Tova was the last to make it off her stool and join in the hugging. "That's so cool. This baby is going to have a giant family and never be alone. I can't wait." She wiped at the corner of her eye. "My hormones are causing the tears, but I'm really happy I met you guys."

"Group hug!" Vienne announced, but only loud enough for us to hear. In this bar, we'd have a few guys trying to join in if they heard.

When we pulled away, Tova dabbed at her eyes again. "Since I'm standing, I have to go to the bathroom. Again."

"I'll go with you," Aggie said. "I'm in the early stages of peeing all the time."

They disappeared, and Vienne and I climbed back onto our seats. Group hugs and more babies, and I got to be part of it all.

Vienne ran her fingers over the silver loops of one of her long necklaces. Tonight was necklace night instead of bracelets. Her critical gaze pinned me in my spot. "*We*, huh?"

Busted. I buried my face in my hands. "How obvious was it?"

She laughed. "You covered well except for looking like you wanted to climb out of your skin." Her smile faded. "You and Wilder are back together?"

Vienne wasn't his sister, but she'd know I was lying to Aggie again—and to her. Would she consider my drama unwelcome? "We're trying a long-distance thing. We just can't..." I lifted my hands and dropped them.

"Star-crossed lovers?"

Emboldened by her understanding expression, I told her the rest. "I, uh, told him I was never interested in getting married again." The words came out sour, but when I thought of getting married, Wilder flashed through my mind, and I couldn't go there again.

She tipped her head, her brow furrowed. "Never?"

"I can't..." I licked my lips. I wasn't usually so open, but she'd kept my confidence when she didn't have to. And she'd do it again. I doubted I even had to ask. I owed her. "My parents treat me like I'm inconsequential. I grew up isolated and alone with cats and game shows to get me through. So when I felt like that with Wilder, I left."

"Oh, Sutton."

"He doesn't make me feel like that when we're doing whatever it is we're doing. But if we marry again?"

"You're back to being that forgotten little girl."

I nodded and drew my thumb over a condensation droplet on the table left by one of the drinks.

"Aggie would understand, you know."

I gave her a regretful smile. "Aggie doesn't need me in her life. My own sister barely talks to me."

"Fuck your sister. This is Aggie."

"I'm scared, Vienne. I thought I was risking your friendship if I told you, he-ey, now we're back on again!" I finished in a falsely chipper tone.

"Sutton, I thrive on the love lives of you and Aggie and Tova. Give me all the juicy details, on again, off again, I don't care." She leaned forward. "I'm not shallow, but it sounds like your family is."

The back of my eyes prickled. "You're a true friend."

"I think that of all of you. I haven't had any until I met Aggie at this very bar one night."

Surprised, I did a double take but her expression was serious. She hadn't had much for friends before us. "I didn't either until I met Aggie. Now I have you and Tova too."

She peeked toward the bathroom. No sign of Tova or Aggie yet. "As for Wilder, you won't know how you two can work if you don't try. And personally, I think it's okay to keep what you're doing under wraps while you figure it out. Just like it'd be okay if you told Aggie."

I took her words to heart. "Eliot figured it out, and he hasn't told the others." Yet. He was probably waiting for the situation to blow up, and then he'd sit back and tell Wilder he told him so. "I think I'm at the point where the longer I wait, the harder it is to tell her. Then I don't know what to say."

Sympathy filled her eyes. "They're not going to cut you off because you and Wilder have a hard time being apart. I don't think they'll blame either one of you for trying to figure out a way to make it work." Her gaze lifted over my shoulder. "I'm going to change the subject. I knew Jake was a bad decision in the making, but I went out with him anyway." She said the last part louder.

"You didn't." Surprise mingled with appreciation. She was putting the spotlight on herself so Aggie and Tova didn't know we were talking about me and Wilder. But also—Jake?

"No, Vienne," Aggie said as she got back in her seat. "Say it ain't so."

"He's temporary, and that's all I want." Vienne lifted her bottle of cider. "And orgasms."

Tova heaved back into her seat. "Did he deliver?"

"One." Vienne pushed up her dark glasses. "Which is more than I got with Theo. So I'm going to make the same mistake twice next weekend because a girl gets tired of batteries."

Aggie chortled. "Some mistakes last longer than others."

"Well, he doesn't, but he can get the O, and that's all I care about. Did you guys hear about the new bakery opening in town?" She slid a glance my way and smiled.

These friends were the real thing. I'd never had women like them in my life. I was grateful every day to have them. I was glad I had all the Knights in my life. I just wasn't sure I could keep the one I wanted.

Wilder

I turned down the highway that'd take me to Aggie's. The sun was sinking low, and it'd be dark in a little over an hour.

Three weeks without Sutton was too long. I was supposed to be on call, but Kaplan had asked me to work next weekend, and I stuck firm on insisting he take call for me this weekend.

Ray was on me about various sheriff's office subjects. He'd wanted to meet this weekend and go over the staffing of the jail. He thought different policies and procedures should change and would help my future election, but all that could fucking wait. I was back to phone sex with Sutton, and it wasn't enough. When Aggie sent me a text inviting me to her get-together with Cody and his family and Vienne and Catherine, I had to use that as an excuse to go to Crocus Valley. I'd be in on family time and meet up with Sutton afterward. I wasn't fucking missing it.

I pulled in behind Eliot's pickup in Aggie's driveway. Cody's truck was there, and Sutton's pickup was parked on the grass. A knot inside my chest released just being this close to her vehicle.

Eliot was by Aggie's front porch, talking to Cody. Ivy clung to his back like a baby monkey. She was in leggings and a long shirt that was probably a dress since that was all she wore.

"Uncle Wilder!" She waved, grinning and looking like a more animated version of her dad.

"What's up, peanut?"

She wiggled until Eliot put her down, and she sprinted for me. I snatched her up and spun her.

She giggled. "I didn't know you were coming."

"I made it work." I set her down, glad I wasn't making excuses over the phone for why I couldn't come.

"Why can't you make it work more? I've hardly seen you *all year*." Ivy's dramatic flair was getting stronger with time.

"What do you mean? I'm here all the time." Wait— No. I wasn't.

"All the time, Wilder?" Eliot crossed his arms and leaned against the corner of the garage. The clever look in his eyes said I was in trouble. "Are you making trips you're not telling us about?"

I shot him a warning glare, but he returned it with a shit-eating grin. "I meant I was just here for Grayson's game."

His grin stayed wide. "But Grayson wasn't the only one you saw."

Cody slid his shrewd gaze between me and Eliot. "Ivy, can you go ask Aunt Aggie what she needs help with?"

"Ugh. Okay, but Grayson's gotta help too." She stomped around the house.

"Something's up," Cody said as soon as she disappeared.

"What gives you that idea?" Eliot drawled.

I glared at Eliot. Not fucking now. Everyone was around, and I didn't want to be on the defensive when my other siblings heard about me and Sutton.

"Exactly." Cody shifted his attention to me.

"He's a shit starter, and he's trying to start shit." I shrugged like I didn't have a care in the world when I cared so damn much. I didn't need Cody's practicality intruding on my almost relationship with Sutton. He'd point out our jobs, the distance, the horrible roads for half the year. He would ask how we thought long distance would work after one year. Two. Then three. Too many valid points Sutton and I didn't have answers for.

I wanted to go look for her, to stand an unsuspicious distance away, and know that I'd be in her bed tonight.

Cody crossed his arms. "I hear I'm talking to the future sheriff of Murphy County."

"That's the plan. For the interim at least." After the last few weeks with Ray, I was tired of discussing the whole sheriff thing.

"It's a miracle Ray's actually retiring in the first place," Eliot said, thankfully dropping the topic of how often I'd really been to Crocus Valley since the night of the street dance.

Cody scoffed. "You're going to get elected and keep getting elected. Everyone's expected you to be the next sheriff since you first pinned on the badge."

"I don't like to take it for granted. Kaplan's shown interest." He commented on being friendly competition last week. I wasn't looking forward to Ray finding out. He'd have me at every single sports event in the county, all the holiday shows, and I'd be sitting on fucking Santa's lap all in the name of community engagement.

"I'm happy for you," Cody said, his stare intensifying. "Since it's what you've always wanted."

"It is." I nodded. My answer rang more hollow than it used to. Getting the top position in the department had motivated me all through high school and college and since my first shift. Every time I put on my uniform, I looked for ways to improve the department, help the officers, and better our presence in the community.

"You'll have Ray in town to give you advice," Cody said. "Or is he moving?"

Eliot snorted. "He's got nowhere to move to."

I shook my head. "His son's in Michigan, and his daughter's in Florida, but I think he plans to stay in Montana." In Buffalo Gully specifically. "He won't quit mentoring just because he hung up his badge."

"What else is he going to do?" Eliot asked. I gave him a *"what is your problem?"* look. He held his hands up like he was under arrest. "I'm just sayin'. He doesn't even really have friends."

"Hello?" I said and poked my chest.

"Do you shoot the shit about divorce and women and your *amazing* family, or do you both sit and talk shop and muse about how if you had unlimited funding, you'd do things so differently?"

I glowered at Eliot, but his words struck home—not the amazing family part. Annoying siblings. Did I talk with Ray about more than work? When I'd told him about the divorce, he'd made a similar comment to what Carla had said to Sutton. *Ah, hell. I'm sorry, Knight. Some women aren't cut out to be a law enforcement spouse. It's a tough job, and you need the support.*

I had needed support—and what Ray said had confirmed it. He'd been the only one to think the failure of my marriage wasn't solely on my shoulders. He'd always wanted what was best for me, and Sutton had needed to do what was right for her.

I had framed the failure as due to Sutton not being right for me. But what if I wasn't right for her?

Then why was I sneaking around with her again so my uptight, oldest brother didn't highlight all the reasons it was a bad idea?

Ansen popped his head around the corner. "How many burgers you guys want? Catherine's going to kidnap the marshmallows and start her own bonfire if we don't eat dinner and start on the s'mores."

Cody started in his direction. "Can't leave the ladies waiting."

"Are you talking to the guy who keeps knocking our sister up?" I asked.

A grin spread across Ansen's face. "As many times as she wants. Who am I to say no?"

"I seriously don't need to hear more," Cody said, back to being grumpy. I laughed. Getting to both of them in one shot was a success.

Eliot followed, and I fell in behind him. That way he wouldn't see me searching for Sutton.

She was sitting in a camp chair by the fire pit, a beer in the cupholder in the armrest, and Ro giggling on her lap. A lovely sight to a man who'd been missing her each day. Tova and Vienne were on either side of her. Ivy was helping Aggie spread out the plates and utensils. Ansen had the grill going on the back deck with an attentive Grayson by his side. Eliot went in his direction, unable to resist the grill.

Cody swung by Tova, kissed the top of her head, and murmured in her ear. She automatically gripped his hand. I doubt she knew she was clinging to him, and she absently rubbed her other hand on her stomach.

I stopped beside Sutton, wishing I could drop a kiss on her mouth. Instead, I squatted and grinned at Ro. "How's my little horse princess?"

She gave me a drooly grin and wiggled, her arms seesawing by her sides. She reached for me. The way my nieces and nephew could make my heart burst got more noticeable after they moved away.

Sutton handed her over with a smile. "I think someone wants her uncle."

I put a knee on the ground and held Ro. Her size and weight brought back memories of Grayson and Ivy. Cody had lived in Buffalo Gully when they were born, but now a new family lived in their home. Cody had sold the house and the five acres around it.

Only Eliot and I were in Buffalo Gully. The thrill of becoming sheriff of the county I grew up in paled when I thought of how much of my family had moved away.

"I've gotta get up," Tova announced. Cody helped her up and was glued to her side as she walked around.

Sutton exchanged a look with Vienne. "You think?"

Vienne cocked a brow a few shades darker than her hair. "Did we really jinx ourselves?"

Sutton turned back to me. "We joked about making the party tonight so she'd go into labor."

Aggie was at my side and leaning over me to talk to

Sutton. "Did I hear you guys say labor?" Ivy had ditched her to practice dance moves in the yard with Catherine. Ro squealed and reached for her mama. Aggie laughed and took her from me. "Sorry to ruin Uncle Wilder's cuddle time." She took off toward Cody and Tova.

I remained kneeling by Sutton, having no damn reason to explain why I was so close to her.

Vienne's lip curled, her eyes mischievous. "If only Wilder got cuddle time."

"Between you and Eliot, I'm not going to survive the night." I took a seat across from them.

"Eliot's already given me shit." Sutton looked around to make sure no one was close to us.

Cody and Tova were making their way back. Aggie was next to them, grinning.

"Well?" Vienne called.

"I think that was a contraction. My water hasn't broken, so I'm having a burger and a s'more first. Then we'd better head to Bismarck." Tova sat, and Cody hovered over her. I'd think she was the one who'd been through the birth of two kids already. "Sutton, are you good with staying at the house tonight?"

"Yes. I can run home and get clothes. Aggie, are you able to take them to Grayson's game?"

"Yes." Aggie glanced to where Ansen and Eliot were getting the burgers off the grill. "Ansen has a horse getting delivered in the morning, and Eliot's staying at our place to help him. I'll have Ro with me."

"It's supposed to be cold and windy tomorrow," Vienne said. "I doubt they'll cancel the game, but I can take Ro. Ivy too."

Aggie pointed to Sutton. "In the morning, you'll wake them to bring them to my place." She aimed at herself. "Then I'll take Ro and Ivy to Vienne." She switched to point at Vienne.

That was a lot of running kids all over town. Sutton went into the clinic early. Grayson and Ivy would be beside themselves waiting for news about their new brother or sister.

Sutton slid her gaze toward me, a question in her eyes. Did I mind? I would've been staying with her tonight. I was disappointed, but I didn't care that she was helping Cody and Tova. I was still in the same zip code as her.

But I also wanted to help, and no one was asking me. They weren't used to counting on me. "I'll take the kids to Grayson's game. I can stay at Cody's instead of heading home tonight." I wouldn't have been driving home, but it's a detail they didn't need to know. "I'll sleep on the couch and take Grayson. I can bring Ivy with me, or she can come here."

Everyone fell quiet and stared at me.

"You'd be okay staying at the house?" Cody asked carefully. "With Sutton?"

Sutton's stare bored into me, stunned, but also waiting to see how the rest would accept my offer.

I was about to laugh, but then I remembered. He didn't know Sutton and I were hot and heavy. "As long as she doesn't mind."

Vienne folded her hands and pretended to wait for Sutton's answer. Good thing Eliot wasn't here, or he'd be chortling, and I'd have some explaining to do.

"It's fine," Sutton answered quickly. Did I hear eagerness too? We used to love having Ivy and Grayson over. "I'd appreciate Wilder's help after the kids are full of chocolate and marshmallows and Aggie's punch."

"The punch isn't spiked," Aggie said. "They'll be

fine. Unlike my brothers, who drank their fair share of spiked punch in high school."

Tova raised a brow at Cody, but he shrugged. "I'm not as guilty as Austen, and I think Eliot learned from us how not to get caught."

Everyone looked at me since Eliot was still by the grill. "Ray scared me straight after he caught me at a pasture party. And Eliot drank on our land, not anyone else's."

"What happens on Knight land," Cody recited, "stays on Knight land."

"Thy Knights' will be done," Ansen said, a plate full of burgers in his hand.

"You learned that the hard way." Eliot snickered.

Ansen's fond gaze touched on his wife.

Aggie's grin was shameless. "I used to hate that saying. Until I got Ansen."

"Yeah, he put up such a fight," Eliot said sarcastically. "Food's ready. Tova called first in line, and I'm not arguing with a woman in labor."

I wasn't either, but I had that woman in labor to thank for getting a sleepover with Cody's kids and Sutton. Something that I had thought would never happen again.

Seventeen

SUTTON

I lay on Ivy's blankets. She was tucked underneath them, doing long blinks, on the brink of succumbing to sleep. "Is Tova going to be okay?"

This wasn't the first time Ivy had asked the same question. "She's had no complications, has a good medical team, and your dad."

"Mommy had a good medical team and Daddy."

My heart broke for the scared little girl. "I know, honey. And I know it doesn't help to tell you this is different, but it's normal to be scared. Having babies is as scary as it is exciting."

She yawned and clutched her blankets. "Are you going to have a baby?"

She'd also asked me the same question when she was younger. The answer used to be that it hadn't happened yet. "I don't think so."

"You don't want one?"

"No, hon. I do. I did. I mean, I would love to, but everyone's bodies are different, and mine doesn't make them as easy as others."

"Oh. Sorry." She leaned over and gave me a kiss on the cheek. "You'd be a good mommy. And Uncle Wilder would be a good daddy."

I exhaled a laugh and hoped she wouldn't continue the conversation.

"If you could make babies easy, would you?"

Oof. She wasn't done with her questions.

"I don't know. I'm getting older, and that usually makes it harder."

"You're not old, Aunt Sutton."

"I'm not married either."

"Tova said you don't have to be married to have babies."

I laughed, an awkward, quiet sound in the room. I often forgot all the explanations and clarifications the kids wanted. "She's right. I guess I planned to be married when I had babies."

"But you and Uncle Wilder are divorced." The dejection in her voice was heavy.

"Yeah," I said, almost as let down as her. "We are."

"But if it was easy, would you?"

Would I? In a perfect world, yes. I'd be married to Wilder. He'd be by my side for every appointment. He'd be so reliable, I wouldn't question his presence. I didn't have a crystal ball, but I saw none of that in my future.

"The only easy part about babies is making them." Oh, crap. What conversations did I just set Cody and Tova up for? I grimaced, grateful the only light was from the hallway. I looked at Ivy, but her eyes were closed and breath puffed out of her lips.

Whew. I cut that one close.

I waited a few moments and then slowly rolled up and snuck out of her room. I stopped at Grayson's door, but only heard his steady breaths. Wilder had seen to his bedtime.

I crept downstairs. A light shone next to the back door. I found Wilder in the laundry room, folding towels. He'd taken his hoodie off and was just in a black T-shirt. His biceps bunched every time he bent his arms. I was here for the arm porn.

I leaned against the door. "Ivy was seconds away from asking me how babies are made before she fell asleep."

"You'd have to tell her we're just the babysitters. Their parents get to teach the birds and the bees after they finish with the repercussions of it."

I moved in to help him fold, enjoying the heavy domesticity we got to experience together.

"There's a load in the dryer, but I saw women's panties and backed all the way out."

I laughed. "Glad to hear you don't shove anyone else's underwear in your pocket."

"Don't think I won't stuff yours in my pocket right now." He tossed his towel on the perfectly folded pile and faced me. "That door has a lock."

I walked backward and closed the door. The lock clicked loudly in the room. "I told Ivy the easiest part about babies was making them."

A slow smile spread across his face. "Doc, are you calling me easy?"

"I happen to be the same way around you, and it's been three weeks since we did anything."

"You got off nice and loud over the phone earlier this

week." He crowded me against the door. "You said you pretended it was my tongue licking your sweet little clit."

My heart beat faster, and heat flooded between my thighs. My hoodie turned stifling, but Wilder would probably take care of that soon.

I twined my arms around his neck and pulled his head down. When his lips landed on mine, I groaned. Three weeks shouldn't feel like forever when it came to Wilder, but it was.

He spun to bump my ass up against the washer. Against his lips, I murmured, "Is it wrong to have sex in your brother's place?"

The desire cleared only slightly in his eyes. "The laundry room is like a neutral zone. It's not right, but it's not wrong." He slid his hand up my ass and skimmed around until he was undoing my zipper.

"Good enough." I rose up on my tiptoes to capture his mouth again. As long as we didn't get caught, I wouldn't feel bad. If Tova and Cody got busy against my washing machine, I'd cheer them on. Another thought occurred to me, and I pulled back. "What if they have cameras?"

"They don't. I checked." His sexy smile made my knees weak.

"Sometimes your law enforcement background comes in handy." I pulled him close to me again so we could continue to do something not quite right, but also not wrong.

✦

Wilder

· · ·

After a full day with Grayson and Ivy, we were all exhausted and sprawled across the basement floor in the family room. A movie was paused, and the kids were talking to Cody and Tova.

"How many fingers and toes does Charlie have?" Ivy asked. She was lying on her belly, the phone on speaker between her and Grayson. Sutton and I were sitting behind them. Blankets and pillows were scattered around us, and a half-empty popcorn container was on the couch.

"She has ten fingers and ten toes," Cody said. He sounded tired and elated. This day had to bring a ton of memories back for him from when Grayson and Ivy were born. And it had to be a little trippy since he was making memories with someone new.

Charlie was short for Charlotte, named after Tova's favorite old-style dance, the Charleston, which Grayson had immediately guessed before he demonstrated the entire dance.

"Are you sure you can't tell what color eyes she'll have?" Ivy was kicking her feet behind her. Both kids were already dressed in pajamas.

"Not yet, but they're a darker blue," Tova said. "So maybe brown."

"Can we sing her a lullaby?" Grayson asked, and Ivy enthusiastically nodded.

"Of course," both Tova and Cody answered.

I rested against the couch and tipped my head back. Sutton leaned against me. We were sitting closer than we usually would, but we were tired. She worked all morning, and I ran Grayson and Ivy around. Then they talked me into taking them to Hummingbird's for lunch. Sutton met us in time to order and eat. Afterward, we walked across the street to the park. They wanted to walk by the house Cody had rented when he first moved to Crocus Valley. Aggie invited us over for supper, and of course, the kids had to see the horse Ansen would be training for the next few weeks. Eliot left for the ranch, and I thought that would be the end of the night, but Grayson and Ivy wanted to teach me and Sutton how to do some of their dance moves. The only thing that kept me leaping across Cody's lawn was Sutton's delighted laughter and clapping.

The lullaby wrapped up with what I swore were a few extra ad-libbed verses.

I picked up the phone and took it off speaker. "Glad everything's going okay."

"Thanks," Cody replied. He'd also taken the phone off speaker. "We'll be home, hopefully before lunch, but you never know when they're going to discharge you. Everything's, uh, going okay?"

"It's fine." The biggest problem was that I couldn't sleep in the same bed with Sutton without raising questions. "We're planning a lazy morning, or do you have accounting spreadsheets you want them to go through?"

"Ha ha, jackass. I have plenty of spreadsheets—anytime, Wilder. They're yours."

"I'd hate to take a job from someone who really needs it."

"Right. Bookkeeping doesn't come with a badge or advertising on the side of the car."

"Now who's being the jack—" I had little ears around. "Jackwagon."

He chuckled. "I'll have the phone on me if you need anything. Otherwise, I'll see you tomorrow."

"Good night. Can't wait to meet little Charlie."

I hung up and tossed my phone on the end table. The kids were focused on the TV. I slung an arm along the back of the couch. Sutton scooted in a little more.

"This is really nice," she said quietly. "Remember when we had them for sleepovers?"

"Yes." I used to enjoy their visits, but Sutton had been all in. She'd helped with Grayson and Ivy when Cody had to travel to doctors' visits with his late wife, Meg. Then Meg's parents had stayed to help with the kids. I'd had to work during a lot of the kids' visits, but I'd still gotten in on meals and movies and playtime. I hadn't realized how much I missed them until Cody moved and then Sutton moved.

"What if they fall asleep out here?"

I squeezed her to me. "We can be part of the slumber party," I whispered in her ear. "Then we can sleep beside each other instead of in separate rooms."

By the time the movie finished, the kids were asleep in their respective nests of blankets and pillows.

"Looks like you're stuck on the floor with me," I told Sutton.

"Oh, darn." She grinned and spread a blanket out over the both of us.

Sutton arranged the pillows. I shut the TV off, and we were bathed in darkness. The only light was from the yard lamp filtering through the lower-level windows. We'd be sleeping side by side, fully dressed, the next best thing to having her alone and naked.

I cuddled her into me, and she came willingly.

"This has been a good weekend," I said against her hair.

"Yeah. Real nice." She buried her face in my chest,

then pushed up to her elbows. "When should we tell the rest of your family?"

My chest puffed out just a little. She wanted to tell my siblings. Seemed a step in the right direction. I wasn't a dirty secret, and this long-distance business could really work. "Soon. Let Cody and Tova get settled with their baby. Aggie shared her good news a couple of weeks ago."

"You're right. I can tell Aggie and Tova at darts."

"Then Eliot can quit giving me hell."

"He'll find something else."

"I'm sure he'll be relentless when I become sheriff too." He was barely tolerable about my job as it was. Saying things like *"Going a little fast on that dirt road, weren't you, Deputy?"* Or *"I can't let you into the house without a warrant."* And one of his favorites—*"I know you don't frisk me because you're intimidated to find out how much bigger I am than you."*

Sutton didn't respond. I thought she'd make some comment about how Eliot behaved, but it was like the word sheriff sucked the fun out of the night. I'd take it back if I could. I'd take a lot back.

I drifted off to sleep wondering if she'd always gotten quiet when I talked about my future aspirations and if I'd been too self-absorbed to notice.

Eighteen

SUTTON

I finished loading the dishes. Wilder was vacuuming up the evidence of popcorn and movie night downstairs. The kids were outside. They'd come up with some game that involved both dance moves and playing catch with the football. Their dog was thrilled to be involved.

We'd just eaten breakfast, which was actually lunch because it was after noon.

I rested my elbows on the counter and watched them play. I could go outside, but I needed a moment to soak it all in. When would there be another time that Wilder and I could tag-team niece and nephew duties?

Would there be a time when Wilder and I could be open together at family functions? Vienne knew. Eliot knew, and he hadn't treated us differently. Other than an initial cursory glance, he'd been the same old Eliot.

I dug out my phone and tapped out a message to Aggie.

I need to talk to you.

Her reply was almost immediate.

Sure. All okay? Was it the night with
Wilder?

The night was fine, but I have to
discuss something with you.

Come over when Tova and Cody get
back.

Once we told everyone about us being sort of back together, then we could plan sleepovers at my place. My excitement rose, then it dipped.

What if he canceled? What if his work or the weather had different ideas? Would we slip and slide down the same path and come to the same conclusion?

The wall of heat enveloped me before strong hands slid around my hips from behind. I rose and turned my face to him. He nuzzled his nose along the nape of my neck. "Mmm, you smell like Ivory dish soap and coconut pineapple."

"It's a special pheromone combination."

He wrapped his arms all the way around me. I was hugged tight against his body. I soaked it all in, unsure when we'd connect next.

I kept an eye out the window, content to be snug against Wilder's front, but also making sure the kids didn't see us attached to each other. By the time we'd all woken up, each of us was pointing in a different direction of the family room. The kids didn't know I went to sleep secure in Wilder's embrace. Their parents should know first, and Cody and Tova had a lot going on right now.

"I have to go soon, and I, uh, don't know when my next day off will be." He'd been reading my mind. I let air leak out of me. He was back on call this evening. A sinking feeling that this was the beginning of the end hung over my mood. "I got the okay from the lawyer to hire another employee for Eliot using some of my inheritance money, but it won't happen in time for all the fall work. I switched some days to help Eliot with working and moving cattle, then the horses. Are you coming out for that?"

I didn't miss the hope in his question. I wasn't opposed to going to Buffalo Gully. When we didn't have to hide anymore, I'd go to the house we'd built and shared and see people who knew us as a married and divorced couple. I wasn't looking forward to it. The talk. The gossip. What would reach Wilder? How would it affect him? More importantly, what would Ray say? That was who Wilder would listen to, and if Ray saw me as a distraction, he'd encourage Wilder to concentrate on the future election.

So I'd be a lot like him, sneaking in and out, unless I was going to the ranch.

While my schedule was more predictable, I'd have similar constraints to his. "I can't take the time off. Ranchers are working cattle here, too, and I've committed to being around and open on the weekends until snowfall. I've also planned a heavier schedule the two months before my camping trip." A trip I was excited about but also ignoring that I'd most likely be alone.

"We'll find a way."

"I know." Except I didn't, and I wasn't going to ruminate on the topic today. Wilder was right. This had been a good weekend. I checked on the kids one more time. Their laughter rang through the air like they were playing right next to the siding. I spun in Wilder's arms. "We can sneak one kiss before you have to go."

"Agreed."

His hold tightened when our lips met. I let myself get lost for one heartbeat, maybe two, when a guy cleared his throat.

"Holy shit!" Aggie's voice resounded in the kitchen.

I jerked away, but Wilder didn't let go. We both turned our heads and found Cody and Tova crowded by the door to the garage on the other side of the dining room. A baby carrier hung from Cody's hand. Aggie was behind them, a tote bag in her hand, her eyes wide.

"Don't let us stop you." A smile played across Tova's face. Fatigue hung around her eyes, and her dark hair was in a sloppy bun that still looked trendy. She wore baggy gray pajama pants and what I suspected was an old sweater of Cody's.

"Shit. Sorry." Wilder didn't shove me away but changed his position to keep an arm wrapped around my back.

Aggie's wide gaze met mine. I was living the worst-case scenario, and I had to look like I was a deer with a semi bearing down on me.

She blinked, then her expression went neutral, and she set the bag on the floor. "Here are the toys they left at my place. I don't want to intrude."

"Aggie—"

"Talk to you later." She gave Tova's arm a squeeze. "Thanks for letting me meet Charlie."

"Thanks for dropping those off," Tova said. Aggie

rushed out, and Tova and Cody turned their attention to me and Wilder. Cody was scowling.

Shit, shit, shit. I messed up. She had to have seen the shock and dismay on my face and known I was lying to her. And now Tova would think I was shirking my babysitting duties. Wilder gave me a squeeze as if he sensed my tumultuous thoughts.

"We're watching the kids, I promise." My pulse kicked up. I couldn't have people I admired, a couple of the people I was closest to in the world, think I was making out instead of watching the children they trusted me with.

Cody's scowl deepened.

Tova's smile widened. "If we didn't know how a person can keep an eye on kids and still get some, we wouldn't have just had a baby."

"What's going on?" Cody asked.

"Is he the reason you've got a spring in your step lately?" Tova asked. For a woman who just had a baby, she looked delighted to dive into other people's business.

Heat flooded my cheeks. Was it that noticeable I was getting laid regularly? "We wanted to wait until you got home and had a chance to adjust to being a family of five before we told people we're seeing each other again."

Cody's gaze danced between us. "One of you is moving?"

"No," we both said, and Cody arched a brow. Tova's smile turned to a grimace.

Wilder cleared his throat. "I'll go grab Grayson and Ivy. They should meet Charlie before us."

"Or you can wait and elaborate. Charlie's sleeping anyway." Cody turned the carrier to show us the tiny little face peeking out from a blanket. Dark fuzzy hair covered her head, and she was the perfect mix of Cody and Tova.

"She's gorgeous," I gushed. Another little niece.

"She's cute. Good thing she takes after Tova." Wilder smirked, clearly loving the glare he got from his brother. "All right, all right. We're doing long distance. We know we have different lives, but we don't want to see anyone else."

Furrows formed along Cody's brow. "How long has this been going on?"

I exchanged a look with Wilder. Where did we begin?

"Aw." Tova pouted. "I thought little Charlie's arrival sprinkled love dust in the air and helped you two cross a divide."

Wilder smirked at his brother. "We crossed a divide in your laundry room, if that helps."

Cody's lips went flat, and Tova barked out a laugh.

"Yes," she hissed, grinning.

Mortified, I lightly swatted Wilder's hard stomach. "I asked you if it was wrong."

"Gettin' my brother back is never wrong," Wilder replied.

Tova looked up at Cody, interest lighting her blue eyes. "I can't wait to hear that story."

"One"—Cody shoved a finger in Wilder's direction—"shut up. And two, it was a kiss."

"That's not what she said," Wilder countered.

Tova smirked. "More impressing girls?"

Fondness took over Cody's expression. "I told you it was all practice so I could impress you."

She visibly melted against him. "You always know the right thing to say." They both turned their attention to us.

"How long?" Cody asked.

"Since the street dance," I answered, wanting to be open and honest. I peeked out the window. The kids were sitting in the grass with Buster. "I'm so sorry I didn't say anything. I was afraid you and Aggie would be upset with me."

"And I didn't want you in my business," Wilder said simply.

Cody's scowl returned. "I don't get in your business."

"You aren't dying to list all the reasons why this isn't practical?"

Tova snickered, then let out a tired sigh. Cody's attention instantly shifted to his wife. "Let's get the kids in to say hi and then you need to lie down."

She shook her head, her hair bouncing. "There's laundry and—"

"Folded," Wilder said.

"We cleaned—everything." I ran my lower lip through my teeth. Oh, god, I was awful. "Sorry, the kids were asleep, but we shouldn't have—"

"Oh, no, you should've," she argued. "The laundry room is a completely acceptable place to bang in someone else's house."

Cody's expression said he wasn't sure he agreed, but he would because she was okay with it.

A spark of envy ignited inside me. I'd never thought twice about him and Meg. They'd been...compatible. But he was a different man with Tova. He'd found the love of his life, and he'd do anything for her.

I hadn't been lying to myself about not getting married again. But I would if I had a guy who'd do the same for me.

"We're family," Tova said simply. "I don't have any

siblings, but sex pranks seem to be a thing between the Knight brothers." She adopted a fatigued grin. "You can ask Austen what Cody and I were able to do when we went stargazing."

"No, don't ask Austen," Cody said. "God help me if he finds out we actually used the condoms."

"All of them," Tova whispered conspiratorially.

"We just want time and space," Wilder said. "And if everything goes to shit, don't blame Sutton."

Tova's lips turned down. "Is that what you were afraid of?"

I nodded, my cheeks warming. The admission wasn't better than the hiding. "You all are really important to me, and I'm afraid I trashed things with Aggie."

"Then you'd better go talk to her," Cody said, steering Tova away from the door while gingerly maneuvering Charlie's carrier. "I've got a wife to convince to get some rest."

✦

I parked in front of Aggie's garage. Wilder had left for home after the kids had each gotten their turn holding Charlie. He and I had been next and then we'd left the tired and excited family to rest and bond.

I blew out a hard breath. A hunk of lead sat in my gut. Everyone had taken the news of Wilder and me in stride, but I didn't have quite the history with them that I had with Aggie.

I found her in the barn, cuddling with her six-pack of cats and sitting on an overturned five-gallon pail. Ansen and Ro were probably in the house.

"I'm sorry," I said in lieu of a greeting.

"You looked so upset to see me." She scratched a cat behind the ears and frowned at me. "Is that what you wanted to talk to me about? To tell me something happened between you and Wilder?"

"I had to tell you I'm a horrible friend." I dropped to my knees and picked up a tortie cat with prominent orange. Fanta. Her purr ramped up in my arms. My sweater would be covered with fur, but the little creature was my emotional anchor.

"How so?" She flattened her hand on Root Beer like she was preparing herself for bad news.

"I've been sort of lying to you."

She arched a brow, the hurt increasing in her hazel eyes.

My stomach started to hurt. Shame. She'd been with me through everything, and I'd left her out. "I've been sleeping with Wilder since the street dance."

She recoiled, and the cat darted from her lap. She scanned the barn, rapidly blinking like she was trying to see the world clearly. "That was months ago."

I nodded and sat back on my heels. I clutched Fanta. He was my lifeline. "I didn't know how to tell my best friend I was sneaking around with her brother, who I divorced, since she was incredibly supportive through the whole process. At first we were just messing around, and I was afraid to upset you..."

"At first?"

I told her about the movies, a PG-rated version of what really happened. "Vienne figured it out. I'm really sorry. Then Wilder and I quit, but we couldn't stop."

Her brows lifted at the reveal that Vienne had known. "And now?"

"We're trying a long-distance relationship, and we were going to wait to tell anyone until we thought it would actually work, but then Eliot figured it out when we were camping in Medora."

"Eliot knows, too?" Her mouth dropped open with a gasp. "Wilder was with you?"

"He invited himself. Showed up just as I was leaving and got into the pickup." I braced myself. I wanted her to know the whole truth. "Wilder was actually at the house when you picked me up to go thrifting." I squeezed my eyes shut. "I'm so sorry I didn't tell you."

"You were hiding my brother? In your house while I was in it?" Her scandalized tone made it all seem so much worse.

"I was terrified. I knew I made a mistake, but I wasn't regretting it, and that was wrong, and we planned to keep doing it. But we know what little chance we have." My throat suddenly grew thick. Our odds sucked. I set Fanta down and brushed my sweater off as if it'd do any good. "We were going to tell everyone, but we didn't want to overshadow your announcement or Charlie's birth, but... it's just excuses. You're really important to me, Aggie. I'd say you're like a sister to me, but my sister's practically a stranger."

She snagged another cat to cuddle, her forehead furrowed. "I know that ultimately, you and Wilder aren't my business."

"But he's your—"

"You know what my first thought was when I walked in on you?" When I shook my head, she dropped a kiss on the cat's head. "I thought, great, you and Wilder are back together, and you're going to move." She let out a scornful laugh. "How selfish is that? You two looked so good together, and I was worried about darts night. And how I'd have to have Dr. Jake as my vet again." We exchanged an *oh no* look and both started laughing. "I'm so selfish."

"No, *I've* been selfish. I've been thinking about how bad I want my ex-husband, and anyone who I thought wouldn't like it wasn't allowed to know."

Her curls flew as she shook her head. "I want to be happy for you, but I admit I'm relieved to hear you might not move."

"You were really upset I might leave Crocus Valley?"

"Yeah." She dropped her gaze to the straw-packed barn floor. "I'll confess my feelings are hurt learning Eliot and Vienne knew. If I wasn't dropping off toys, Tova and Cody would've beaten me too. You know how left out of family business I used to be."

She still was, but she chose to do her own thing now. If I realized why not telling her would hurt her, I would've swung open the bedroom door that morning. "I didn't think of that. I was too deep in my own abandonment issues."

"You're not getting rid of me that easily. Neither is my brother. If you and Wilder don't work out and end up despising each other, you're going to have to figure out a schedule for who gets to go to the family gatherings. I also would've never forgiven you if Austen found out before me."

A smile played over my lips. I never should've doubted her. "Have I told you lately how awesome you are?"

"Hold that thought because I'm going to ask a hard

question." The way her stare bored into me made me squirm. "Are you happy with long distance?"

Her question sucked the air out of my lungs. I would be honest with her when I hadn't been with myself. "I'm...content. I wish he'd give everything up and be with me, but he's not going to. And honestly, I'm not either."

"Sutton." The heartbreak in her voice was almost too much. I wanted to run.

"I know. He's made his choice, and I made mine. But we've found a middle ground, and it's good." I lifted my gaze to hers. "It's enough."

"For how long?"

Wasn't that the haunting question? I shrugged. "You should've seen him on that camping trip. He was a Wilder I hadn't witnessed before. We went hiking. We got ice cream. He wasn't being stopped in the grocery store to rescue someone's cat or help look for a runaway dog. There was no getting called out. It was perfect. I mean, if I get that once in a while, that's good." I swallowed a mysterious lump in my throat.

"Oh, Sutton," she said sadly. "I wish I could whack some sense into my brother."

"No. He let me go because he knew I wanted to open my own clinic, and I couldn't do it in Buffalo Gully. I let him go because being sheriff is his childhood dream. Getting that position will make up for your dad's bad behavior and redeem him in his own eyes. We both have career goals that define us, and they can't be accomplished in the same place."

She flattened her hands on her knees. "Okay, then. We're good, as long as you know that you can come to me with anything. Wilder is my brother, and that means I love you both, but if anyone knows what it's like to be unable to kick feelings for a guy when she knows better, it's me."

I nodded and smiled and stopped the words on the tip of my tongue. *Yeah, but it worked out for you.*

Nineteen

WILDER

I got out of my SUV and went into the sheriff's office. My stomach was rumbling like it knew it was Thanksgiving and it was missing out on a giant feast at my sister's house. Austen was staying in Crocus Valley with Aggie. Eliot had gone down for the day. Sutton would be there too. They'd have turkey, stuffing, mashed potatoes, probably the most unhealthy sweet potatoes known to man, and pie. A lot of damn pie.

I was working. And I'd be working the whole weekend.

"Next weekend, Doc." I juggled the phone as I navigated the hallways to the break room. The courthouse side of the building was dark and would stay that way until Monday.

Savory smells of turkey and stuffing filtered in. Brenda was the dispatcher on duty for the day, and she made sure we were taken care of. The church with the quilting club she belonged to had cooked for us yesterday, and Brenda had been reheating the food. The day was quiet, and the weather was mild. Unless the wind kicked up and blew around the fine snow we'd gotten over the last week, I shouldn't have to field calls for accidents and stranded vehicles.

"I can't wait." She sighed. "It's been forever."

Between the ranch and regular work, I hadn't been able to get to Crocus Valley all of October. I'd gone to all levels of Buffalo Gully football games, and several times, I'd wished I could be in Crocus Valley to see my nephew's games instead. Then weather had hit like clockwork on my few days off. But since I was working the holiday weekend, I had big plans for Sutton next weekend when I was off.

I stopped before I got to the break room. I put my back to the wall. "Hey, I need to ask you something."

"What's that?" A baby cried in the background. Charlie had a set of lungs on her. She might become the family singer instead of a dancer. Or both.

"I'd like to take you out Saturday night."

"Like, out to eat?"

I stuffed my free hand in my trouser pocket, a sudden case of nerves attacking my stomach. "Yeah. A date. You know, a first date."

I didn't want to spell out that I wanted to be her last first date. Our renewed long-distance dating seemed too new to declare that I'd be her last. Deep in my brain, logic tried to intrude. *You really think long-term long distance can work? You really think this is what she wants? To grow old together in different zip codes? Different area codes? Different states?*

Fuck those thoughts. I didn't know the answer. That

was why we were trying. We each had hope, and that was as good a start as any.

"What are you thinking? For this date?" she asked.

"I know you don't like movies, so just dinner. There's also a band at one of the bars downtown. We can do some dancing."

"A first date?"

"Again." Okay, I could see why her conviction wasn't overflowing. I didn't want her to revisit her anger from the double date when it came to this date. I couldn't tell from her tone if she thought the idea was romantic or a flailing attempt that fell short.

"A first date again. Yeah." This time I heard the smile.

Now I had to find a way to be her last first date.

*

Sutton

I checked the radar. A huge swath of snow crested the western half of the state and much of the eastern part of Montana.

I tossed the phone down. Berry mewed, and I dug my fingers into her fur. "He's going to have to cancel."

Even if Wilder could get to my house, we might have to cancel our date if the wind picked up. He wasn't scheduled to get off work for another hour. I didn't want him on the road if traveling was dangerous. I also wouldn't want him agonizing over whether he might get snowed in. Not my idea of a first date.

There was no way he was making it.

I gently lifted Berry off my lap and went to the

bedroom. I was wearing purple flannel pajama pants and a Knight's Arabians and Cattle Company hoodie, but I had bought a new outfit. My summer dress would get blown up by the cold winter wind, so I'd purchased a long fuzzy sweater to pair with soft gray leggings. Ivy would swear the outfit wasn't a dress, but it was mostly a dress.

A foolish warmth heated my cheeks as I took the hanger down. I tucked the garment safely in my closet.

It's okay. I knew this could happen. He's not skipping out on me because he's choosing work. Sometimes, Mother Nature has the ultimate say.

Affirmations done, I went into the living room. I would be stranded tonight as soon as the storm hit. The house was clean, and I had no projects going on for the winter.

I'll take "Wishing I Had A TV" for five hundred!

Shaking my head at myself, I dug out a puzzle I hadn't put together yet. A landscape image of Glacier National Park. That was next on my big camping trip list, along with Yellowstone, and then Itasca State Park in Minnesota. The Dells in Wisconsin. The Turtle Mountains in northeast North Dakota. I'd have to take more time off if I branched out farther, but someday.

I dumped out the puzzle just as a flash of headlights speared through the front window. Frowning, I got up and went to peer out the glass. Who else could be here? Coolness radiated from the window. Snow flurries made it hard to see, but they weren't heavy yet.

Wilder's pickup was in the driveway. I ran to the front door like it was already Christmas, and he was my only present and whipped it open.

He tipped his head down and jogged toward me. He

had on his black winter coat and blue jeans, but no cowboy hat or ball cap. His hair was neatly brushed to the side.

"What are you doing?" I called, leaning out.

"I traded with Kaplan so I could get off early."

Kaplan would likely ask for an unfair swap, and Wilder would have to give more time than Kaplan had given him. But that was a worry for another day. I went to step out, but I had only socks on, and an inch of snow layered the landing in front of the door.

Wilder approached the stairs and grinned, taking in my pajama pants and sweater. "I'm here to pick up my date. It's a little early, but I can make it work."

My excitement flared to life. That dress would get some use after all. "I'll be right back."

I rushed to the bedroom. Grateful I only had to add curls to my hair, I dressed and frantically put some body in my straight strands. When I was done, I took a good look at myself. My eyes were bright, a natural flush tinted my cheeks thanks to the man waiting inside the entry, and I flashed back to my real first date with Wilder.

It'd been at the same horse show, but he'd come to my hotel room and was a gentleman the entire night. He'd been charming and sweet and interested in me. I had thought I could spend the rest of my life with a man like this.

Nothing had changed. Maybe our arrangement wasn't what younger Sutton had thought it'd be, but Wilder was making an effort.

Would he still make an effort ten years from now?

Would I?

Tonight wasn't the night to worry about the future. It was our first date. Again.

He was waiting by the door, Berry in his arms, when I returned. She had a pleased look on her face, and she shoved her head into him. That cat and I had a lot in common. I ducked into the kitchen to grab my coat by the door to the garage. "I've been waiting to tell you she hates people."

He scratched her chin. "I'm not people." His gaze stroked down my body. "Lookin' good, Doc."

He'd said the same on our real first date. "Same goes for you, cowboy." Also what I had said to him all those years ago.

Desire filled his eyes, but he held the door open for me.

We loaded into his still-running pickup. The cab was toasty, and his smoky-whiskey-with-hints-of-vanilla smell infused the space.

"The roads won't be bad going to town, but we probably don't want to linger," I said.

"As long as we get this date in, we'll leave whenever you want."

"The band was canceled. I checked."

He smiled at me as he pulled onto the highway. "Don't worry. I have a backup plan."

This wasn't the Wilder I was used to. He was good at going with the flow. He adapted or dropped what he was doing according to others' needs, but I wasn't accustomed to being the reason.

Although, I'd been the reason a lot lately. Since the night of the street dance. But getting stranded in another state during a bad storm was another level of flow. "What if you get snowed in?" He might miss work. Had Wilder ever missed a shift? He'd done acrobatics to get coverage, but he'd never even been late.

He lifted a shoulder. "I'll figure it out then."

I snuck a peek at him. His shoulders were relaxed, and he wasn't clenching his jaw. This wasn't the reaction I was expecting. I'd actually expected him to skip the date altogether so he could be in Buffalo Gully to help with the storm. "Are you really not bothered about getting snowed in?"

We were entering town, and the streetlights highlighted his chiseled profile. "It's a worry. But I've covered enough for other guys who got stranded out of town in the winter."

The warm glow he was causing inside me was going to turn permanent if he kept this up. And I kind of hoped that was exactly what he'd do.

Twenty

WILDER

The restaurant was busier than expected. Everyone in town wanted to grab a good meal before getting snowed in. The workers probably wanted a chance to get last-minute groceries and hunker down.

As much as I'd have loved to stay and enjoy Sutton's company, I also wanted to get her home safe. And tuck myself in with her. It'd been too damn long.

What if you get snowed in?

Was I a bad guy to admit that I hoped I got snowed in? I wanted the winter storm to turn into a blizzard and dump two feet of snow on western North Dakota and eastern Montana so for once in the time since I'd known Sutton, I wouldn't be out in some of the most dangerous weather Mother Nature had to offer. I wouldn't be rescuing stranded motorists out of half-buried cars, freezing my ass, my feet, and my nose off, praying I wasn't the next to be buried by either snow or an out-of-control vehicle. What was it like to be a normal guy, hanging out in a warm house with my girl, putting puzzles together, and cuddling with the cat and the dog Sutton would surely bring inside once it got bad out?

Sutton finished the last of her pasta and pushed the plate to the side. She peered out the window. "The snow's getting heavier."

"Sure is." I was silently cheering for more. "Want dessert?"

She rolled her eyes toward me. "You know I always do."

"Triple chocolate cake or the lava cake with ice cream? We can take both to go."

She groaned and pressed her hand against her stomach. "You're going to get me so full I won't be too active tonight."

I read into her meaning. "I'll do all the work."

She laughed but shook her head. "I'd love the lava cake." She dropped her gaze and picked up the wrapper that had been around the napkin and silverware. She'd gotten halfway through making a tiny paper airplane. "I didn't think you'd make it, and I wouldn't have been upset. You can't help the weather," she rushed to tack on.

"I know." I plucked the small airplane from her grip and lightly launched it at her. I would've fucking walked if necessary. I wasn't canceling a first date.

She giggled and batted the plane away. "I'm really glad you're here."

"Me too." I soaked her in.

Her hair was down, cascading behind her shoulders, soft and shiny. I envisioned wrapping the whole curtain of silk around my hand and drawing her to me.

"Hey, Sutton."

She glanced up. A fond smile graced her face. "Hi, Jennings."

The man I'd practically elbowed out of the way during the street dance stood a few feet from the booth. A curious expression was on his face, but he didn't shoot me glares. "The roads are getting slick. Thought I should warn people."

"Thank you." She gestured to me. "You didn't officially get to meet Wilder."

I stuck my hand out. "Wilder Knight. Sorry for our first meeting. I was on a mission."

"Yeah." Jennings's laugh was good-natured. "That was obvious." He nodded toward the younger hostess who'd seated us. "I came to pick up my girlfriend. Her car's shit on the roads."

"Glad you're looking out for her." Sutton gave him a smile that would've made me hate the guy before I'd gotten her beneath me the night of the dance. "Thanks for the warning, Jennings. We were going to get dessert, but we should go."

He ducked his head and stuffed his hands in the pockets of his jeans. "I've been meaning to thank you, but I haven't been out much since getting together with Freya. But thanks, you know, for being honest. I would've been too busy chasing you to see that Freya's hints about liking to dance were her being too shy to ask me out."

Sutton's grin turned wide and radiant. "That's awesome. If it wasn't for you dancing with me, this guy wouldn't have let his caveman brain take over and cut in."

Jennings laughed, and I wasn't sure if I should join in or not. Her description was accurate. I should listen to that part of my brain more often.

Jennings gave each of us a nod. "You two have a good night—and a safe drive."

Sutton and I got our coats on and were ready to go by the time the server returned with the ticket. The roads were getting slippery and snow-covered. As I turned down the driveway, a gust of wind kicked up. Snow filled the air, temporarily blocking the view of the garage. In town driving would be worse, but doable. Any longer and out-of-town driving would be treacherous. Jennings was right to warn us.

"I guess I'll forgive Jennings for putting his hands on you."

She barked out a laugh. "It was dancing, Wilder. You're the only man who's seduced me in the back seat."

"I can seduce you in the front seat, too, just to make sure." I parked behind her spot outside the garage.

"Maybe another time, cowboy. I have a warm house and a big bed that you fit in."

Her camper was getting hard to see in the snow. In four months, she'd be pulling out for her Black Hills trip.

I had four months to figure out how to take off the first two weeks that I'd officially be sheriff. I didn't have to tell Ray to know he'd worry that being on vacation right when I took over could be used against me in a competitor's campaign.

Could I get away for a few days?

Sutton got out of the pickup, a gust of frigid wind blowing in, and called for Oreo. He loped around the garage, used to the winter weather but also knowing it was a one-way ticket for an outside dog to get inside.

"I'm going to put him in the garage to dry off," she called over the increasing wind.

I opened the garage door for them, then closed us in.

The wind and snow were blocked out, bathing us in quiet. Oreo rushed to me, and I gave him lots of pets. Sutton wasn't the only one I missed since last being in Crocus Valley.

He trotted to the fluffy dog bed Sutton kept for him during storms, and Sutton and I piled inside. I helped her take her winter coat off and hung it up. Mine went next to it, and I took an extra second to look at our garments hung side by side. How fucking right was that?

Sutton pushed her hair back. Her cheeks were red from the few minutes in the cold, and her eyes were still glowing. I hadn't seen this Sutton in a long time. It was like her light had faded a little more each year she lived with me. I'd been oblivious.

"How about hot chocolate since we missed dessert?" She crossed to the cupboard. No packets for Sutton. She made homemade as often as possible. I realized now her parents hadn't wasted expenses on processed foods to afford figure skating lessons for her sister.

"I'll help."

This was also new. With no TV, I didn't park myself in front of ESPN and try to forget about the demands of the job. I'd rather be taking Sutton out every night off.

She smiled at me and handed me the milk. "Three cups in a saucepan, please."

Once we prepared the hot chocolate and our mugs were full of the steamy drink, I pulled up a playlist on my phone and hit play. A slow country song filled the air.

Sutton was about to sit at her kitchen table, but she paused and looked up.

I held a hand out. "Would you like to dance?"

A smile curved her lips. "Your plan B?"

I nodded. "Any excuse to get you in my arms."

She rolled her eyes, but the grin didn't go away. "Careful, or I'm going to fall head over heels in love with you."

She froze, and my outstretched arm wavered. Wasn't she in love with me? I'd been trying to win her back, to earn any time with her, but neither of us had said the L word. How could I not have considered where her heart was? Did I take her love for granted?

"I already am," she said quietly and took my hand. "I didn't mean for that to sound like I wasn't."

I tugged her to me, keeping her hand in mine and snaking an arm around her waist. I spoke against her hair as I swayed us to the beat of the music. "I love you, too, Sutton. I've never not been in love with you."

"Wilder." She crowded closer, letting me take over and spin us around between the table and counters.

"I took you for granted."

She lifted her head to meet my gaze. "Maybe I took you for granted too."

"No. You didn't. You kept working, kept trying. And I kept assuming you'd always be there."

The corners of her mouth pulled down. "Even after we divorced?"

"No. Maybe?" I swayed us around in a lazy circle. A new song started, just as slow and romantic, but also the perfect melody to keep me talking. "I let you walk out because I wasn't going to be like Barns."

The admission came out of nowhere. Had my father been the excuse for why I let Sutton go?

Her eyes flickered. "How could you think you'd ever be like him?"

"I wasn't going to try to trap you if you weren't

happy. You might leave and never want to think about me again."

"Like your mama did?"

My nod was jerky. Barns had kept talking Mama into baby after baby, but he wasn't willing to put the work in to win and keep Mama's love fairly. And she'd been so defeated, so fed up when she left, she wanted little to do with boys who reminded her of him. Boys like me.

She stopped the dance and released my hand to cup my face. "You're not like Barns, and you can quit compensating for him. You don't owe anyone anything because of how he behaved."

Not long ago, I would've brushed her off. This time, her statement sunk in like footprints in fresh snow. Had I been compensating for my dad and wrecking my most important relationships because of it?

But my life wasn't just about me. I wasn't selfish like Barns. "The town helped me when he wouldn't."

"Ray helped you, and his aid came with high expectations. It's *your* life, Wilder. If you want to be sheriff, do it. If you don't...that's okay too."

I hooked her hand and started a slow two-step with her. I was about to tell her being sheriff was what I always wanted, but she'd heard it before. This time, I was also worried the words would still feel hollow when I said them.

Twenty-One

WILDER

A phone was buzzing. I didn't open my eyes. I had a round ass nudged into my side. "That your phone?" I mumbled, trying to clear the sleep fog and remember whether she said she was fielding calls this weekend.

"It's yours," came her sleepy reply.

I picked up my phone. Ray's name flashed on the screen. I squinted at the time. "It's four a.m. his time."

"He doesn't care." She didn't have to look to know who I referred to.

I rolled out of bed. A displeased grunt came from the cat at Sutton's feet but neither Berry nor Sutton moved.

In the hallway, I answered. "Knight."

"Wilder, we need more bodies out there. Everyone tried getting somewhere else instead of staying hunkered down during the lull we got."

"I'm not at home." I had hoped to miss this conversation, for it to be unneeded. I certainly didn't want to have it before dawn.

"Whenever you get here. We need you."

Of course they did. The department always needed help. It'd been Ray's mantra. The consummate politician in him, continuously pointing out the faults in the system so it'd stay in the back of the county board's mind and that of the voters. "I'm out of town, Ray. I'm…" I hadn't told him yet. My gut suspected he'd have advice that went against making things work with Sutton. I sank onto the edge of the couch, dreading the reveal. "I'm in Crocus Valley."

"You're…" He made a disgruntled noise. "Deputy Knight, there was a clear winter storm warning that we knew would cause issues. What if you can't get back later today?"

"I'll keep an eye on the road reports." I hadn't thought to look yet. I was off for the weekend. It shouldn't matter where I was. But I knew it would. I'd have come anyway, and even though I was on the phone with my boss, I didn't regret the trip. I didn't have an ounce of anxiety over being stranded with Sutton, only at Ray's reaction to it.

"The roads are closed to the border. I'm sure it's the same where you are."

Probably. "I'll get back when I can."

"What good is that going to do the people on the road now?"

Irritation was chasing away the lingering sleepiness. "Ray, I'm trying to work things out with my wife."

"Your wi—" Silence fell. Pieces were probably clicking into place for him. The times I was out of town and didn't give him details. How I wasn't as giddy about learning every facet of his job. "Am I wrong, but didn't the divorce already happen?"

My body tensed so tight I thought I'd get a charley horse in my back. "It's a big problem I'm trying to fix."

"She's moving back? I thought she opened her own clinic. You know the Cleavers have all the business for a hundred miles, and they won't hire her."

"Fuck the Cleavers."

"Don't let one single person hear you say that. If any family has the ability to tank your campaign, it's them. You know they don't want a Knight in charge of anything outside of the boundaries of Knight land. That bothers them enough. Did you hear Kaplan's thinking about running against you when it's election time?"

"I'm not worried about Kaplan." I'd already put over fifteen years into my run for sheriff. I could take a little time to myself right now.

"You should be. Kaplan's going to be out there getting pictures to share with the newspaper. People are going to remember this storm, but you're not here for them to remember."

Everything he was saying was true. My history had less meaning than what I did now that Ray had announced his retirement. Each day, I would be studied by those who didn't want me in office who would use what they saw against me in the next election. The Cleavers had the power to do that, and they'd back Kaplan if only because he wasn't a Knight. With their vet clinic, they could network with families I'd never be able to reach. A real grassroots movement.

But goddamn. Just one storm to not be involved in wasn't asking for too much, was it?

He let out another grunt. "Look, Wilder, it took me

by surprise is all. So Sutton's thinking of returning to Buffalo Gully?"

"She's not moving."

He went quiet. I could hear his unspoken question, "*What's the point, then?*"

I scrubbed my face with my free hand. "I'll keep an eye on the roads. As soon as they're open, I'll take off."

"I wish you were here. We're short out there. We have two semis wedged in a ditch and at least five motorists stranded. There was about twenty minutes when the wind let up, and everyone made a break for it. You know how it is."

He did too. Yet he wouldn't plan for another storm. He'd rely on calling everyone out who was home with their families, especially me. The lack of planning for forecasted weather emergencies was on my list of things to deal with.

"I'll let you know when I'm back."

"Wilder." His grave tone gave me pause. "You deserve someone who supports you. You've dreamed of taking office for a long time."

I thought of all the ways Sutton had sacrificed her dreams and goals for me for years. "She always had my back, Ray. I'll keep you updated." I hung up.

He probably thought I meant I'd keep him posted on how things were going with Sutton. I'd been talking about the weather. I laid my phone on the end table, left it there, returned to the bed, and wrapped myself around the woman I still wanted as my wife.

✶

Sutton

When I woke and saw all the roads closed in the state and passing into Montana, I worried Wilder would be climbing the walls. He'd told me about his call with Ray and how disappointed his boss was. Then he'd fallen back asleep as if he hadn't done something completely unheard of in his entire career—upset his boss.

All day, he'd acted like he wasn't keeping close tabs on the roads. As soon as the wind died down and the plows got out, he'd have to go, no matter how treacherous. Yet, he'd helped me make meatloaf—a double batch so he could take some home with him to freeze for future meals.

We were 450 pieces into a 500-piece puzzle of a cardinal. Berry was delighted she had two warm bodies to lie on while we worked on the puzzle.

My gaze dropped to his phone, lying ignored on the arm of the couch next to him. I was sitting on the floor to keep from disturbing the snoozing tabby at his side.

Wilder snapped a piece in place. "I'm not looking at the radar until we finish this thing."

He'd noticed me noticing. "I'm just... This is different. Today is different."

"I know."

Unexpected relief blew through me like I was next to the drafty picture window. He wasn't going to deny how he usually behaved. He used to pace the floor, waiting for the call, any call, to help. Or he'd just go. Get dressed and call himself in. Ray never cared if Wilder or any of his other deputies worked too much, just like he never correlated the overtime with the short-staffing. "Ray's going to be more upset because you told him about me."

"He might be, but it's not his business."

A phrase I never thought Wilder would utter. "You're going to turn me on if you keep acting rebellious like that."

He chuckled, and Berry raised her head to mew. She went right back to sleep when he petted her. "Sutton likes the bad boys."

"No, but I like when you act naughty." I picked up a red puzzle piece I knew was part of a feather, but rotated it in my fingers. "I know you said it's none of his business, but what if he, like, pressures you to find someone else?" I pushed the piece in place like it was Ray's face. He'd never been warm with me, and I always got the impression he would've preferred someone completely subservient to Wilder. An unquestioning, undemanding woman. Which told me a lot about why Ray was divorced.

"Well, I heard Carla's hooking up with a guy from out of town, and I already turned down Jodi, in a way."

My heart skipped. "Jodi? Your high school ex?" I'd met her a few times. She was nice, but I'd never been intimidated. Until now. They were both single. Well, technically, Wilder was no longer single. We'd gone on an official date.

He nudged a piece of the beak in place. "Yep. Eliot tried to get me to hit on her before he knew you and I were a thing." He lifted his gaze to mine. I searched his brown eyes, unsure of what I wanted to see. "I wasn't interested, and she sensed it. Guess she's living in Sidney."

Oh. Sidney wasn't far from Buffalo Gully. Not at all. And Jodi was exactly who Ray would prefer. She was from Buffalo Gully.

"Sutton."

I jerked. I was no longer looking at him but at the wall. "What?"

"Not. Interested. Okay?"

I nodded, finally letting my gaze stroke over the scruff on his jaw. "Okay. But...why didn't you tell me?"

"Because she didn't hit on me. Eliot was pushing me to do something, anything. And I was sleeping with you."

"Is it too much to hope she finds a nice, out-of-town guy to hook up with like Carla?"

The corner of his mouth crooked up. "Go wild. As long as I can hope Jennings is so madly in love with Freya he proposes soon and is completely off the market."

"That poor girl's toes are never going to survive their wedding dance."

We finished the puzzle. As soon as the last piece was in place, Berry woke up, stretched, and walked over it. I was laughing when Wilder checked the road reports on his phone. His jaw clenched.

"You have to go?" Today had been as nice as camping. Today would also make solo snow days harder to weather without Wilder.

"Yeah. The roads are open, but they're not good." He stood and held his hand out to help me up. When I was on my feet, he pulled me close. "Maybe I should give them another half hour to improve?"

Warmth spread through my body and went deeper than where I was pressed against him. "Hmm." I pretended to think. "However could we pass the time?"

He carried me to the bedroom. I was laughing, but deep inside, down in a place I would ignore thanks to moments like this, the question popped up asking whether what we were doing was worth it. Would these blissful moments that showed me what life could've been like with Wilder be enough to justify continuously parting ways?

A more important question took precedence. When would I see him again?

Twenty-Two

SUTTON

Christmas and the New Year had passed, and each holiday had been Wilder-free. I spent Christmas at Aggie's and sent two pans of frozen meatloaf home with Eliot as Wilder's gift. Wilder had sent a small box with a note that told me to open it while alone. I had and found a red, lacy pair of underwear. While he'd been working on New Year's Eve, he'd still called me at the stroke of midnight and told me his plans for taking that underwear off me and pocketing it.

January didn't hold any more promises of getting together. He had a free weekend coming up, but he wasn't confident he could get away. The closer Ray's retirement was getting, the more demanding he was of Wilder's time.

I wiped down the exam table. My vet tech had taken off early to get her daughter to basketball practice. Wilder would be going to basketball games in Buffalo Gully too.

Ivy talked about trying basketball, and I was looking forward to seeing her games. I hoped I could see them with Wilder. We'd sat apart for the one game of Grayson's we'd gone to together.

The irony was that Cody, Austen, Eliot, and Aggie all knew about us now, and we hadn't had a chance to be a couple around them.

My phone started vibrating. Wilder. My thoughts had summoned him, but he was also on my mind all the time. Since the clinic was closed and the doors were locked, I put my phone next to the keyboard on the counter and hit speaker. "Hi. You're on speaker, but I'm the only one here. There is a loopy Dachshund in the back who might eavesdrop. She thought the road was a good place to go for a stroll today, and she's still medicated after surgery."

"She gonna be okay?"

"Yes, thankfully. She was lucky." I always liked how Wilder asked about my work and cared about my patients. I put the disinfectant away. "How's it going?"

"Ray's in a mood. I don't know if he regrets his decision or if he's doubting me, but he's...being a dick."

I'd always found Ray a little dickish, but I never thought I'd hear Wilder say something similar. "You only have a few more months."

Wilder's chuckle was dry. "I might get this office, but I don't know how long it'll take him to actually leave. He heard talk the Cleavers were going to encourage a family friend of theirs to run next year. A guy from Great Falls who's been a detective for years. So that's got Ray fired up."

"But not you?"

"Eh, it is what it is. If my time here hasn't spoken for itself, I'm not going to do tricks in front of the crowd."

Wilder never used to talk like this. I thought he was ready to do what it took, but then that was what he'd been doing all along. "Isn't that why they call this stuff a 'dog and pony' show?"

"I've gotten my share of horses ready for a show, and I'm not interested in switching places with them." He blew out a hard breath. "Whatever. I'll worry about it when the time comes. The interest in this position took him off guard, and he's paranoid. I'm more concerned with learning what I need to know to do a good job."

Ray was probably stressing that he wouldn't be in charge of all the things soon. He was finally having to put up or shut up, but I also had a lingering animosity toward Wilder's boss. I recalled all the times the guy had been dismissive when Wilder had talked to him about getting the schedule out in a more timely manner so spouses could plan their lives around call time. Ray had dilly-dallied longer. Why the hell had he been doing the schedule anyway? Once Wilder quit asking, then Ray handed the job off to one of the jailers-slash-dispatchers. The schedule was only one example of how Ray didn't support his deputies beyond the job.

"Anyway," Wilder continued, "I'm calling to say that I don't know when I'm going to be down next."

My hope sank like a stone. "We knew the winter would be hard." And once spring hit, he'd be in his new job position. Our time together wouldn't increase once the snow decreased.

"It'll get better. I promise."

Would he have held my gaze if he was here? Or would there have been a slight dip? He'd never made that promise before, so he must mean it. I ran what I knew of his schedule through my head. "What about Valentine's Day?"

God, that was a little over a month away.

"About that...we just had someone resign. She's done at the end of the month. Got a job in Billings with more pay and no call time."

"Oh." I knew all too well resignations meant overtime and more call trying to patch the gap an empty slot made. "That sucks."

"I know." His answer held dejection that had never been there before.

I wasn't surprised, but my disappointment rang through me clear as a church bell. Dong. More challenges. Dong. He tried, and it still wasn't enough.

I'd like to phone a friend. Complain and whine. That friend would be Aggie, but nothing would be accomplished other than finding an outlet for my upset. I could go home and hug a cat. After, I'd start tearing carpet out of the upstairs rooms in my house. I needed a project after all. "And here I was trying to lure you down to help me refinish the original hardwood floors in the bedrooms upstairs."

"I'm sorry," he said. "Save some backbreaking work for me?"

"Changing light fixtures is all yours, cowboy."

His chuckle prompted a smile. "I have a lot of vacation time, Sutton. I plan to use it."

"I look forward to it."

I believed he'd actually take his vacation this time, and I couldn't wait. In the weeks since the snowstorm, I'd grown accustomed to being alone, and I'd come to a decision. Long-distance dating Wilder was better than being divorced from him. He said things would get better, and my days were already better than they had been this time last year. I couldn't help but worry that things would change once he was sheriff, and for us, I wasn't sure it'd be for the better. But I was willing to two-step with another heartbreak to find out.

✴

Wilder

It was goddamn Valentine's Day, and I wasn't with Sutton. Last year for Valentine's Day, I'd made sure I was working, and it was a shift where I slacked. I had parked in the trees and prayed no one came speeding by. I had wanted to be left the fuck alone.

This year was different, should be different, and yet I was facing a gruff old man instead of the woman I'd rather be deep inside.

Ray had papers scattered in front of him. "So that's the jail and courthouse security. As you can see, there's room for improvement. I've been trying to justify more technology for years, but voters don't like to feel like their tax dollars are being spent on prisoners even if it's spent on systems we use for scheduling and appointments and meetings."

He hadn't covered anything I didn't know. We'd had long talks over these issues, sometimes at the lake with a few beers during the rare times we were both off duty. "Got it."

Whatever he saw in my expression—boredom, frustration, both—made him shake his head. "It's been a long week. Go home. Get some rest. We'll revisit this tomorrow and cover my duties as coroner."

Great. Didn't everyone want to talk about dead bodies on a Saturday? "Sure thing."

He shoved the papers at me. "Take these. Go over them tonight."

I stacked the budget reports and scheduling lists for the jail over the new department headshot for me as sheriff and concept for a logo for when election season started.

Fuck's sake. I had a logo.

I knew being sheriff was political, but the reality reared up on me like a spooked horse, all striking hooves and unpredictable behavior. Had Ray made it look easy, or had I taken for granted the office was mine?

Ray had scoured the shift calendar and arranged meetups every free weekend until he was done in April, which wasn't many, since the department was working short. Ray had taken several more field shifts than he normally did. His extra hours didn't bode well for getting more free weekends after I took his position. I'd never planned to leave the field, but long days combined with extra shifts and call during short-staffed times weren't uncommon in this department.

Fuck.

"Going to the game tomorrow night?" he asked.

Ray loved basketball season. I enjoyed watching the kids and not being in an empty house, but since Ray's retirement announcement, I'd been to a lot of damn games. None had included my niece or nephew. I was showing my face everywhere except for Sutton's house. "Isn't it out of town?"

"They're playing an invitational in King's Creek."

That'd be a two-hour drive one way plus the game, but all I heard was tomorrow would be a short day with Ray. "I have to catch up at home." There was nothing I had to do, but if Ray cut out early enough, I could make a quick turnaround trip to Crocus Valley.

"You and Sutton, uh…"

Prickles skated along the back of my neck. Since the snowstorm, he hadn't mentioned Sutton, but he'd made damn sure my head was on work and not her, as if that was possible. "Yes."

"How's it going?" He tapped his fingers against the back of his hand.

"Good." A strong word, but she answered my calls, we had phone sex, and she didn't tell me we were done. Good enough.

The rhythmic finger tapping continued. "Who all knows you two are a thing again?"

"My family."

He studied me, and I couldn't get a read on what he was thinking. "It might not be a good look."

"What?" I didn't want to hear the answer.

"You with your ex-wife who lives in another state. Residents of the county might worry that if they elect you in, they'll be faced with an interim sheriff shortly after. They might worry you're going to leave to be with her."

"They might worry?" I echoed, disbelief swirling inside my chest, followed by dismay. He was right. The Cleavers would start the speculation themselves.

He dipped his chin. "Kaplan's happily married. He's lived in Buffalo Gully for years with his family. He'll be seen as more dedicated."

"The election isn't until next year."

"I told you campaigning starts—"

"What are you saying, Ray?" I snapped. The job might've run my life, but the election was taking over when I was a year out from even entering my name as a candidate. I would be interim for over a year before the election.

He sat forward, leaning his elbows on his desk, his face a mask of calm. "I'm saying that Sutton is a liability."

Was Ray so focused on helping me attain my career aspirations, he'd forgotten I was also a man? He'd been teaching me how to be a politician. Time to say what he wanted to hear so I didn't have to justify my private life to him. "Ray, I appreciate everything you've done for me. I know you're concerned about me and how things with my ex-wife will affect my time in office. I promise you this job is on my mind at all times." Like a magnet stuck inside my skull.

He studied me again, his gaze contemplative. That damn tapping continued. "Good to hear. You'd better make the next game. The kids notice when you're gone— and so do their parents."

I took my out to leave his office, otherwise he'd start on the coroner side of his job tonight, and usually when he did that, he bitched about lawyers and the legal aspects of the job beyond what I dealt with as a deputy, and that wasn't a conversation for this late at night.

I'd rather go home and find out if I could call and catch Sutton in the bathtub. I got the best sleep when I drifted off after having her breathy moans in my ear.

Snow had been falling while I'd been in Ray's office. My work boots crunched through the untouched layer. It was almost ten. Ray had ordered a pizza from the gas station. I had passed on a slice. Since seeing Sutton again,

I'd taken better care of myself. I hadn't realized how much gas station pizza I'd been consuming or that I rarely had more than beer and cereal in my kitchen.

Instead of meandering through a few blocks to see if anyone needed a hand, I went straight home. My nights were for cooking and talking with Sutton.

I pulled into the garage. Inside, the house was empty as usual. I dropped the papers on the table in a spot neither Sutton nor I had ever sat in and went through my routine, hanging up my vest, locking up my sidearm, and putting my uniform in the wash. I wasn't officially on this weekend, and I wouldn't wear the damn thing when I met with Ray tomorrow and Sunday.

As I was veering into the kitchen, my doorbell rang. My stomach sank. Did someone go in the ditch and need a tow? Being hit up for aid at my house wasn't an uncommon occurrence. I swung the front door open without looking and was met with the most beautiful sight.

Sutton gave me a nervous finger wave. "Hey."

She was here. In the house she'd left. I tugged her to me, pulling her flush with my body.

"Does that mean you don't mind me dropping in?" Her voice was muffled pressed against my shoulder. Her coat was puffy around her, and her stocking hat tickled my nose, but I didn't fucking care. She was here.

"Hell no, I don't mind." I kissed her and lifted her, backing up so I could shut the door and block out the cold air. Her weight in my arms felt so right.

Holding her in this house was...odd. We couldn't return to how we had been, but I hadn't realized how cozy her house was. How much I missed the natural clutter that came with it. My place was always clean. Always organized.

I pulled away to give us both air. "Hey."

Her smile was everything I needed now. It'd been over two months since I'd seen her last, and video calls only did so much.

"Catherine and Vienne are going to take care of Berry and Oreo, and Catherine's fascinated by Sylvester. Well, I'm paying Catherine, but Vienne's going to oversee the job and make sure no crickets escape."

She'd planned a getaway. To a place I never thought she'd return to. "Why'd you come?"

She flattened her still-gloved hands on my chest. "You've been making all the trips, and everyone important to us knows we're seeing each other again. So, I figured why not? I told my tech and admin that we're taking the weekend off and to change the voicemail."

She was willing to miss out on business to spend the day with me. A deep part of my brain suggested she might move back in, but the rest of me didn't feel right. This place wasn't her. She wouldn't have stories about Walter, the Maine coon, or corgis that peed when they were excited.

"I'll be in meetings all weekend. Coroner duties and lawyers."

She lifted a brow. "A rollicking fun weekend."

"None of it's new. Nothing I wouldn't have learned otherwise." Or figured out for myself. Work was the last thing I wanted to discuss. I pressed another kiss to her lips and stroked a thumb over her cheek. "Give me your keys. I'll park your pickup in the garage. Have you eaten yet?"

"I figured you'd be working late, and I deliberated about letting myself in, so I had a sandwich after work."

"Come in whenever you want. I won't complain about finding you naked in bed." I could haul her straight to the bedroom, but once I had her naked, I wasn't going to stop and feed myself. "I was just going to make something."

"I'll eat with you. What were you going to cook?"

Good thing I had more than beer and cereal. "I have a lasagna to throw in, but I add more cheese. Be right back."

I ran out and moved her pickup. I closed the garage from the outside and jogged to the front steps. Another car pulled up. A little red convertible with the top up.

If I'd had the pizza in Ray's office, I'd have heaved it up. What the hell was Carla doing at my house?

She parked on the curb and got out, a round container in her hands. "Yoo-hoo, *Sheriff*!"

I looked around. Was I being pranked? No way the first time Sutton visited me Carla showed up. "Is something wrong?" Maybe she was stopping to ask me to help someone else.

"Does something have to be wrong for me to visit you?" she purred. A white stocking hat was on her head, but the rest of her wasn't dressed for winter weather unless she was doing snow yoga. She didn't have a coat on either.

Acid was going to claw its way through my abdomen. Wasn't she off the market? Why had I thought that meant she'd quit trying to sleep with me? "Carla, I can't talk right now."

"Oh, hush, Deputy. It's Valentine's Day, and it's just been *eating* me up that you're celebrating alone."

"Aren't you seeing someone?"

Her grin widened. Shit. She mistook my question for interest. "I'm as single as can be, Sheriff."

The front door creaked open, and Sutton stepped out looking like my own personal snow bunny. She'd taken her winter coat off and had her -40-degree-rated boots on over her leggings, a clingy long-sleeved top that hugged her bust and hips, and her stocking hat still on her head with her light hair streaming out. The two women looked like they would both do snow yoga, but I knew which ass in leggings I'd be watching.

Carla glanced over, did a double take, and her eyes bulged out.

"Who said I'm alone?" I bit back a smile. Then shot Sutton an *I had no idea, you've gotta believe me* look.

"Carla," Sutton greeted, dropping the temperature a few more degrees with her coolness.

"Sutton. Oh my god." Carla swung her wide gaze toward me. "Oh, I didn't know—" A switch flipped, and she adopted a cunning gleam in her eye. She shifted her gaze back to Sutton. "I thought I'd check on our future sheriff here. It's not like I come by *every* night."

Fuck's sake. I'd already told this woman I wasn't interested, and she was still trying to get into my bed even when Sutton was on my doorstep. I opened my mouth to deny, deny, deny and pray that Sutton believed I'd never seriously considered Carla as a bed buddy. I shouldn't have used the woman to tempt Sutton into hooking up again.

"I know you don't," Sutton said. She came down the steps and stopped next to me, her hands on my arm. A twinkle of mirth danced in her gray eyes. "When he's got a free night, he's either on the phone with me or he's inside me."

A grin spread across my face.

Carla stuttered through a surprised "O-oh."

"What can I say? I'm a weak man around her. Good thing I got myself a strong woman. Someone who understands me so much she knows when to walk away. I needed the wake-up slap."

Sutton's grip on me tightened. So did Carla's gloves around the tray of whatever dessert she had brought for me. Her smile was forced. "Aren't you two sweet?"

Sutton rested her head on my shoulder. "Night, Carla. Happy Valentine's Day."

I smiled down at Sutton, then wrapped my arm around her and left Carla behind. The confrontation was like tying a loose end. Sutton got some closure with a woman who'd intentionally hurt her feelings, Buffalo Gully would learn about my rekindled relationship by dawn, and I'd be left with the most important woman in my life.

Ray's words in the office rose like unwelcome smoke. Carla would tell people. The chatter would start. Word would make it back to Ray. He might double down on me even more. I only had to endure his overzealousness until the middle of April. As for the small-town grapevine, I tried to find a fuck to give, and I couldn't. Too much had interfered with me and Sutton. There would be limits this time.

Twenty–Three

SUTTON

Knight for Sheriff.

A solid black statement against the faint outline of an Arabian's head over the shape of a badge, written in serif font. I walked my fingers over the flat poster. The papers were scattered across the table, unusual for Wilder. I might've bypassed them if they were in a neat stack.

A larger poster was underneath a few papers that had different versions of the logo and taglines.

Wilder Knight, a hometown boy who really cares.

Deputy Knight, duty, loyalty, honor.

Deputy Knight knows what it takes to keep your neighborhoods safe.

One of the papers had a color image on it. A picture of Wilder in his duty hat. He wasn't smiling, and his chin was lifted. Pride shone from his face. His rugged handsomeness was undeniable. The picture was recent. The lines I liked to trace were in the corners of his eyes.

Wilder came out of the kitchen, lobbing a dish towel on the counter behind him. He'd put a thawed lasagna in the oven and had even tossed together lettuce and cucumbers and tomatoes for a quick salad.

Being here was weird. Facing Carla when I didn't have to play nice with her because I lived in this town was liberating, yet the brief high faded when we came inside. This house used to be my home. Old feelings and resentments threatened to pile onto my shoulders. I wouldn't let them.

I knew coming here for the first time would be a mental trip. Eating, sleeping, doing normal daily stuff I used to always do, but doing them now as a visitor. As his girlfriend. I hated that word to describe us, but it was no longer wife, so what was I left with? We were more than exes with benefits, but we weren't husband and wife.

To keep from dwelling on why I could never get married to a man who couldn't live in the same zip code as me when he knew how important it was, I pointed to his logo. "Am I going to have to ask for your autograph?"

His brows pinched together before his gaze landed on the campaign materials. "Jesus, Sutton. You're going to make me blush."

I laughed and pointed to the sheet with the logo on it. "It's nice."

He made a disgruntled sound. "How did I not know all this shit went into campaigning?"

"Because Ray's run the same campaign every time."

He spread a few of the papers out. "Those taglines are cringe, as the kids would say."

"'On god,' as Catherine would say." I put my arm on his. No matter how odd being in my old house was, I was glad I was here. "I'm really happy this is happening for you." I might not have been his boss's number one fan, but Ray was retiring, so Wilder could be interim sheriff. It'd be harder for another candidate to oust him from the office than it would be for two new candidates to compete. Ray had known what he was doing.

"You really mean that?" He took my hand in his.

"Of course. You're going to give everything to that job, just like you do now. You really have worked hard for this."

"You of all people would know." He feathered his lips over my knuckles.

The touch of his mouth made it hard to keep my clothes on. "I might need to get a copy of that photo."

"You gonna hang it across from your bed for when I call?"

"Probably, but it's better when I've got the real thing between my legs." Yet, the thought of going to the bedroom, the one devoid of everything but a pair of underwear he'd taken months ago, messed with my mind. I wanted to be intimate with him, but I didn't want the dynamics between us to change. I didn't want the lonely kid inside me to insist that he was still in Buffalo Gully because I wasn't good enough.

No, I couldn't go there, but I needed his touch to root me to this moment, to how it was *now* between us. I spun him around so his ass hit the table, and I lowered myself to my knees.

I gazed up at him, loving the way his eyes darkened seeing me on my knees. "Remember when we first got this table?"

I had imagined a large family gathered around the solid hickory plank, and we commemorated the purchase by stripping down and having sex on it. We hadn't used the table for much more than sex and an occasional meal together after that, making this a good spot for our first intimate experience in this house as a divorced couple who were dating. Long distance.

I flicked open his fly.

His knuckles turned white as he gripped the beveled wooden edge. "I think of it every time I sit in my spot. The way I spread you open like my very own four-course meal."

"It was three courses if I remember correctly. I'm going to have the fourth course now, cowboy." I fisted my hand around his sweltering erection and pulled him free.

"We're not stopping there—" He cut off with a groan. I licked across his tip, tasting the familiar saltiness of his skin. "Fuck, Sutton."

I closed my lips around his broad tip and sucked him in. A ragged groan left him. I knew exactly what he liked. The pressure, the rhythm, the way I cupped his balls. I hit every one of his preferences like I was proving we could still be us. Our circumstances might be different, but we were a part of each other.

Perhaps I was staking a little bit of a claim. Showing him there was a reason to keep turning down Carla. That long distance didn't mean we couldn't connect. Didn't mean we would grow apart but also that our past wouldn't ruin our future together. Again.

"Shit." He buried a hand in my loose hair. "I'm not going to last long if you keep doing that."

I was sucking him off with more pressure than normal, and I eased. I gazed up at him, knowing he liked seeing my caved cheeks and my lips around his cock. Also knowing I was more raw about finding the posters than I was about the town flirt trying to worm her way into his warm house.

He gently pulled himself out of my mouth and lifted me to my feet. He wrapped a hand around the back of my neck and put his lips on mine.

"I fucking love you." He spun us more smoothly than if we were on the dance floor. Next, it was my ass up against the edge of the table and Wilder kneeling to take my leggings off.

When he stood, he shoved his pants down farther and hitched my legs around his waist. Was he feeling the same, or was this all physical for him? Was his head continually trying to yank him out of the moment with insidious doubts and insecurities?

"I'm going to have my favorite dessert after we eat, but I've got to be inside you before the oven timer goes off." His urgency had to be more than biological. Being unable to physically touch for months hadn't been easy for him either.

The steady thrum between my legs needed him inside me too. I gripped his slick shaft and guided him in. When he was close enough to thrust, he tipped me back until I had to grip his shoulders to keep from falling backward, and he buried himself to the hilt.

"Wilder," I moaned. He'd hardly touched me, and I was about to explode. My peak was right there, and I was ready to careen over.

"We're going to fuck on this table for fifty more years, aren't we?" He pulled out and thrust in, the sound of our slapping skin filling the room.

His question moved the climax further away. "Fifty?"

"Fifty." He scooted me closer to the edge and penetrated deeper.

My brain gladly clung to the pleasure.

"You're mine."

I hugged my legs tighter and let the energy between us build until I didn't care to know where I ended, and he began. The explosion that catapulted through me carried the echoes of *fifty years* and the questions of how that length of time would be possible living apart. He grunted and released inside me, going rigid in my arms.

I said I wouldn't marry Wilder again, but I was in a committed relationship with him. Committed. To commuting. To trying to connect when we had a free night or day. To scaring other interested men and women off so they could find someone to spend fifty years with.

But we weren't committed to each other. Not completely.

Did I want fifty years of that?

If not, what was I willing to give up to get what I wanted?

Wilder

A switch had flipped in Sutton. I'd narrowed the time to when we were having sex the first night she was in town. Her ass had been on the campaign logo sheet. The rest of the weekend, if I wasn't with Ray, then I had my phones in a drawer by the dining room table and was with Sutton.

There hadn't been much time. Yesterday had gone

long. Instead of going to the out-of-town basketball game, Ray had stuck around. Had he heard Sutton was in Buffalo Gully and at my house?

Sutton hadn't sat around the house while I was gone. No, not her. She'd packed her kit and went to the ranch to help Eliot for the day. She'd done the same today, too, but I'd cut Ray off early, telling him I had to get my beauty sleep for a week of night shifts. I needed to be home when Sutton started for Crocus Valley.

I needed to see her walk out the door and know she'd be back.

"Thanks for letting me crash." She hugged herself, and we were back to being an awkward divorced couple. She was dressed similarly to when she'd arrived, back to being my snow angel—and melting out of my life.

I frowned. Where had that thought come from?

I scratched the back of my neck. "So, next time. I'm not sure when that'll be."

She gave me a regretful smile. "We knew this time of year would be busy for you, and now it is for me."

She was working more before her vacation, the camping trip where she'd be farther away and gone longer.

"Maybe I can get a few days off and hunt you and Oreo down at camp."

Her eyes lit, and a bright smile began and then dimmed. "That'd be cool. But do you really think you're going to get away? There's going to be calving too."

One problem that had been solved. "Eliot said the new guy is doing really well."

She rose on her tiptoes and kissed me. "I'm not getting my hopes up, Wilder. If we have a free day, we'll try to hook up. I'll call you when I get home."

Home. A home that wasn't fucking here.

I walked her to her pickup. The condensation from our breaths mingled between us in the cold air.

She opened the driver's door and smiled up at me. The distance was back in her eyes. "I'll take a lot of pictures on my trip if you can't make it."

"I have two months to figure something out." I placed a kiss on her lips and deepened it until a shiver ran through her body. Since it was probably from the temperature and not me, I loaded her into the toasty cab.

I hung in the open door. I couldn't let her leave like this. If she didn't talk to me, then we were doomed, and if we were over, then the sacrifices we had made were for nothing. "What'd I say? Friday night when you arrived. What'd I say to make you go quiet?"

She opened her mouth, closed it, then ran her lower lip through her teeth. "You asked if we'd still be doing this in fifty years."

The wind racing behind me wasn't the reason for my chill. "You don't think so?"

"Ten years? Twenty? How long will this work?" She twisted her hands together. "I don't know. It made me wonder if we were better left as an unfinished memory."

An unfinished memory was the best way to describe why the divorce had felt so wrong. Like I'd taken a wrong turn and didn't know how to get back, and every road led back to the same incorrect spot. "If I believe that, then it means we're over, and that's unacceptable."

"Unacceptable? Or unavoidable?"

"Lots of couples manage. Military." Austen hadn't had high recommendations based on what he'd seen during his time in the Army, but I sure as shit wasn't going to mention that right now. "Oil field workers. Railroad crew."

Her hands were still on me, but she was wearing her gloves. The distance the material created might as well be as thick as a mountain range. I saw the question in the warm depths of her gray eyes. *For decades?*

I didn't have an answer for her.

Twenty-Four

WILDER

The date taunted me. Sun shone through the window. The start to spring had been irritatingly mild, and the daily temperatures had been unseasonably warm. No freezing rain to shut down roads. No winter blizzards in the forecast to make people prepare to hunker down. Nothing but gorgeous days for the next two weeks.

Perfect for a spring camping trip. Starting tomorrow. On April 16.

I glared out the window. She'd be leaving tomorrow. All alone. She and that camper with the boxed-in bed. My dog. And no one else. To make matters worse, we hadn't been able to see each other for two months.

"Wilder?" Ray's voice cut through my ruminations. We were at his retirement party. His time with the Murphy County Sheriff's Office was almost over, but as per usual, he wanted to meet with me after the party. To go over more items. One last time.

We'd been through a lot of last times.

I'd be sworn in at nine a.m. Ray had wanted everyone fresh-faced and in attendance. Tomorrow would be a big day. Huge.

Yes, that date echoed through my head. April 16.

He ducked his head, concern knitting his bushy brows together.

"Yeah? Sorry, what?"

He shook his head. "I thought I lost you there."

"No, uh…" I had to get his attention off me. He'd ask if I was nervous, and that'd draw out his *one last thing* even longer. "Nice turnout, huh?"

Ray nodded like how many people showed didn't matter. "Free food. Always gets them."

Except all the dispatchers who weren't working had come in. Same with the other deputies. Even the ones out on patrol had stopped in. Jeremy Miller had brought his twins over and joked that we didn't even have to tow a car for him. Teachers, and Annie, the school librarian, roamed around the city hall conference room.

Brenda had decorated during the hours she wasn't working. In the corners were black and blue balloons, and a giant banner that read "Thank you for all your years" was attached to the back wall.

Lawyers and judges—even the ones Ray notoriously rubbed the wrong way—had stopped in. Grocery store and gas station employees. Local business owners. The guy who tips Ray off on the best fishing locations and types of bait to use. All of them stopped in.

Who didn't I see? His kids. His grandkids.

"Your kids couldn't make it?" I was being intrusive, but I couldn't help it. Sheriff was his role, but he was a dad. A grandpa. Had those other roles fallen by the wayside until at the end, he didn't even have his job anymore?

"Eh, you know how it goes."

I was afraid I was beginning to.

"Long flights. It's in the middle of tax season for my daughter."

"They coming out later now that you'll have all the free time?"

His dry laughter was empty. "Doubt it. They're city kids now. Montana ain't got nothing for them." He slapped me on the back. "Ready for the big day?"

My gut clenched, and the piece of store-bought marble cake with extra foamy frosting threatened to come up. "Yeah," I said weakly.

"Don't be nervous. You were made for this job."

I had been molded for the job. Was I made for it? "You taught me well." And he had. He'd been a dedicated mentor. A sheriff loyal to his county. But not a devoted husband or father.

"Sutton going to, uh, be there tomorrow?"

I studied him. His question was probing, but I could tell he hoped the answer was no. In an odd turn of events, I wished I could disappoint him. "No. She's got things to do." Places to be. Ones that wouldn't include me.

We were both embarking on the start of new adventures.

A question that had crossed my mind once retraced its path. When I retired, who did I want at my goodbye party?

✳

I wished the balloons and banners hadn't been cleared away, and I could pretend it wasn't April sixteenth yet. But I couldn't escape reality. The party today was for me. As many people as had shown up to Ray's retirement party had come to my swearing-in ceremony. More, if I counted Eliot, who hadn't been around last night, and Cody and Tova, who'd made the trip with their kids. Aggie, Ansen, and Ro were here as well. Austen couldn't get leave.

Having them present when I took my oath of office meant the world. So why was a lingering sadness surrounding me like a fog? My heart held a dread that wouldn't leave. Trepidation. Fear. All the negative emotions and none of the relief and elation I thought I'd experience.

Cody stopped next to me. "Quite the crowd."

His comment reminded me of how I'd made a similar statement to Ray. "Good turnout." I didn't have kids to blow off a big moment in my life. But there was one person missing. One person who'd be hooking up her camper and checking off her packing list this very minute. I hadn't invited her to attend, and she hadn't offered. Today would be uncomfortable for her, to be among my coworkers and the community as the ex-wife I was dating. I'd never ask her to postpone the trip she had planned for months, when in reality, she'd put it off for years because of me.

The county commissioner sidled between me and Cody. Cody left to wander through the crowd to where Tova and the kids were at the fringes. I was tempted to call him back, to tell him I needed his advice, but I didn't know what for.

The commissioner had a huge smile on her face. She

was in full maroon pantsuit glory, just like I was dressed more for a policeman's ball than a traffic stop. "We're so excited to be involved in the swearing-in of a new sheriff." She nudged me. "Can't wait to do it for a full term."

I forced the political side of me to the forefront and let out a good-natured laugh. I had to embrace the new job. "It's an honor."

Ray came up and slapped me on the back. "He's ready for it."

My stomach churned.

"It's time." She grasped my hand, then went to the front of the room. People started filling in the seats. Tables from last night had been moved out as well. Nothing but a sea of faces would greet me when I was called to the front.

I'd take the oath of office in a few minutes.

Soon I'd be exactly where I'd planned to be most of my life. I could finally prove to myself I was worth something.

Fuck's sake.

Sutton had been right. I was chasing a feeling. An inner need only I could fill. One I'd ignored and in pursuit of which I'd chased away the one person I'd wanted by my side at any damn party.

"If everyone could take their seats, we'll get started," the commissioner announced.

My back was pressed against the wall, cold leaching through my uniform. Ray came to stand beside me, my support. Only he hadn't been. When I'd needed the most support, he'd steered me in the direction he preferred I go. Sutton had left me—for herself, but also because she knew how important this position was to me. She even knew why. Ray had only known his wants and needs. She sacrificed, and I hadn't.

I was selfish. I was worse than her parents. I'd sworn to Sutton that I'd be there through sickness and through health, and she'd known me better than me. She'd known I wouldn't live up to my vows.

Those were the only oaths I was concerned about anymore.

"It's an exciting day for all of us..." The room went quiet while the commissioner talked.

I'd rather be with Sutton than be in this uniform.

I'd rather be with Sutton than spend one more minute in this building.

I'd rather be with Sutton and find out how much better life could get when I lived in the same place as her.

I blew out a hard breath. I'd rather be with Sutton. For the next fifty years.

Becoming sheriff had represented all the power and recognition I thought I didn't have growing up. I had been in Cody's shadow. Then in Ray's. Waiting. Like Sutton waited on me.

She wasn't waiting anymore. And I no longer cared about shadows. She was my sunshine. If my life was a game show, I'd take the deal. I'd come on down. *I'll take "Making Sutton Mine for Fifty Years" for eight hundred thousand!*

Frantically I looked around. I caught Aggie and Cody watching me. Eliot lifted a brow. Out of the entire room, only they sensed something was wrong.

Cody dipped his head barely enough to notice. But I did, and it was enough.

"I can't do this."

The commissioner stopped, her mouth open mid

word. I hadn't heard a thing she said. All eyes were on me. Confusion and murmurs went through the crowd. I hooked on Aggie's bright stare. She was biting her lower lip like she was trying not to grin. I summoned the words to finish what I started. To finish my career.

While I did, I hoped Sutton would wait on me just a little longer.

<h1 style="text-align:center">*Twenty–Five*</h1>

SUTTON

I looked through the camper and made sure all the interior latches were secure. Oreo had followed me in. I petted his head as I looked around.

I was wasting time. Stalling.

It was time to leave.

I smothered the aching disappointment in my chest and led Oreo out. I locked the camper door and checked over the connections one last time.

I'll take "Who's Stalling Again" for one hundred!

Irritated at myself, I opened the back door. "Load up, Oreo."

He jumped in and took his normal spot in the back seat.

I walked around to my door. The April sun was bright, and big fluffy clouds drifted across the robin-egg-blue sky. The weather was supposed to be just as gorgeous in South Dakota. April sixteenth wasn't the perfect date mentioned in *Miss Congeniality*, but it still wasn't hot, and it wasn't too cold. I'd have minimal wind for the drive, and no major storms were on the horizon. Perfect camping weather.

I got into the driver's seat and pulled away. I reached the end of the driveway. No cars were coming, but I kept my foot on the brake for a minute. And then another. The road on either side of my driveway was clear in all directions. In the distance, a pickup crested a hill. My heart rate spiked and then slammed down. A white pickup. Not Wilder.

He wasn't getting here in the nick of time. Today was his big day. Guilt ate at me that I wasn't there, but the feeling was better than the searing anxiety at the thought of standing among his coworkers and acting like my presence wasn't a spectacle. The day was about him. Not us.

I had to continue with my dream, and he'd live his.

What about the next time I drove to the end of my driveway and looked for his pickup? How long would I wait?

I blinked back sudden tears. Aggie's words streamed through my head. I could talk to her about anything related to Wilder, and I really needed to phone a friend now. I put the pickup in park and called her.

She didn't answer.

Right. Wilder was getting sworn in.

He'd already have taken the oath. Wilder Knight. Murphy County Sheriff.

His life was cemented in Buffalo Gully. Mine was in Crocus Valley.

My breathing kicked up. The tears burned hotter. How important was my life in Crocus Valley?

No. I wasn't giving up everything I'd worked for.

But did I work for Wilder? *Really* work? Or did I sit around and wait for him to change like I'd done with my parents? Had I withdrawn and not been completely honest about what I was feeling? We'd talked, but I also hadn't been as transparent as I should've been. I had thought I shouldn't need to be.

Wilder was achieving something he'd worked almost half his life for, and I wasn't there. I'd been determined to lead my own life. I wasn't waiting on anyone. Now I wasn't there for him either.

Was fucking Carla at the swearing-in ceremony?

I growled, and Oreo popped his head up in the back. "Sorry," I muttered. I rubbed my face and pulled my hands back. My cheeks were wet. I let out a frustrated breath. "Did I fuck up, Oreo?"

He thumped his tail against the seat.

"What do I do?"

Light flashed off a vehicle that was turning. My pulse jumped, but it was Aggie's pickup.

Wait—Aggie?

When she approached, I frowned. Ansen was driving, and she was in the passenger seat. Why weren't she and Ansen at the ceremony? In *Montana*? Ansen pulled in front of my pickup, a giant grin that matched Aggie's on his face. The back door opened, and Wilder hopped out.

I blinked. "Wilder?" I opened the door and climbed out before I could figure out what the hell was going on.

"Hey, Doc."

I stared at him, bewildered. Why was he here *now*?

Ansen hopped out, grabbed a bag out of the back, and tossed it on the driveway. Then he got back in. Aggie rolled down the window. "Call me later!"

Ansen backed up and sped away. As if I wasn't confused enough.

"You what? How are you here? Where's your pickup, and what—"

He yanked me to him and crushed his mouth to mine. I whimpered and wrapped my arms around him. I wasn't any more informed than before. My brain registered Wilder's presence when I was missing him the most. When I felt like I'd let him down the most.

I pulled away. "I'm sorry. I should've been at the ceremony."

"No, you shouldn't have."

"I made a huge mistake, and I think I know what I have to do."

"Sutton." He pressed his finger against my mouth. Oreo barked from inside the pickup.

"Nice to see you again, Oreo," he said without taking his eyes off me. His grin was sheepish. "I should've called, but I was too worried about missing you. I caught a ride with Ansen and Aggie so you'd be forced to take me on as a passenger wherever I caught you. We were going straight to the Black Hills if we missed you."

"You got vacation?"

"A long one." His grin spread. "So long you might get sick of me. I quit."

Words I never thought I'd hear him say. I must've misunderstood. "You quit? Your *job*?"

"Yes. I quit the department. I quit putting work first. I quit disrespecting what makes you feel safe and what you fear. I quit letting others dominate my time." Gently, he took my hand. "You're the most important thing in my life. Period. I'll spend my life making it up to you if you'll let me."

Euphoria was spreading through me, like my body understood what he said before my brain comprehended. He was choosing me. Over everything. I couldn't believe it. "You're moving?"

"My place is here. I don't want a career with no family at the end to show for it. Sure, my siblings were there, but how many more times would they come out to support me if I continued to work the way I had been? But more importantly, you weren't there. And I finally realized that being your husband is what I really want to do."

I really missed being his wife.

Tears gathered in my eyes. Concern took over his expression. The tears fell, and he brushed them away. "Hey," he said softly. "Tell me what's going through that sharp mind of yours. Were you really considering giving up your life in Crocus Valley?"

I let out a shaky laugh. "I'll take 'Desperate Women Do Desperate Things' for eight hundred. I love you, Wilder Knight, and this long-distance shit is too much of a roller coaster. I want to be where you are."

"Lucky for you, I love you so much I'm going to be right where you are instead, Doc." His smile was utterly devastating. It was the same one he'd flashed me after we first met. The same grin that made me wish I could rope me a cowboy like him. "As long as you forgive me for being a little slow on the uptake."

"What about your career? It wasn't all Ray—a large part of you wanted to be sheriff." What if he grew to resent me like I'd resented him before the divorce?

"I wanted something that was my own. That was you. What I do now? I don't care. I'll do some paperwork for Cody to lighten his load. He can boss me around if he's paying me. I'll still make runs to the ranch and earn my inheritance. I'm going to be useful to my family like I always wanted." He gripped my arms. "If you don't want to get married again, I'm not going to pressure you. I messed up once, and—"

"God, Wilder. Of course I'll marry you again." My flimsy resolution didn't hold up when he quit his dream job before he started to be with me in the Black Hills. I'd definitely marry a guy who moved mountains for me.

His sexy smile was back, devastating and unfurling all the desire I'd built up since I first laid eyes on a confident deputy and let him steal my heart. "You mean that? I don't have a real job. I don't even have a ring, but I can polish those hardwood floors of yours really well."

"I happen to have a ring I like a lot that was given to me by this cocky cowboy I met at a horse show."

"I love you, Sutton Knight." He tilted my chin up and captured my lips. I threw my arms around him and drank him in. A low rumble of laughter left his chest. He pulled back and placed a simple kiss on my mouth. "If we keep doing that, I won't be able to call Aggie back to tell her to give everyone the go-ahead."

"Excuse me?" Was the shock of the day the reason I wasn't tracking? Who was everyone, and what were they planning?

"You said you liked our big family grill-outs, so I asked Aggie if she and Tova and Vienne would be willing to do one in the Black Hills. They're all for it. Kids and everything." He lifted a shoulder. "Cody's too pragmatic to drag his family on a trip before you agree to the idea. Aggie and Ansen thought they could do with a vacation anyway. They're going home to pack. And I think Vienne needed to arrange time off work. If you're okay with it, you and I head down today, then tomorrow we party."

He'd never planned a family get-together. Ever. Until now. For me. I was more in love with him than ever. "Cowboy, I'm not sure I can wait until we're in our campsite to do what I want to you."

His eyes went dark. "How about we duck into the camper? I won't need more than a couple of minutes to have you screaming my name."

"Survey says...yes!"

I was on my third s'more. The picnic table that was part of my campsite was full of different ingredients for all the renditions of s'mores we could come up with. And there were a lot of us here to come up with ideas.

Ansen was following Ro as she toddled around. Aggie was sitting in a camp chair with her feet up on the cooler, her hand over her seven-month-pregnant belly. Grayson and Ivy were walking Oreo around the campground, and Cody was following them with little Charlie strapped into a baby carrier on his front. Tova was sitting between me and Aggie. Vienne and Catherine were making peanut butter cup s'mores.

Wilder hadn't left my side since we arrived. I would've been content to stay in bed all night and day, but Wilder dragged me out for an afternoon hike with Oreo. My ex-husband fiancé refused to let me miss out on the trip I planned.

My mind was continuing to wrap around the sharp left turn my life had taken back to the direction I had been going. I was delighted. Giddy. Ecstatic. Still scared. But the more I saw Wilder relaxed, the more I was confident he'd made the right decision for himself. I'd gotten so used to seeing the weight of expectation on his shoulders that I started assuming it was permanent.

"When's the wedding?" Catherine asked after crushing her peanut butter cup with a roasted marshmallow and graham cracker.

"Catherine," Vienne chided. Catherine shot her a "*God, Mom. What?*" look, and Vienne shook her head. "Sorry."

"We haven't talked about that yet," I answered with a smile.

"It's not talking they've been doing," Aggie said and snickered. Tova giggled and fist-bumped her.

"Gross," Catherine said, her mouth full of s'mores.

Grayson and Ivy ran into the campsite with Oreo. "Guess who we found!"

Cody grinned behind them. "A couple of weary travelers drove up."

A black pickup coasted to a stop in front of the camper. Austen poked his head out the window. "Heard you were going to try to have a party without us."

This trip got better and better. My entire family was here.

"You weren't invited," Wilder snapped and grinned at Eliot behind the wheel.

Eliot scratched the side of his face with his middle finger.

Wilder shook his head, a smile playing over his lips. "Glad you two troublemakers could make it."

Austen's grin was wide as usual. "You tell me you quit and are having a party? I'm not missing out."

He and Eliot hopped out of the pickup.

"How'd you get leave so fast, Austen?" Aggie asked. Her husband came to a stop beside them, Ro on his hip.

Austen's trademark lazy grin was wide. "I'm retired. Surprise. I had to rush a few things when Eliot told me what was going on, but I made it happen."

Delight ran through me. I had enjoyed Austen's visits, more because of the way he could draw out Wilder's lighter side. Austen was the only brother he hadn't been in competition with.

"The real surprise is that Austen kept a secret," Wilder grumbled, but he rose and slapped his brother's back.

Austen let go of Wilder and held his arms out. It was like the guys had all woken up and coordinated their outfits. Jeans, boots, and a hoodie with the name of one of the Knight family companies. "Sutton, bring it in. You made him squirm, and I'm sad to say I missed most of it."

"Jackass," Wilder muttered under his breath.

I gave Austen a hug. He lifted me and squeezed. He was as big as his brothers, but he had a strength that didn't show in his lanky body. "Glad to have you back, second sis."

"Nice you could make it." I patted his back after he let me go. "Cody and Aggie brought a ton of chairs. Pull one up."

Wilder sat back down and pulled me on top of him. I happily settled on his lap.

Austen took the seat next to me and nodded to Tova and Ansen. "Hey." He switched his gaze to Vienne. She was fiddling with the jangles on her wrist. "Hey, V."

She gave him a polite grin. "Austen. Nice to see you again."

"KitKat," he said in a teasing tone, and Catherine fought to keep her lips shut around her mouthful as she grinned. She wiggled her finger in greeting. "Or should I say 'Howdy, neighbors?'"

Vienne's eyes widened. "Neighbor?" She'd always been aloof around Austen. He'd flirted with her as much as he did every woman who crossed his path. She'd never said a thing about him, and I assumed she'd kept her distance since Aggie was his sister, and Tova and I were second and third sisters. She wasn't interested, and she didn't want us to think she was.

He kicked his long legs out. "I bought the house Cody used to rent."

She tightened her fingers around a metal band. "It was for sale?"

"Nope. Cody hooked me up with the owners, and I made an offer."

"Oh." Vienne sat back.

"Yep." Austen adjusted his ball cap. His hair was longer than he usually kept it. How long had he been retired? "It's gonna need a lot of work."

A choking sound came from Vienne. "That house is over one hundred and twenty-five years old. It's one of the original houses in Crocus Valley."

"Yeah." He chuckled. "It's pretty damn old."

Her eyes flared wider. I exchanged a look with Aggie and then Tova, who was already peeking at us to see if we noticed the same thing. Vienne was not happy about the house getting purchased by Austen, and she didn't seem to be thrilled with her new neighbor.

Austen swiveled his attention to me and Wilder, oblivious or uncaring about Vienne's house angst. "When's the wedding?"

Catherine snorted, and Vienne shot her a warning look.

I threaded my fingers through Wilder's. "I think we should commemorate the one-year anniversary of getting back together." I twisted to look at Wilder. His expression was pleased. "What do you think? We'll swing by the courthouse at the end of July?"

"I'll be there." He kissed my knuckles. "I won't change my mind by then."

By July, I might actually believe this was real.

Twenty-Six

SUTTON

"I now pronounce you husband and wife. Again." The justice of the peace grinned. Johanna was a woman the same age as me and Wilder and had heard the whole story while we had filled out paperwork.

Wilder yanked me to him and planted a kiss on my lips, bending me backward. I giggled and clasped my arms around his neck. Clapping filled the air.

"I'm so happy for you two!" Aggie said.

Wilder set me upright, and I grinned at our two witnesses.

Aggie's eyes misted over, and she sniffled. She wore a loose dress, and her hair was frizzier than usual, but then she'd been short on sleep since giving birth to her second child, a son. Tripp was only six weeks old, but she refused to sit out being my witness. Tripp was with Ansen for the day. Aggie was going home right after. Wilder and I had to leave town.

She waved a hand in front of her face. "Oh my gosh, these postnatal emotions are out of control."

Johanna smiled and set a pen by a document on the edge of her desk. "If the two witnesses can sign, we'll get everything finalized."

Aggie bent to sign the document that would complete our nuptials. Wilder kept an arm around my shoulders.

Cody slapped Wilder on the back and gave me a quick hug. "Congrats, guys." He stepped to the desk to sign after Aggie was done.

"All right." Johanna smiled. "You all have made my week. I could do this every Monday."

"I'm not usually in courthouses for these reasons," Wilder joked. He'd had to return to Buffalo Gully a few times for court for cases he'd worked on and to help Eliot. I'd even gone with him once, and we'd finished moving or selling the items in the house and put it up for sale.

New buyers would move in next week.

"Thank you," I said.

Wilder led me out of the office and through the wide hallways and outside. Aggie and Cody followed. The summer sun was already heating up the pavement, and the air was muggy, but Wilder and I would be in an air-conditioned car for our drive to Bismarck.

"Good luck with everything." Cody slid his aviator shades in place.

I nodded, nerves fluttering in my stomach.

Aggie wrapped me in a hard hug. "It's going to go so well, and I can't wait to hear about it."

"Thank you."

They were off, each walking to their respective vehicles, going back home to their spouses and kids. Wilder and I would be going to an appointment to see if we were able to have kids. The first opening I could get in just happened to be the day we were also getting married. Seemed fitting. I'd closed the clinic, and Wilder had guarded this day like the world depended on it.

His commitment warmed me from my head to my toes, but no matter the outcome of today's doctor visit, even if it was the first of many appointments or the last of any, we'd be fine.

Like the night of the street dance, Wilder was there when I needed him.

He slid his hand into mine, and our fingers twined together. "Ready?"

"I am."

<h1 style="text-align:center">Epilogue</h1>

WILDER

10 years later...

The trees towered over our campsite. The large fifth-wheel camper we hauled beamed in the fading sunlight, its shine a testament to how fucking expensive it was. The pickup had been upgraded to a bigger model too. We were back in the Black Hills this year, our first time back since I'd followed Sutton that day and declared I was hers forever.

Forever was turning out to be pretty darn good.

I turned my head in time to save my eye from being poked out. "Whoa, Alex. You're going to skewer someone if you aren't careful."

My eight-year-old son blinked at me. His hair was darker than his mom's but constantly messy like his uncle Austen's. "There's a marshmallow on it."

"Is it made of body armor?" I asked.

"That'd be cool!" Alex's twin, Drew, said from where he was bent with his roasting skewer over the fire. Sutton hovered next to him because the two boys tended to forget that fire could severely harm them. They forgot a lot of what could harm them—or didn't care.

"When's Tripp getting here?" Alex asked, swinging around and nearly sticking his mom in the ass.

I snorted, and she shot me a playful glare. The woman was as beautiful as ever with her hair tied back in a simple ponytail. When the boys were born, the whole braiding thing went out the window. Someday, our lives would slow down, and she said she'd start again, but we both enjoyed the fast pace.

She'd grown her vet clinic to four veterinarians total, including her. Plenty of coverage for the family vacations we took every year, twice a year, and for the long weekends and spontaneous days off.

I was her resident handyman and stay-at-home dad. I kept busy with projects in the house and the clinic. Our little hobby farm was for the boys to learn how to care for animals and tend to the land. Right now, it was more work for me, but I fucking loved it. And we had free vet care from the sexiest vet around. I coached the boys' baseball, and somehow I ended up learning how to play fucking soccer so the kids had a coach for that too.

Cody threw some work my way, but he'd also caught me up on everything Knight's Oil Wells so he wasn't the only one in the know. I continued to go to the ranch for the busiest times of the year. None of us would tire of our family trips to Buffalo Gully.

The only other time I went back was for Ray's funeral. He hadn't talked to me since I quit, and that day had shown me I'd made the right decision. It'd been like losing a father all over again, but I'd had Sutton and my siblings to fill in the emptiness Ray left behind. Turned out, he'd never been there for the real me, just who he wanted me to be.

Even Kaplan had talked to me after he'd pinned on the sheriff badge. He said he was sad to see me leave but relieved that I'd gotten my head out of my ass about Sutton. Kaplan was still the sheriff.

To say Ray's funeral was a simple affair would put it mildly. The church wasn't packed like one would've thought when the man had worked in the county for most of his life. His kids and grandkids hadn't attended the memorial, and those people who did were only able to talk about Ray in a working role. Nothing personal.

"Dad? Tripp?" Alex repeated.

Right. I couldn't get lost in my head with these two. They'd tear the house down while I was daydreaming. Tripp was Aggie and Ansen's son and the closest cousin in age to the boys. "He's coming tomorrow."

"We're celebrating with a day on our own, just like the last time we were here." Sutton backed up, and I tugged her down onto my lap. She settled in. The kids were used to seeing us all over each other—in a kid-friendly way, of course. "All the rest of the family will come tomorrow."

This weekend was a big family reunion. All of us gathering in one spot—happened all the time these days, but this was the first time taking our gathering out of town since I had quit the sheriff's department.

"Remember how we spent the night before everyone arrived?" I asked her quietly.

"Vividly." She pressed a kiss to my cheek. "We'll have to settle for our memories tonight."

I put my mouth close to her ear and whispered, "I'm willing to test out the door to our bedroom after they're asleep."

She giggled, and Drew looked back at us. Sutton had been relegated to bed for the last three months of her pregnancy—after giggle-crying when she heard the medical staff refer to her as a geriatric mother. She'd broken down and asked me to get a TV. For three months, she'd watched reruns of some of the game shows she'd watched as a kid, and she caught up on some of the new hosts. She made peace with how she grew up by naming the kids after a couple of the hosts.

I made my peace with how I acted the first eleven years after we married by being the most present and dedicated husband and dad I could be.

I tightened my embrace as we watched the boys scoot their graham crackers across the table trying to assemble a s'more. "I love you, Doc."

She put her hands over mine. "I love you too, cowboy."

She'd wondered once if we were better left an unfinished memory. We showed each other we weren't. Our present was full of memories in the making.

———

Thanks for reading!

What happens when Vienne gets locked out of her house in nothing but a short towel? Good thing she has a

super helpful new neighbor who's good with his hands in
A Fearless Memory.

If you'd love a glimpse into Sutton and Wilder during her
days of bed rest and when the babies finally arrive, you
can find it when you sign up for my newsletter at
mariejohnstonwriter.com.

About the Author

Marie Johnston writes paranormal and contemporary romance and has collected several awards in both genres. Before she was a writer, she was a microbiologist. Depending on the situation, she can be oddly unconcerned about germs or weirdly phobic. She's also a licensed medical technician and has worked as a public health microbiologist and as a lab tech in hospital and clinic labs. Marie's been a volunteer EMT, a college instructor, a security guard, a phlebotomist, a hotel clerk, and a coffee pourer in a bingo hall. All fodder for a writer!! She has four kids, cats, and a half blind Corgie.

mariejohnstonwriter.com

Follow me:

Also by Marie Johnston

<u>Return to Coal Haven</u>

Violet Promises

Daisy Whispers

Poppy Kisses

<u>Crocus Valley</u>

A Reckless Memory

A Temporary Memory

An Unfinished Memory

A Fearless Memory

An Endless Memory

<u>Coal Haven</u>

Make Me Whole

Make Me Shiver

Make Me Blush

Make Me Dream

Make Me Exhale

<u>King's Creek</u>

King's Crown

King's Ransom

King's Treasure

King's Country

King's Queen